"Baseball novels are a staple of literature. Something about the game captures our imagination, maybe because we view the players as better versions of ourselves, chasing a dream we once harbored. Like the game itself, we lose ourselves in the rhythms and bounces of it. Every pitch is an opportunity, every swing a herculean effort, every throw from the outfield the pursuit of a low probability shot at changing everything.

In Darin Gibby's new novel *Gil*, this sense of the dream is given breath through vivid detail and the vicarious immediacy of strapping on the cleats and staring down a batter. Love, dreams, bitter disappointment, heroic effort—it's all here and it will break your heart as it takes you back to a time when you believed anything is possible. You don't have to love baseball to love *Gil*, but if you do, you'll be back on the field. Being in the game is everything, and *Gil* takes us there with a full count and a shot at glory."

—Larry Brooks, former minor league player

"At 44 years of age, Gil Gilbert places his seemingly superhuman ability to pitch a baseball at unheard of speed on display with the Colorado Rockies. The decision has its fans and detractors, even within his family. With the ultimate prize within reach, Gil must decide if it's worth the sacrifices he must make. *Gil* is a well-told tale about the personal costs of pursuing a dream and the far-reaching, unintended consequences it can bring. A mesmerizing tale about much more than baseball, *Gil* will have you cheering while turning pages. Baseball fan or not, you'll love *Gil*."

—Ron McManus, award-winning author of *Libido's Twist* and *The Drone Enigma*

"*Gil* captures the imagination, and presents questions that linger long after the reading is done. Very well written with realistically drawn characters, it is a compelling portrait of a man torn between the two North Stars in his life: baseball and family. Even though this is a baseball tale, readers who are not baseball fans, like me, will find *Gil* relatable and enjoyable, because *Gil* speaks to universal themes that haunt us all—the choices that we make in life, and the "truths" that we thought were inviolate, but turn out to be just a set of individual points of view."

—Maria Granovsky, Ph.D., J.D., author of *Poison Pill*

Gil
by Darin Gibby

ISBN 978-1-63393-363-7

Published by

 köehlerbooks ™

210 60th Street
Virginia Beach, VA 23451
800-435-4811
www.koehlerbooks.com

Gil

some gifts come with a price

DARIN GIBBY

VIRGINIA BEACH
CAPE CHARLES

In loving memory of Melvelene,
whose courage, compassion,
and love of life inspired me
to include her story here.

1

GIL HURLED THE baseball as hard as he could at the backstop. He needed to blow off steam and calm himself before he did something stupid, or regrettable. He picked up another ball from the fluorescent-orange five-gallon bucket, and concentrated on his form.

He was consumed with frustration, and was venting with the baseball instead of with his fists or mouth. He tried concentrating on his form instead of his woes. Gil could control his pitches, but not his destiny. He was good, but not good enough. At age forty-four, Gil knew he was well past his prime and was trying to accept the inevitability of unfulfilled dreams.

He reached again into the bucket beside him on the mound and grabbed another ball. Focusing his form, he hurled another, and then another. *Arm back; elbow bent,* he told himself. He threw once again, then he looked up, and saw his buddy and assistant coach, Peck, making his way over to him from a series of disjointed brown brick buildings, the campus of the Prairie Ridge High School Coyotes.

"First strike I've seen you throw all night. What gives, Gil?"

Gil kept his foot lodged against the rubber on the pitcher's mound then stooped down and plucked up another baseball.

With a quick windup, another of his pitches cut the thin Colorado air and hammered the fence.

"Okay," Peck interrupted, stepping between the mound and home plate. "That's enough, Gil. We need to talk before you ruin a whole bucket of balls—and your arm. With these budget cuts we'll be lucky if we get enough for the season." He turned and made his way to the backstop, tugging on two balls lodged in the wire lattice. Peck yanked one out and ran his fingers across the torn leather.

"Holy crap," he muttered to himself, shaking his head.

Gil flippantly tossed the ball back into the orange bucket.

"What's got you so pissed off?" Peck asked.

Gil slid the back of his worn leather glove across his brow. "I've got my reasons."

"Like?"

"All my life I've worked so hard, tried to do the right thing, and look what it's gotten me."

Peck lifted up his ball cap and smoothed back his brown wavy hair, letting his burly hand glide over his six-inch mullet.

"Are you kidding me? You've got the hottest wife this side of the Mississippi, two of the most well-mannered kids I've ever met, and you're one of the most highly respected high school coaches in the state. And you're still playing ball—and coaching it. Most guys your age gave it up long ago. What's with the self-pity?"

"My age, exactly," Gil huffed. "What I've really got is some loser job that is going nowhere fast."

"Shoot, Gil. I'm your assistant. What does that make me? A double loser?"

Peck made his way to the mound, his tattooed arms folded, like a coach ready to talk some sense into his rattled starter, or else make a decision to yank him before the other team could do any more damage.

"How so?"

"We don't need to go into this, not now."

Peck continued rolling the ball in his hands, digging his fingernail into the sliced leather. "Oh, I think we do. You know, with the strike, all the major league teams are looking for replacement players. You could try out for the Rockies."

Gil grunted. "That's not going to last. The owners will cave before the season starts and all those replacement players will be back on the streets. Besides, I gave up that dream—and I'm too old. All I've been doing is messing around in the rec leagues for years. I'd get creamed, even by replacement players."

"Not from what I've seen. You can still throw in the eighties, and you have a big breaking ball. I've seen it. No way, I bet you were just firing at least eighty-five," said Peck, looking at one of the scarred balls he plucked from the fence. "That's better than most minor leaguers."

"You never told me why you didn't try to play professionally," Peck continued. "You must have had one rocket of an arm when you were younger."

"Unlike you, I didn't stand a chance," Gil snapped back.

"That's not what I heard. And not with what I just watched you throw. What gives?"

"It's really complicated."

"Try me."

Gil hung his head and breathed out deeply.

"Well, when I was playing for ASU, a lot of scouts were looking at me. I had to make a decision."

"Like?"

"Being a responsible adult and finishing my degree, or being flighty and chasing some harebrained idea that I was good enough to play professional baseball."

"I take it you were offered a contract?"

Gil nodded.

"You never told me that. So why didn't you sign?"

"Some things came up, and getting a degree seemed like a better choice than wasting my life away in the minors."

"Easy there. Remember who you're talking to."

"You had a real chance, Peck—if you hadn't had those elbow problems. Not so with me. Do you know how many twenty-year-olds can throw a ninety-mile-an-hour fastball?"

Peck shrugged.

"A whole bunch." Gil adjusted his cap. "It's water under the bridge. My life is in the history books. I made my bed and all that stuff. I've lived a very mediocre life. Four years of misery to get a physics degree. I was too much of a loser to even try to get a masters degree. I took a job as a lousy high school teacher making fifty thousand a year, coaching on the side. What kind of loser career is that?"

"Again, Gil, consider your audience. At least you are the head coach. Look at me. I'd kill for your job."

Gil spit and covered up the spittle with a kick of his toe. "You know I didn't mean that."

"But seriously. How can you say it is a loser job? With all the talk of your science fair this year—and another season in the playoffs—you could easily get teacher of the year. How many people can brag about that? And the kids here love you to death. You are the coolest teacher ever. How many high school students beg to have their science teacher play at their prom? You can sing *Sunday Bloody Sunday* better than Bono."

"When I get to play him! The only gigs I get anymore are overplayed country songs about some guy finding religion. Have I ever written one of my own?"

Peck shrugged. "I'll bet you have."

"Well maybe, but you'll never hear it on the radio. Just good ol' Gil. Friend to everyone, foe to no one. That's all I am."

"Well tell me this, if teaching is such a loser job as you say, then why did you choose it?"

Gil shook his head. "I don't want to go there."

Peck hopped up beside his friend and shoved him back, enough to dislodge Gil's foot from the rubber. "With the energy you were putting into that ball, I think we need to go there. Come clean with me. How long have we been together?"

Gil's jaw muscles clenched, and he slapped his glove against his thigh then looked up into the fading sky. "Alright, I'll tell you, if you really want to know. I did the honorable thing and married her, then dumped any dream of playing pro ball. I took a teaching job to pay for the baby. Would you believe that I met her at a frat party? You know when you go to those dinner parties and everyone has to tell how they met? I couldn't do it. I made up some story about how I picked her out of the crowd when we were playing UCLA."

"Whoa, wait a minute. Way too much information. I didn't mean to pry like that."

"She was pregnant. My plans for baseball were over. And

don't you ever mention it to anyone—my kids don't know."

Peck reached out and put a hand on Gil's broad shoulder. "How was that a bad thing? Look at what it got you."

"Yeah, a beautiful family that I can't even support. Not now—not now that I am going to lose everything."

"Gil, what exactly are you talking about?"

"The little turd is suing me, that's what."

"Are you drinking, man?"

"Do I ever drink? I am the clean-cut all-American parent. Except that now I am getting hauled into court."

"For what? Wait, for when Zach was screwing around after practice and thunked Shaila in the head?"

"Yes, they're suing the school and me personally. Two million bucks. Claiming the ball cracked her skull and caused brain damage."

"If you ask me, the ditz already had brain damage."

"Yeah, well tell that to a jury. They are going to wipe me out."

"They can ask for anything, you know that. Besides that, the school district is required to defend you."

"That's what I thought, but it's not that clear. What if they don't? I can't afford a lawyer. You know how much I make. What am I going to do?"

Peck also spit and shook his head. "I see now." Then he went and fished a catcher's mitt from the equipment bag. "Okay, at least throw the rest at me so we don't destroy any more balls. And don't worry, they won't fire you. Can you imagine the protests? You've had a winning season for fifteen straight years."

Gil went into a full windup and whipped the ball at his catcher, each pitch slamming into the glove with a loud smack. Peck bolted up and tossed down the mitt, shaking his stinging hand.

"Holy crap! What is going on here? You taking some kind of performance cocktail? Your gut is gone, your chest looks like a bulldog's, and you are solid as a rock."

A hint of a smile crept onto Gil's weathered face. "Drugs? Never did them—not being the son of a preacher."

"Then what? You don't just all of the sudden hurl like that."

"Mid-life crisis is all. Lots of stress builds the physique... and I've been working out some."

"No, man. What kind of drugs are you on? I've caught for a

lot of pitchers, but nothing like this. You gotta be throwing in the nineties, pushing a hundred. I've got to get a speed gun on you, Gil. What is the record these days?"

"The fastest pitch? Some say Bob Feller threw a one-hundred-and-seven-mile-an-hour fastball, but who knows? Most of those guys were full of themselves. That was before radar, so it is all speculation."

"You are the science guy. You should know."

"Since modern speed guns came around, there has been a few clocked at one hundred and four, and in 2010 Aroldis Chapmin was officially measured at one hundred and five. But it's hard to say. Feller thought Satchel Paige was the fastest pitcher alive. So, could he throw faster than one hundred and seven?"

"What were you in college?"

"Fastest was ninety-one."

"Then that confirms it—you are all screwed up my friend. A forty-four-year-old man can't throw like that, not without a whole lotta dope."

"No drugs, man. You're just getting old. Bad eyesight and soft hands. Still getting those manicures?"

"Hey, the last time was with you. Come on Gil. Let's be honest here. This is crazy stuff. Those balls I pulled out of the fence—the leather was completely torn through. Let's try one more, just as a sanity check. Let me have it. Get really pissed off. Imagine you are throwing at that lawyer's face."

Peck backpedaled to the plate and pounded his fist into his glove. "Give me all you've got."

This time the ball whizzed into Peck's glove with the same familiar smack. Peck removed his hand from the glove. The palm was red.

"I think that confirms it," he said, shaking his head. "Tomorrow I am going to make a few calls."

2

RAY RATCLIFF, MANAGER of the Colorado Rockies, scratched his gray whiskers and shook his head as he watched his rotation of pitchers loosen up in their last practice before heading off to Arizona for spring training. His bullpen should have been practicing in Arizona beginning the third week in February, but with the strike, they were scattered across a continent. This season, nothing would be normal.

The players' contracts had expired at the end of the World Series last October and, despite prolonged negotiations, no progress had been made in getting the players onto the fields for spring training. Normally, preseason started in early March, with the teams playing around thirty games before opening day on April 6. This year, the fields in Arizona and Florida remained vacant and the bleachers empty. Both sides started getting nervous, but the major league owners, convinced revenues would continue to decline, held firm. The players felt ripped off, even though most of them made more money than they could ever spend. By the third week in March, the owners and general managers got together and made a decision: If the players refused to accept the current offer, they'd hire replacement players. The striking players laughed, assuming the fans would boycott mediocre talent. Not even minor league players would take the field, because they too were bound by the fate of MLB—Major League Baseball.

The owners were ready to gamble that a new generation of fans might not care about seeing the pampered, overpaid pros. Most people earn forty, maybe fifty grand a year. These spoiled ballplayers were making millions a season. How sympathetic would the average fan be? Trying out for a major league team could become a great fascination and make for great TV, the owners calculated. Fans would almost certainly empathize with these underdogs who, like them, were fighting for a break in life. When the players insisted they deserved more and rejected the final offer, the owners decided to play ball without the pros. Each team had until the end of March to fill its roster. They'd play a ten-game preseason, then the regular season would proceed as normal.

Playing baseball in Colorado in March was just wrong. Training indoors at the rented local community college was a downright embarrassment, but with a blinding blizzard outside and gaping holes in his lineup, the Colorado Rockies had no choice. The manager needed to round out his team before heading off to warmer climates. In the heart of the Rockies, a sudden storm could slip over the high peaks, changing a mild February day into a winter wonderland in a matter of minutes.

Last year should have been Ratcliff's last, but he sweet-talked his way into one more season. If the Rockies didn't win the pennant, he promised to resign, or, more likely, retire. The real reason he wasn't laid off was because Ratcliff was a master at playing Billy Ball, finding the right young talent at the right price. That was critical for a small-market team like Denver, which lacked the big-dollar budgets of major-market teams like the Yanks, Dodgers, Cubs, Giants, and even the Red Sox. Billy Ball was named after Yankees manager Billy Martin, who had perfected the idea of trading for players with the best on-base percentage—and the lowest salaries. The idea was to find players who know how to get on base, not who swing for the long ball.

Ratcliff won several pennants, nearly always posted a winning record, and his scrappy style of playing ball was enough to keep ticket sales respectable. But he'd never won the World

Series, at least not as a coach. Just when his young players became stars, they reached free agency and the Rockies could no longer keep them on and still make payroll. So, Ratcliff was in a constant state of finding undiscovered talent.

Ratcliff cut his own salary down to the bare minimum, hoping to save a few scarce dollars for a lucky pre-season trade. Ratcliff didn't need the money—he had made plenty. Taking the pay cut would be part of the story and a way to show fans and players that the game came before the money. Ratcliff's face was stoic as he studied the rag-tag team the GM had thrown together, an assortment of retired players and third-tier minor leaguers. Nobody with a real shot at the majors would even consider crossing the picket lines. Minor league players with promising careers assumed the strike would soon be over and they didn't want to be labeled a scab. That left a spattering of lackluster players to field a team.

"We are going to get booed out of the stadium with this motley crew."

Ratcliff looked over at his pitching coach, Adrian Connor. "They're . . . different, that's for sure, but I think they are going to surprise us."

"You say that every year—it's always going to be our year."

"Have to be an optimist in this business, otherwise it will eat you alive. Spring comes around every year for a reason." Yet Ratcliff knew he had a serious problem.

"This tryout thing is a damn joke. It's not going to work," Connor said.

"The owners think it will," Ratcliff said.

"Based on what? Show me one scintilla of evidence this cockeyed scheme is going to work."

"They want to appeal to a new audience. There's a different generation of fans out there. They want to see the underdog, the undeveloped talent discovered, like on *The Voice*."

"Yeah, but this is baseball, not some TV circus for the Millennial crowd. There's absolutely no precedence. They'll screw up a hundred years worth of history."

Ratcliff tipped his cap. "What about the teams fielded during WWII? The owners claim those teams were just as popular, if not more so."

"Yeah, until the war was over. Then baseball really exploded. The golden decade of the fifties."

"That's their point. They need to shake things up, get some new blood into the game. Then, when the strike is over, baseball will be more popular than ever. Let's face it—baseball has been beat up. Tarnished with drug scandals, overpaid players, commercialism, you name it. The game could use a fresh start."

"Maybe, but I don't think we're the ones to be the guinea pigs. We're too old."

"I hear you, and this bit about tryouts and reality television is crossing the line," Ratcliff said. "You may be right. This whole charade could be over before it starts."

"I hope so. The last thing I need is for my life to be scrutinized like the Kardashians."

Ratcliff grunted. "My wife used to watch that show. Imagine us on a reality show. Could be kind of fun humiliating some of those replacements on national TV."

"Right now I'd settle for three more pitchers."

Ratcliff mentally went down the list of what they had so far conjured together for a pitching staff, more than a little concerned his promise of a successful season would be anything but prophetic. He'd been handed an equal mix of lefties and right-handers, but with little professional experience.

So far, his two most promising starters were DeJesus, the Cutting Cuban, because of his nasty cutter fastball, and Melendez, who'd eked out a respectable fifteen wins in his third and final year in the majors, making him the most likely candidate for this year's ace. Each had his own set of issues. DeJesus had spent most of his career in the minors. He'd been called up to the majors once, but after three games blew out his arm. He'd recovered, but lingered in the minors until he finally threw in the towel. Melendez lost his will to play, and rather than face the humiliation of going back to the minors, he retired and took a job as a baseball announcer. He regretted the decision almost as soon as he made it.

Ratcliff needed at least three more pitchers to round out his starting rotation. And he needed to firm up the bullpen. He had a mediocre set of mid-relievers, and the only option for a closer was Tajima, whom he found hard to understand because he had a strong Japanese accent.

He had what he called a generation-gap team. There were lots of over-the-hill veterans he was calling back and the rest were greenies. Yes, the old timers could give their sage advice and wisdom, but that advice usually fell on deaf ears. Youth always favors experimentation.

Ratcliff's assistant, Connor, was well past his prime too. The two had been together for more than thirty years. Connor was a drunk with alimony payments from two failed marriages. He didn't enjoy the game much anymore, but he needed the money. Wherever Ratcliff went, Connor followed.

"I hate this crappy weather," Connor said, changing the subject from lousy pitching. "Can't wait until we get to Arizona. Let's just hope the snow is gone by Monday so we can have tryouts in a real ballpark."

3

RON GILBERT, KNOWN to his parishioners as Pastor Ron, had been a mainstay of the Centerpoint Church of Christ for more than three decades. The Gilbert family home, a single-story rambler with a carport, was a short two-minute walk away from the church. The Shady Brook subdivision was constructed two years before the church, and was now truly shady with its soaring maples and blue spruce trees. It was Gil's only childhood home.

Gil pulled the family car onto the driveway as Pastor Ron, navy tie swaying with his stride, crossed the front lawn. Sunday dinners following Pastor Ron's sermon were a weekly ritual rarely missed. Keri, Gil's wife, didn't mind because she didn't have to fix dinner and none of her close relatives lived in Colorado. Austin, Keri and Gil's son, had the habit of slipping into Pastor Ron's recliner and watching whatever sporting event he could find.

Keri reached over and slid her hand over his. They had a good life together. Keri's life was just how she wanted it. It wasn't without challenges, but they were all within what she could handle. Their oldest child, Alicia, now a junior at CU in Boulder, was pulling straight A's, had a serious boyfriend, knew she wanted to go to medical school, and had already taken two prep classes for the MCAT. Except for the typical high school irritability, Alicia had been the easy one, the model child. Austin was their challenge. Although fourteen, he was still in middle school. Based on his age, he should have been a freshman at Prairie Ridge, but Keri and Gil had held him back because of how he struggled with school, and he was even more socially behind than academically. It was only Austin's involvement with sports that ended up saving him. What he lacked in academics, he more than made up for on the court, or the gridiron, or the ice, or the field. Gil wasn't the only coach at Prairie Ridge waiting for Austin to become a freshman. But they all knew that baseball would take priority.

Austin swung open the door and stumbled out onto the grass. He ran up and hugged his grandfather.

"How was the first week of baseball?"

"Okay."

Ron pointed to the front window. "I still remember when your dad broke that window with one of his fastballs."

Keri, now beside her husband, gave him a wink. Gil couldn't remember how many times the story had been repeated.

Austin scampered ahead and swung the door open, holding it ajar as his grandfather, assisted with the handrail, ascended the stairs.

Sandra, Gil's mother, already had the table set. Steam was rising from the mashed potatoes, and she lifted a silver lid from the pot roast.

They were seated, and Pastor Ron said grace before Austin dove in. Keri had long given up trying to tame his table manners.

"Nice sermon," Keri said.

"Thank you. After all these years, hopefully I can get it right."

"You've reached a lot of people during your ministry."

"Speaking of . . . I'm looking forward to presenting that scholarship at your science fair this week."

Ever since Gil started his science fair, the church had garnered donations to support the cause. The pot was now up to twenty-five hundred dollars for the winning project.

"Keri has gone way over the top this year," Gil said. "We're focusing on opposites in nature, and Keri has been very creative in her decorations."

"When hasn't she gone the extra mile? And Gil, we can't say just how very proud we are of you and what you've done at Prairie Ridge."

Austin took this as his cue, hopped up and turned on the TV. Keri coughed loudly.

"Oh yeah, thanks Grandma." Austin scooped up his plate and slipped it into the sink before plopping himself into the recliner.

The rest of the family finished their meal with ESPN blaring from the other room. Pastor Ron slipped behind his grandson, listening to the latest update on the baseball strike.

"This is awesome," Austin said as he looked up behind him. "Every team is going to have tryouts on TV to find the best players. It's like *American Idol* or *America's Got Talent.*"

Pastor Ron shook his head. "These times are a changing. Seems like a crazy idea to me."

"I think it's a great idea. I hope they still do it when I get old enough," said Austin. "I'd love to try out. Every team has to have playoffs for at least one starting position. They are going to show the playoffs on TV, and the fans get to vote for their favorite player."

"And that's who starts?"

"No, the teams decide on their own, but everyone sees the vote, so it would look really bad if all the fans wanted a player but the manager picked someone else."

"That might be interesting," Pastor Ron said.

"The Rockies say they may do more than one player. The reporter said they hardly have a pitching staff right now."

"Well, good pitchers are hard to find."

"Dad," Austin turned to the kitchen. "I wish you had played. Grandpa, tell me what happened? Dad always says we'll talk about it later. I know he was good enough to play, but why didn't he?"

"Because he met your mother and had two beautiful kids. Isn't that good enough?"

"But lots of baseball players have families. Why couldn't he do both?"

"I think God had another path for him, and look at what he's done with it."

4

ROOM 203, BETTER known as Gil's lab, was where Prairie High students got their fill of earth science, chemistry and, for the lucky few who got accepted, physics. Or, as most of the kids called it, *Gil's Show and Tell*. "If you can't see it, you can't understand it," Gil would tell his students the first day of class. "And, you are going to understand everything I show you."

Physics was meant to be physical, and that meant Gil had to come up with a contraption to physically demonstrate every law of physics that the district expected him to teach. The room was dotted with lab stations, large enough for eight students to huddle around watching their Bunsen burners bake away some concoction, or their scales swing in and out of balance.

Today, all of that equipment was gone, stored away in some back cabinets. In their place, the countertops were cluttered with all sorts of science projects, awaiting Gil's final inspections before the official fair opened, when they would be showcased in the gymnasium for eager parents to gawk over and for the local media and scientists to cast their votes.

Gil was perched over a kind of winged contraption, fiddling with a round knob.

"Don't break it, Mr. Gil." A heavy-set teenager with a bright yellow T-shirt lumbered forward. "Here, let me show you how it works."

The rotund boy twisted the knob and a stream of high-pressure air hissed out of a nozzle that was pointed straight at the suspended wing. Just as the air came out, the wing rose about four inches.

"I call it fast and slow. It's based on Bernoulli's Principle. The wing is curved just like an airplane. I suspended the wing so it can move up and down on this vertical track. The curved surface on the top of the wing causes the air to cross the top of the wing faster than the bottom. And that causes a lift, just like a plane taking off." The boy folded his arms with an air of satisfaction. "Uh huh. Fast and slow, it gets you to fly, higher than a kite," the boy said proudly.

"Nice job, fat boy," someone called out. "Too bad you'll never be light enough to fly."

Gil whipped around in search of the loudmouth who spouted off the insult. His reaction only caused hushed laughter among his class.

"Hey, Gil."

The awkward silence was broken by Peck, his large shoulders filling the doorframe. "Class is over. Got to go."

"What's that?"

"Got you that appointment. Come on, let's go," Peck said.

"Appointment. *What appointment*?" Gil said.

"Just, wrap up this dog-and-pony show and come with me," Peck huffed.

"You guys hang out for a few minutes until the lunch bell rings. And don't think of skipping out early. I have this place under surveillance."

Peck grabbed Gil's arm and pulled him toward the door.

"Can you tell me what this is all about? What *appointment* were you talking about?"

"Just get in my car," Peck snorted. "There's a lawyer downtown who says he'll handle your case for free. He called it pro bono."

They drove for nearly fifteen minutes, with Gil occasionally looking down at his watch.

"Don't worry, you've got an hour lunch break, then your off-period. We have two hours. I'll get you back on time," Peck said.

"But all the way downtown? That's more than thirty minutes away, if there's no traffic."

"Trust me, Gil. Have I ever steered you wrong?"

"You're asking the wrong question. Have you ever steered me right?"

Peck exited the freeway and turned toward the line of skyscrapers. Just then, Peck swerved the car into a nearly overflowing parking lot; one reserved for Rockies baseball games. News vans intermixed with hundreds of other vehicles from future Rockies hopefuls filled the lot. The previous week's snow was dissolving in the hot sun.

"Peck, I don't like this. Not one bit. I know where we are, and the Rockies aren't in the business of defending people. You can't be serious. I'm not going to clown around with these guys."

"Ah come on, Gil. The Rockies need pitchers. Today is the first day of tryouts. You can't pass this up. Besides, I know the trainer. He said he could get you to the front of the line. It's the only way I could get you to come here. Trust me. Fate is on your side with this one."

"No way. Just turn this boat around and sail back home. I need a lawyer, not to be made fun of on some outlandish reality television show."

Peck shut down the engine and popped out of his seat. "They're waiting for you. Don't let him down. Last year the Rockies donated five thousand bucks to our athletic department. You owe it to them."

Gil slowly got out and slammed his door shut. "Owe them what? A thank you, yes, but free entertainment? Of all the stupid ideas." Gil hesitated and reopened the car door, slipping his foot inside. "Peck, I am forty-four years old. That's an old man in baseball. I am not going to make a fool out of myself."

"I'm just doing this for you. It's about time you stopped feeling sorry for yourself and did something about it. What have you got to lose? If it doesn't work out, you can cross over to singing country music and write a sad song about it. Then you will have an album of your own. Seriously, Gil, this is what you have always wanted, and for some freaky reason it's being handed to you. A gift from the gods I think."

Peck had hit him right where it counted. Gil knew he couldn't turn back. He clapped the door shut and started for the main gate of the stadium.

"You know this is absolutely crazy. How many forty-four-year-old pitchers have ever played in the big leagues? Maybe two?"

"But there's never been anyone who can throw a one-hundred-and-ten-mile-per-hour fastball."

"Peck, don't exaggerate. I wasn't throwing that fast."

"That's what we're all about to find out."

Gil hesitated, not sure whether he wanted to follow Peck through the giant metal gates. His head started spinning with "what ifs." What if this baseball thing is for real? I couldn't just leave Prairie Ridge. Peck is out of his mind. This is nothing but a pipe dream, he thought. Even if I can throw fast, I need a full package—curve ball, slider, change-up. I haven't thrown those for twenty years.

Gil wondered—and worried—most about the recent changes in his body. He was getting stronger, his muscles firmer, and his thoughts clearer. But why?

He suddenly felt a wave of nausea. None of this was real.

Peck grabbed Gil's shirtsleeve and pulled him in the direction of the shortest line. The main concourse looked as full as on opening day. Thousands of people were milling about, with baseball hopefuls queued up in two-dozen lines, while staff in white and purple Rockies T-shirts collected application and waiver forms.

TV reporters posed and pontificated in front of the cameras, some interviewing would-be players about their dreams. A pretty blonde approached Gil.

"Excuse me, sir, you tryin' out?"

Gil nodded yes.

"Mind if we ask you a few questions on camera?"

I'm never going to get back to class in time, Gil thought.

"Thanks, but no thanks," Gil told the reporter, walking away.

"Ah, he's too old anyway," the cameraman told the reporter. "Probably doesn't want to embarrass himself."

Gil heard the wisecrack, looked over his shoulder at the guy, and kept walking.

What a circus, he thought.

"Forget them," said Peck, "and just follow me. We don't have time to be messing with them anyway."

Peck pointed Gil to a line of men who had already filled out their tryout forms.

"But I haven't filled out any—"

"I told you not to worry." Peck pulled a wad of papers out of his jeans pocket and began unfolding them. "It's all taken care of."

Peck handed the attendant the forms while Gil nervously waited with his arms folded.

"This you?" she said.

"Naw, they're for my buddy, Gil. I'm his agent."

"I see," she said. "Well, I need Gil to sign on the last page, then go ahead and be seated in section one twenty-three. They'll call your name."

She shoved a pen in Gil's direction. He snatched it and scribbled on the highlighted line. Before he knew it, they were in the bright sun, looking over the green infield grass. Peck escorted them down the stairs and onto the field.

"Wait," Gil said. "She said to wait in the seats."

"Get warmed up. I've got it all worked out. And keep quiet out there. The cameras are rolling."

Peck disappeared, leaving Gil in left field, his mitt dangling from his finger.

When he returned, Gil was heaving some long tosses with another pitcher. Gil blinked his eyes twice. Connor, the Rockies' pitching coach, was at his side. "I know, I know," Peck said, "but you've got to see Gil pitch. Trust me, you don't want to miss out on this."

"This better be good," Connor spat back. "You warmed up? All these people have been waiting in line for hours."

"Need a catcher," Gil said.

Connor's eyes narrowed as he turned to Peck. "You said he was warmed up."

Peck shrugged. "It will be worth it. Just get him on the mound."

Connor mumbled a few profanities and turned toward the bullpen. With Gil in tow, Peck followed.

Connor stood, arms folded, until one of the mounds became available. Connor pointed to the mound, fumbled with his watch, and said, "Get warmed up. The last thing I need is another grandpa throwing out his arm. We've already had three this morning."

As Gil began throwing, a woman with a ponytail and a purple Rockies T-shirt tapped something into her iPad. "So here are the rules: He gets ten pitches of his own, then Connor asks for five of his own. We clock all of them. Placement and control are usually better than speed."

Even hurrying his warm-up, it took Gil ten minutes until he felt confident he could put on the heat. He nodded at Connor.

"Okay, get the cameras rolling," said the assistant with the ponytail. "You, Peck, can you look into the camera and tell your friend's story?"

The light on the camera shone red and Peck froze. "Yeah, sure," he finally stammered. "Gil here is the baseball coach for Prairie Ridge High. He's been a closet pitcher for years. What nobody knows is that he may have the fastest fastball in professional baseball."

Connor stared at the ground and shook his head.

"Well, that's quite the claim. Let's have a looksee. Is the speed clock on? I think it is, and I think we are ready for Master Gil to show us his stuff."

"Go ahead," Connor said.

"Wait," Peck said, lunging forward. "Is it okay if I catch for him?"

"As you wish," Connor said. "We've already wasted thirty minutes—what's another thirty more?"

Gil flung his arms back and forth, while Peck took over catching duties. He then reached into the bucket and pulled out a brand-new white baseball with deep red laces and let out a deep breath. The display screen cleared and Gil knew it was live. *This is crazy.* Gil kicked the dirt in front of the rubber, secured his hind foot and took a full windup and let the ball fly. He casually looked at the red numbers: *72.* That was horrible. He was right. He shouldn't be here.

This time he put everything he had into it. As soon as he let go, he knew he was in trouble. Everything felt off, like a golfer who can't find his swing. He didn't dare look.

Peck saved him from the bother. "Come on, Gil. Eighty-one. You are throwing like a granny. Come on, get mad like you were the other day."

Gil shook his head and gave Peck a mean stare. *The old coot . . . This is embarrassing,* he thought. Gil barely eked out a windup and flung the ball at Peck. This time the clock read 85. That wasn't a big-league throw.

He didn't dare make eye contact with Connor, who said nothing and shook his head.

"Dammit, Gil," Peck grunted through gritted teeth, "get pissed off. Think about how much you are going to have to pay that lawyer."

Connor raised his eyes then moved his gaze from catcher to pitcher.

"Speeding ticket. Okay then, just think about the entire student body of Prairie Ridge cheering for you."

"Peck, just clam it, okay," Gil said.

Gil collected himself. Maybe he should get ticked off, work up his anger to a boil. He flashed back to what had happened on the practice field just two weeks ago.

It was all innocent enough. The day was warm, one of those freakish March days in Colorado when the temperature spikes to near eighty, usually right before a massive blizzard is about to strike. Gil had taken the team outside for practice. He handled infield practice while Peck took the outfielders and pitchers. Gil stood at home plate, bat in one hand and glove in the other. He would hit a grounder, wait for the throw to first, and then catch the ball when it was thrown back. The trick was being able to toss the ball from his glove to just the right location in front of him so that he could sharply hit a grounder.

The practice was routine until Peck called him over to help explain how to throw a curve ball. Gil turned over the batting to the catcher, Trent Bushman.

"I need to go work with the pitchers. Keep things going, Trent."

Gil walked toward the outfield.

The girl's tennis team had just finished practice and they were lackadaisically skipping toward the baseball field from the tennis courts. Gil saw them coming and didn't want the distraction. He called out to the approaching tennis players: "Please, ladies. We're practicing. I'm sure the boys will be happy to mingle when we're done."

He hadn't noticed that one of the players, Shaila, had slipped around the fence and dashed toward first base, waving her racket.

"I want a turn. I want to hit a home run." Instead of getting a turn at the plate, she was tagged in the face with a shot from Bushman's bat, an apparent attempt to scare her that did more than just that. Gil heard the scream, a bloodcurdling cry before she collapsed to the ground.

Flashing back to that moment made Gil sick. *Stupid Bushman; that no-brained idiot,* he thought. *If I'd been paying attention, Shaila would never have been hit.* Gil grew angry with himself and the situation that now had him on the receiving end of a major lawsuit.

Gil took a full windup and in a rage threw the baseball directly at Peck's unprotected face. The speed gun clicked 87. Peck's glove popped enough to get Connor's attention.

Gil wiped his upper lip with his forearm and hung his head.

Connor made his way to the mound. Gil jerked to life when Connor put his hand on Gil's shoulder, then gently squeezed it.

"Just as I thought. You are wound up tighter than my ex-wife's ass. Come on, just loosen up and relax. I am going to go over and turn that machine off and you just throw like you are having fun. Isn't that what you tell your own players, to have fun?"

Connor's gentle hand instilled a new sense of determination.

Unconsciously Gil wound up, letting his mind go. Make the team or not, just having the chance to throw a ball was the real satisfaction. At least he had the chance to throw on a pro team's field. Gil brought his arm back, then let it fly, allowing his body to take control and effortlessly project the ball.

His follow-through was so complete, his arm was a mere few inches from the ground. Gil didn't see the ball strike his glove, but he did hear the sharp smack of leather on leather. How fast was it? It was impossible to tell with the radar turned off. Gil wasn't thinking of that, only how good it felt for his body to flow so smoothly, like a gently meandering stream. The serene moment didn't last.

"Holy shit!" Connor threw his hat down.

The exclamation jerked Gil to attention, back into reality. Then he saw why, the moment he glanced at the set of numbers emblazoned on the screen. Connor had intentionally left on the radar. But it wasn't the glowing red numbers alone that bolted him upright out of his recovery stance. It was that he could see an extra digit. On the clock were three numbers, not two.

It had to be wrong, he thought. "Keep throwing Gil . . . Just relax," he called out.

The ball thwapped into Peck's mitt. "Damn!" he shouted. "You're gonna blow a hole in my hand." The speed clock read 105.

"I can't believe it!" Connor sputtered.

Peck rose from his crouch and stood speechless. All pitching on the adjacent mounds came to a screeching halt, and an eerie silence fell over the bullpen. Then, a few fans in the stands who could see the clock began clapping.

Connor hitched up his sweatpants, shuffled over to the clock, and ran his index finger along each number, slowly tracing out a one, then a zero and finally a five, shaking his head each time. "Okay, cut the cameras. You heard what I said, cut them. Now!"

The cameraman flipped a switch and let the camera slide off his shoulder.

"Take another." He flipped the switch and the red LEDs went dark.

A smile crept on Gil's face. This was for real. Whatever was happening to turn his muscles rock solid, it was turning his arm into a superhuman pitching machine. He was being given a new chance at life. Gil plucked up another ball and rubbed it like he was polishing an apple. *Okay, this time I'll really show him*, he told himself. Another full windup, a mental release of all his worries, followed by a lightning-fast rocket. Gil didn't bother looking at his clocked speed. He knew this one was even faster. He had felt it.

"One-oh-eight," Peck said. "This kid is for real. Nobody has ever been clocked that fast."

Connor hurried and cleared the screen, then he made a beeline straight to the mound.

"So tell me this—have you always pitched this fast?"

"That's a hard question. I haven't been clocked since I pitched in college."

"Don't make a fool out of me, Gil. What is really going on here?"

Gil shrugged. "I really don't know. I have noticed that I'm getting stronger. For kicks, I put up a two eighty-five on the bench the other day."

Connor folded him arms. "How am I going to explain this?" he muttered.

"If it helps, my wife is kind of baffled too, especially with how much I eat."

"How do you feel? Any fatigue? Insomnia? Shortness of breath?"

"Great. Fantastic, actually. Maybe a little tight every now and then, but I figured just regular soreness. At forty-four, my body doesn't recover as fast after messing around with the team in the weight room." That was a lie. Besides a few reps on the bench or challenging his players to a squat contest, the most he had going on exercise-wise was a mild routine of pushups, sit-ups, and light jogging. Gil massaged his chest and let out a breath. His arm did feel a little tight.

Connor stepped closer and poked his finger into Gil's chest. "You've got the bicep of a twenty-five-year-old. What gives? What kind of new steroid are you on?"

Gil shrugged. "Unless the city is putting something in the water, nothing is going into this body."

"Not bullshitting me?"

"Swear on the Bible."

"Alright, stay right here. I can't believe I am doing this."

A few minutes later Connor returned with Ratcliff at his side. The two were having a heated argument, with Ratcliff's mouth only a few inches from Connor's ear.

"Well hurry up and throw it. I don't have all day," Ratcliff said, still twenty yards away.

Now it really was fun. Gil let another one rip, and it registered at 105.

Ratcliff whispered something in Connor's ear and approached the mound.

"I want to know what you are taking, even if it is prescribed."

Peck sprung up, threw down his glove and sprinted toward his friend. "Gil, we don't need this kind of harassment. We'll just go find another team."

Ratcliff held up his hand as if he were a policeman halting traffic. His eyes were both foggy and bloodshot. "These days we've got to ask the question. Just keep your shirt on."

"Look," Connor said, "we've got this three-ring circus going on, and the last thing we need is some sensational story to get leaked. So here's what we're going to do: I want you to throw another and I want to catch it, see your control. Fastball, a little high and inside. Brush away pitch. And turn off that clock."

Gil watched as Connor snatched the catcher's glove from Peck then squatted his wiry frame behind the plate. Gil wondered whether it had enough mass to stop the momentum of his throw.

Another pitch, high and inside.

"Never caught a pitch that fast before. Really not on drugs?" Connor said, standing up straight and shaking his glove.

"That's not, Gil. He's clean. He'll take any drug test you want. He doesn't even drink alcohol," Peck said with a glare.

"Would you submit to a physical?"

"Anything you want," Gil said, "but in case you don't already know, I'm a high school teacher. I don't do drugs."

"*Was* a high school teacher," Connor said. "You've pitched before?"

"Four years at ASU."

"What years?"

"Early nineties."

"With an arm like that, how come nobody has ever heard of you?" Connor asked.

Ratcliff remained silent and looked straight at Gil.

"It's a long story," Gil said, "and I need to get back to the school."

"Connor, see when Dr. Chavez has an opening," Ratcliff said.

They all waited in silence as Connor whipped out his phone and placed a quick call.

"Ten tomorrow morning. That work?" Connor asked.

"Perfect," Peck said, holding out his hand. "I will have him there."

"Wait," Gil said. "Can we make it another time? I have to

teach my physics class."

Connor shook his head in disbelief. "Most guys would give their left arm for this chance, and you want to negotiate. Alright, when would his royal highness like us to schedule his appointment?"

"School is out at three, but I coach—"

"Of course," Connor said. "Why didn't I think of that?"

Peck stepped between the two men to stop the bantering. "Do you have time to take a look at his slider?"

Connor pushed him aside. "One step at a time. Let's see what the doctor says. And not one word of this to anyone." Connor turned to the other pitchers who were still watching in awe. "That goes for all of you. And that footage better not leak. I'm covering my bases on this one."

5

GIL WATCHED IN silence from the bench as his players practiced taking ground balls. After the afternoon's excitement had worn off, giving up his life at Prairie Ridge didn't seem like such a good idea. He loved watching his players mess around, remembering what it was like to be so carefree. They made him feel young.

"All set for tomorrow?" He felt Peck's massive paw on his shoulder.

"I'm all set for the science fair. Look, I've been thinking since we got back. Yes, I'm flattered the Rockies are seriously looking at me. Yes, I'd love to be on the mound again. Yes, I'd love to be on television and all that stuff, but it's not for me. This whole thing about me being able to pitch like a rocket isn't for real. It can't be. I just want to forget the whole thing and go back to my life. And please don't tell Keri about this silly idea."

"Now you really are crazy. You've *got* to pitch for the Rockies."

Gil shook his head. "No, I've made up my mind. Even if they want me, I'm not going to play. I made my decision nearly two decades ago, and I think it was the right decision . . . I don't need the sound of screaming fans in my ears to fulfill my life."

"That's not how you felt about it yesterday, Gil. Admit it, your life changed the minute you went to that ballpark this afternoon."

"As I recall, you dragged me there on false pretenses."

"No matter. You can't go back. If you tell Connor you're backing out, they are all going to assume you're on the juice. The players will find the film. Trust me. And they'll leak the film to the press, say the replacement players are all a bunch of druggies, and you refusing to take a drug test proves their point. Not to mention what the school district might do. You don't want that."

Gil's jaw muscles tightened. "Don't do this to me. Don't go there."

"I'm not going anywhere." He held up his hands. "If you don't want to play, just say the word. I'll never tell a soul."

Gil pulled down his cap and trotted onto the field. "Hey, Sanders. That's the way to scoop up the ball. Everyone, watch Sanders."

6

GIL'S TEN-YEAR-OLD Ford pickup truck jostled over the cracked driveway as he approached his home, a small three-bedroom ranch with a basement, one that he'd been promising for years to finish. On a teacher's salary and with all the hours spent away at games, plus his weekend gigs with his band, there had been no time or money to do the job right. He imagined what kind of house he could purchase if he landed a contract with the Rockies. He'd get one big enough so that the home theater could hold his entire house.

If tonight were normal, Keri would have dinner already dished out on a plate and covered with foil, a feeble attempt to keep it warm. She'd long given up waiting to eat together. With coaches meetings after practice, it could be dark long before he got home.

He removed the foil and tossed the dried-out chicken breast and baked potato into the microwave, too tired and hungry to care what the plate contained. He'd barely gulped down one bite when Keri slipped into the kitchen. She was already in her pajamas, a loose-fitting T-shirt, and mid-thigh shorts.

From behind, she put her arms around his neck and kissed his cheek. "Long day?"

"Uh huh," he said through another bite.

"So tell me about it," she said, sliding her arms down his square shoulders, pausing as she reached his biceps. "I like this new exercise program you are on. Reminds me of our college days." Keri slipped into the chair beside him, rested her chin on her arm and looked up to him in silence.

"What?" he said, after an uncomfortable silence.

"Nothing, just remembering what it used to be like when you were the star of the team, the big man on campus. Those were fun times."

"Yup."

"You know what's funny, Gil?"

He shrugged and wiped his mouth with the back of his hand.

"All my girlfriends think you are the perfect husband. You know why?"

"Nope, but you're going to tell me anyway."

"Well, it's certainly not because you can read my mind. It's because you are a five-thousand-word husband."

"Now this I've got to hear," he said, shoving his plate back.

"It's because you are a chatterbox. Women need to get in their five thousand words a day, and with you it's easy. Once you get going, there's no stopping you. And on women subjects too—shoes, purses, even laser hair removal. You've got an opinion on everything."

"And that makes me adorable?"

"That, and all that muscle you've recently put on. Yeah, the girls can't wait for the pool to open. The Gaudreys even invited us to Hawaii this summer. He has extra airline miles and hotel points. It would be a free trip."

Gil slipped his eyes down to her bare thighs. She'd had bird legs when they first met. Over the years they had filled in nicely, after the kids got older and she got hooked on running. First a few 5k races, then a 10k. She skipped the half-marathon and went straight to the full. He imagined her in a swimming suit, slathered with oil. Her naturally blonde hair that first caught his gaze at the frat party was now streaked with brown and cut shoulder length. He knew she'd have it pulled back into a ponytail, and she'd be nice and tan. That part would be nice. The neighbors he could do without.

"I think we'll pass. Hawaii sounds good, but not with the Gaudreys," Gil quipped.

"Oh come on, it would be fun," Keri pleaded. Gil shot her a look, shaking his head.

"Okay, I'll drop it," she relented. "So, give me my five-thousand-word fix. Have anything you want to tell me?"

"Crap," Gil muttered. Keri obviously knew. "So, Peck opened his big mouth? He just can't keep a secret."

"Gil Gilbert. Why are you keepin' secrets from me, especially big ones?"

"I was going to tell you, honest. But I needed to know for sure before I said anything."

"So what is going to happen to us? What about the house?"

"New house," he said. "I promise, first thing I will do."

Keri burst out crying. "Gil, that isn't funny. We could lose everything. You know how much lawyers cost?"

Gil immediately recognized his blunder. With all the excitement about the Rockies, he'd completely forgotten about the lawsuit. *Keri was asking about the lawsuit.*

He slipped his arm around her and pulled her body close to his, getting a fresh whiff of her night cream. "I'm sorry," he said, tucking her hair behind her ear. "I should have told you, but I didn't want you to worry about it, or at least I didn't want to deal with it until the fair was over." He reached out and took her hand. "What have you heard?"

"That her family is after big money, and they are using you to get it."

"I honestly don't get it. The kids were just messing around after practice. It was just an unfortunate accident. The object of baseball is to hit the ball. I can't help it if she got too close."

"Well, people are saying that it wasn't just an accident, and that they have some evidence that proves the injury could have been avoided."

"That's news to me."

"They say it is something you don't want in the papers, and that it will force you and the school district to settle before going to trial."

Gil shrugged. "I still have no idea. We were just winding up practice, and I was teaching the guys a few pitches. Not sure how that would be something I was trying to hide. Even then, so what? You know as well as I do that we don't have any money. Why sue me?"

"I called Gaudreys' attorney. He said the school is required to defend you and that the only way they could come after you personally is if you completely disregarded district policies."

"There are no district policies on this kind of stuff. It's all nonsense, and you should stop worrying about it."

"But what if the school district has to pay up? Are you going to get fired?"

"Stuff like this happens. Nobody did anything wrong!"

She leaned forward and kissed him. "I guess you're right. It could be worse. Could be one of those sexual harassment charges that are flying around."

"That's not funny."

She stood up and he pulled her beside him.

"Now what else aren't you telling me?"

He had never lied to her, at least not about anything that mattered, and he didn't want to start now. But his pitching escapade needed to stay a secret until he was sure it was for real, so he changed the subject. "So your friends really want to see me with my shirt off?"

She reached around and pinched him from behind. "You know what I think? I think you are sneaking off and going to the gym. This thing is as hard as a rock." Then she rubbed her hands across his chest. "Your pecks are bigger than mine."

"Just making sure you don't have any incentive to run off with the milkman."

"I just hope you are doing this for me, and not some fling. You would tell me if you start going through some midlife crisis, right? I just read this magazine that says now is the time for most men."

He pulled her tight, feeling her body mold to his. "No chance of that. I'm not that stupid."

That prompted a kiss.

"Go watch *SportsCenter*. I know that's what you want. And don't forget about lunch tomorrow. Wait until you see my idea for this year. I think you are going to like it."

With all that was going on, he had forgotten. It was a tradition between them. On the day of the fair she always came to school for lunch then stayed the rest of the day to oversee decoration of the gym before the students arrived.

"Right," he said. "At noon, just like always."

He found Austin doing homework in front of the TV, watching *SportsCenter* highlights. They were winding down a story about how March Madness was just around the corner, and then went on to a segment on the developments with baseball tryouts. Gil paused, hoping the big media teams, like the Yankees or Giants, would lead the story.

"Hey, Dad," Austin said without looking up.

"I see you're getting a lot of studying done."

"Enough. Hey, did you know someone threw a hundred-and-five pitch today at the Rockies tryouts? Said it was some old guy."

"Didn't hear," Gil said. "How was practice today?"

"Boring. I wish I was a freshman, then you'd be my coach."

"No. Coach Peck runs the freshman team."

"Yeah, but you'd be on the next field."

"You need to get into high school first, so hit the books."

"Okay, but I want you to coach me. You gotta get me ready to play for the Yankees. I'm gonna get a contract for ten million bucks, and then I'm gonna buy you and Mom a new house."

"We don't need a new house, but I'll help you get that big contract, sport. Now hit the books."

7

THE MEDICAL OFFICE of Dr. Michael Chavez was located in a low-rise in the heart of Cherry Creek, near the posh shopping mall and mansions. That's where all the athletes chose to settle down, amid country clubs and quaint boutiques where their wives could spend their money. Chavez was more than just an orthopedic surgeon; he was the first point of contact for any medical issue facing Rockies players. From strep tests to migraines, all the players went to Chavez, the best in the business. The other professional teams used his services as well. Football and hockey injuries kept him busy most of the year. Once you are the official doctor of a sports team, everyone wants you, from weekend warriors with a blown ACL to high school kids with broken limbs. Gil nervously fidgeted in the waiting room, studying the signed jerseys and sports memorabilia, from autographed footballs encased in glass to photos of Denver's most memorable victories. Alone, he could sense the gaze of the receptionist, an obvious patron of the plastic surgeon's services next door, with pouty lips, a petite nose, and an oversized chest— one that even his couldn't compete with.

If all went well, Gil would be back at school by lunch, ready to help out organizing the science fair tables in the gym while

Keri took care of the decorations; then baseball practice, a quick change of clothing, and back to the gym for a final review before the guests arrived. Dinner would happen when he got home.

"Mr. Gilbert?"

Gil looked up, expecting to see an attendant ready to escort him in. Instead, he was greeted by a middle-aged man with a deeply tanned face, devoid of wrinkles. He was wearing a crisply pressed light-blue shirt and a yellow patterned tie. He was holding out his hand.

"I am Dr. Chavez."

Gil shook his hand. "You can call me Gil, everyone else does."

Dr. Chavez escorted him into a small room with a reclining table and stool. "Have a seat," he said, watching as Gil shimmied himself onto the tissue-covered table, then sat himself on the round stool.

"Okay, here are the ground rules. We are both busy men, and there is no need to waste each other's time or the team's money. As a doctor, everything between you and me is confidential, at least for now. Before I begin the examination, I am going to require you to sign a release so that anything I discover, or anything you disclose to me, goes straight to the front office. But for now, it is all off the record. Comprehend?"

"Look, if you think I am on drugs, I can save you a bunch of time."

Dr. Chavez raised his hand. "No need to take offense. I have been in the business a long time. I ask everyone, no exceptions. You could be the NBA MVP and I would still ask. I have been burned too many times."

Gil flashed a warm smile. "Oh, I understand. You should teach high school. The excuses those kids come up with." Gil looked at his watch. "I have nothing to hide. Let's get going. I will sign anything."

"We will start with you reviewing and executing the paperwork. Then, I will do a full physical. After that, the lab work."

"And you can do that here?"

"Yes, the initial urine and blood samples we take here, then send them over to the lab. The results will be in by tomorrow."

"Then I guess I am ready."

Gil was supplied with a mountain of papers—waiver and consent forms that were so hard to decipher he felt like he should have brought an attorney. He pretended to read each page, shuffling through them like he'd seen his own students do when they weren't prepared for a test and were merely going through the motions. Then he signed them all.

Dr. Chavez had him strip down to his underwear, then ran a routine physical, poking him, feeling his prostate and listening to his breathing through a stethoscope, all in silence.

"Have you always been in this good of shape?"

"I try to keep fit, being a coach and all."

"I understand, but you have the physique of a man half your age. To maintain this level of conditioning takes a lot of work."

"Well, I have been a little more intense the last several weeks."

"Like? Be a little more specific."

"Lots of push-ups and sit-ups, and I have been throwing a lot more in practice."

Dr. Chavez frowned. "Tell me about how you are feeling. Any changes in health, illnesses, do your bowels move every day?"

"I'm good, really."

Dr. Chavez ripped off his stethoscope. "Gil, you need to understand something—you and I are on the same team here. I'm not the enemy."

"I understand, but I am not hiding anything, even if you do control my destiny."

"That I do, but believe me, with the strike and the Rockies' desperate need for a starting rotation, I would love to do anything to help them. You see, you have got to give me something to work with here. I can't go back to Connor without some kind of explanation on how you out of the blue start throwing a baseball faster than anyone on the planet. I've seen the film maybe fifty times. Your mechanics are solid, but I am here to tell you as a sports doctor that the human arm was not made to throw that fast. With the kinds of forces you are generating, bones snap and tendons tear. If you aren't doing drugs, then what on God's planet is going on inside of your body?"

Gil slumped his shoulders. "Honestly?"

"I've got to know the truth. Otherwise, I can't let you within five hundred miles of training camp. When the press hears about a guy throwing close to one-ten, they are going to swarm here like flies on crap, and we've got to have something to tell them. And if it isn't drugs, then we'd better have a darn good story . . . I need the truth."

"The truth is that I have no clue what is happening to me."

Dr. Chavez grabbed a writing pad and slipped a pen out of his shirt pocket. "Continue."

"Four or five months ago, I started noticing changes; I started to gain muscle all over." Gil gestured with his hands as he spoke, making curvy lines all over his body. "You know, like when old people start growing hair in unwanted places? But for me it was muscles. It was weird. I've stepped up my push-up and sit-up routine, run a little more and things like that, but that's all. I am baffled, and frankly, a little bit scared. There is no way I can tell Keri."

"Your wife? I can't believe she hasn't noticed."

"Oh, she's noticed, her and half the women in the neighborhood. My wife thinks I have been hanging out in the gym, some sort of mid-life crisis, but that's not true. I can't explain it. Frankly, one of the reasons I agreed to meet you was because I need some answers."

"Tell me anything out of the ordinary, besides the muscle growth."

"There's not much to tell. Maybe a little tightness in the chest, but nothing a normal body wouldn't experience. Feels kind of like the day after a good bench workout. You know, a good kind of stiff, something you would expect. And I probably eat a little more, but I just figured that my appetite tracked my running."

Gil searched the walls for a clock, but realized that doctors never put clocks where patients can see them. He checked his watch. It was almost eleven thirty. If he left now, he would barely make lunch. When he looked up, Dr. Chavez had placed his notepad next to the sink and had crossed his legs. "You've looked at your watch a dozen times."

"Busy day today. I run a science fair. Tonight is the grand finale, parents come, the press send a few notables, and we award some great scholarships."

Dr. Chavez nodded at his file. "I ran a Google search on you.

Didn't realize how popular your science classes were. Lots of local coverage on the science fair."

"I enjoy it, most of the time. Teenagers in America these days are falling behind the rest of the world in math and science. Whatever I can do to help."

"I am going to need to do a CT scan, and I don't have that in my office. Can I get you to run down to the medical center?"

"Right now?"

"I am afraid so. The start of the preseason is just around the corner, and the starting rotation has some gaping holes. The Rockies need to make a decision by tomorrow.

"Before you go, I do have one more matter of business. Go ahead and sit down. I need to know why you want to be a major league pitcher. Are you really ready to turn your life upside down, because, if they sign you, *everything* will change.

"Your life as a teacher and high school coach will be over. You'll be on the road, living in hotels, hanging out with players half your age, most of whom think life owes them a living. There will be temptations, lots of women. And the pressure—the media will uncover every stone, find every skeleton. You think I am hard on you, or that Connor is in your face, just you wait. There will be cries for drug tests before and after every inning you pitch. They'll want a private investigator following you around twenty-four-seven, picking your turds out of the toilet to see what in your system is making you pitch so fast. Think of it. You can't even take a crap in peace. And this is all off the field. Wait until your own fans start booing you, or the catcalls you will get in New York. Can you emotionally handle the life of a big leaguer? Can you keep it together while pitching with the bases loaded, with Connor telling you that you are off the team unless you can pitch yourself out of the inning? Can your wife handle the tabloids? What is she going to do the first time a woman claims she is carrying your baby?"

Gil rubbed his whiskers. He knew about all of this—and it was precisely what ended his baseball career before it began.

Amid all the confusion swirling in his mind, Gil knew Peck was right. He couldn't turn back now. For some unexplained reason, a door had opened. This was his chance; his chance to take back what he'd given up two decades ago. Yes, he'd be giving up his life of safety, but this was his dream. It would be a sacrifice, but with a huge reward. He would realize a dream—his dream on his terms.

Gil's mind swung between good and bad like a playground swing. What if I wash out at spring training, or throw out my arm like Peck? I'd be out of a job. I wouldn't be there to coach Austin.

Gil inhaled deeply and looked the doctor in the eye. "You tell Connor that if the Rockies pick me, I'll give him everything I've got."

"I will have all the data later today, tomorrow at the latest. I'll call you as soon as I get the results . . . Hope you're ready for this, Mr. Gilbert.

8

THE MANAGER AND his pitching coach rested their forearms on the dugout railing, their skin pocked with sunspots and deep wrinkles—coaches' battle scars. Following two weeks of snow, the temperatures shot up into the mid-seventies, and the sun's rays felt good on the old men's stiff joints.

"I am sure going to miss this," Ratcliff said, adjusting his cap.

"Me too."

They watched as DeJesus and Melendez jogged their warm-up lap.

Tajima, who had trouble speaking English instead of Japanese, was their closer, and trailed behind. A last-minute recruit, he'd never played in America. Everything about Tajima revolved around his mother country, except his diet of hamburgers and fries and his size. No sushi for this six-foot-four-inch giant who looked as skinny as Old Abe. He thrived on calories and intensity.

Juarez leaned over to massage his right knee, which was the reason he retired the previous year. He blew out the cartilage and tore tendons. He was healed now, but his speed was gone and fielding tentative. The Rockies hired him for right field mostly because he could still crank the ball into the bleachers and because he'd help fill the seats, maybe. "What a cryin' shame," Ratcliff said of Juarez. "The kid could have been a Hall of Famer if he stayed healthy. After the strike ends he'll never play again in the Bigs."

It was the last day of spring practice before the team headed to Arizona. A few hundred fans showed up to hear the team announce its roster and to cheer the one guy who really was a big league player.

Slider. Slider. Slider.

"Should be calling him Mamma's boy," Ratcliff mumbled under his breath. Ratcliff panned the few spectators in the sparsely occupied bleachers, filled mostly with reporters scouting out this year's teams. Right on the front row, struggling to contain herself, was Mamma Slider, or Mrs. Treyz, Slider's mother. Ratcliff wondered how much of Slider's paycheck went to flying her around the country when he was on the road. Ratcliff recruited Slider straight out of high school, after he promised Ms. Treyz that she could attend every practice. Slider's biological father was out of the picture the day after Slider's conception. That is, until Slider's second year in the league, when he suddenly reappeared. Slider wanted nothing to do with him.

Slider was Ratcliff's best find, a diamond in the rough that could end up breaking half a dozen major league records, including most hits and stolen bases. The kid was fast, an aggressive base runner, and he could hit. He built his reputation by sliding into the bases, head first, the way the great Cincinnati Red Pete Rose had done. In his first year, Slider batted a whopping .386, had 223 hits and stole 66 bases, including home twice. If he kept healthy, kept his nose clean, and stayed focused, he could be a legend. Ratcliff knew it, the fans knew it, and most important, Slider knew it. He already had an attitude and had been less than gracious to fans.

"I play ball, not raise kids," he said one day after refusing to sign autographs for a group of VIP children, all cancer survivors.

The most levelheaded and experienced in Ratcliff's makeshift lineup was Timber Johnson, the veteran catcher and general advice giver. He had retired after nearly a twenty-year career in baseball. When it became apparent that the Rockies needed to field a new team, Ratcliff begged Johnson to come back, at least for a month until they could get the strike settled. Johnson agreed, but only because he'd poorly invested his retirement and needed more of a nest egg. And even if he wouldn't admit it, he missed being part of the game. He followed his teammates in tow, warming up his large, muscular thighs. He had nothing to prove.

"Good old Johnson," Connor said. "Whatever happened to guys like him who came out every day, worked hard, got along with teammates, and stayed out of trouble?"

Ratcliff shrugged.

Johnson, who everyone called The Preacher, or just Preacher, hefted his bulky frame fully upright, still sucking in air from the wind sprint.

"I hope to God he doesn't have a heart attack on us," Connor quipped. "I'm getting too old for this. I'm sarcastic, politically incorrect, and will probably do something to get me thrown out on the street. You should just let me go before I say something stupid and get us all sued."

"Can't do that," Ratcliff said. "Who would I find to replace you? You're the only one I know who will work for free."

"You know how many hungry MBA types would kill to be part of this organization? They'd pull out their computers and run numbers until the cows come home—and would do it for free. We get a handful of resumés every day."

"I don't need a number cruncher. I already rely on them too much. What I need is someone who can manage with his gut, tell me inside of here what I should be doing, when to pull the pitcher, when to hit and run, that kind of stuff. Besides, it's nice to have another old-timer around. The world may have changed and passed us both by, but the game doesn't. Never will. Baseball will always be baseball. Keep wood for the bats, horsehide for balls, and cups to protect the jewels. As long as the distance from the mound to the plate is sixty-five and you have to run ninety between bases, life will be okay."

"And, they don't blow up Fenway," Connor said.

"Right. And they don't blow up Fenway. The day the Green Monster goes, we all go."

Preacher led the rest of the outfield, including Gonzalez, the center fielder rookie they had just obtained from Cal State

Fullerton. Decent bat, worked hard, rifle of an arm, and didn't mind getting advice from Juarez. Boclin, the only Brazilian in the majors, was slated to play left field. He'd been in the States for just under a year, desperately hoping for a career in baseball. After every at bat, Ratcliff swore he was going to cut him. But he never did. He knew he couldn't find anyone better—and he was always good for drawing in a few South American fans to the games.

Besides Johnson and Juarez, the only other player with any real experience was Biondi, who'd been camped at first base for almost a decade. Like Juarez, Biondi had retired the year before, but had come begging for a spot on the roster after he'd discovered his accountant had embezzled his retirement. Ratcliff was only too happy to take him back. His speed was still respectable, but he too could stand to lose a few pounds. In the past two weeks, they had picked up a new second baseman and shortstop. They got Trudeau for a steal from the New York Yankees, which had dumped him at the end of the season when his contract was up. With the strike looming, no team wanted to take a chance on the aging player with a high salary. That all changed with the strike. The Rockies landed Manzi from the White Sox when he was let go after a career-ending sexual scandal in Minneapolis—and after learning the DA's office wasn't going to prosecute. Ratcliff was confident the change of scenery in the Rocky Mountains would pull Trudeau out of his slump and keep Manzi's nose clean, or at least his zipper up.

Ratcliff and Connor watched as his players tossed a few balls, loosening their throwing arms.

"A bunch of misfits," Connors huffed. "Wannabes. Broken-down old men. Gimps, hotheads, criminals, and a mamma's boy."

"I'll be glad when tonight's over," Ratcliff said. "We need to fill our final spot and get down to Arizona."

"What's the story with that miracle man, Gil?" Connor asked. "He for real? Or did doc find out he's juicing?"

"The preliminary test all came back clean, and trust me, we ran everything. Scoured his urine, tore apart his every red and white blood cell, even took a tissue sample. All clean. But the whole thing is weird as hell. How can some middle-age guy suddenly start throwing like that?"

"Think he's on something undetectable?"

"He didn't strike me that way, but you never know these days. Still, the tests all came back negative. Chavez wants him to see a specialist, but says from a liability point of view we are okay to bring him on."

"A specialist?"

"He said we don't need to worry about getting blindsided. He is more interested in seeing if he can find a reason for this guy's strength. Maybe be wants to do some genetic testing. The guy's a freak."

"So what are you thinking?" Connor asked.

"I'm thinking we've got a pathetic pitching staff, our attendance is as low as it's ever been, and now I've got a guy to fill some seats. I really don't care if this Gil guy is some kinda mutant . . . and I certainly don't want to know. Ignorance can be bliss. We'll just put a clause in his contract that if he can't pitch, he's out. And if we find he's on drugs, gone. Not much different than how we treat all the other players."

"So I guess we have nothing to lose. Float him a few hundred grand for the season. Even if he washes out, it wouldn't matter. We spend more than that on players we don't even want."

"Good point."

9

KERI ARRIVED A few minutes before noon. She liked being early, as much as being neat and tidy. It was a way to control her life. It was fine if Gil's life pulled him from baseball field to Saturday night gigs, but she preferred routine: morning exercise, get Austin off to school, pick up around the house, take care of a few bills, run some errands, wait for Austin to come home, and then deal with Gil. She could be spontaneous and strike up a conversation with anyone about anything. Teenagers loved her, especially Gil's players. She was outgoing, seemed cool, and she was hot, especially for a middle-age mom. She had been a cheerleader in high school, a social butterfly, and in her mind nothing had changed since then. Her arms were still toned, she bore no wrinkles, and she could still do a string of backflips.

Keri's social calendar only got busier when she attended ASU. Her first two years she majored in boys, dating, hanging out, and barely scraping by in classes. At the beginning of sophomore year, she had to declare a major and picked business, but it could just have easily been political science or art history.

She checked her watch. Five minutes past noon. *Gil's late again,* she thought. He always had his reasons: a student needing help with homework, a problem with his lineup, a gig that went late. A group of about ten girls were huddled about the first table, shoving fries into their mouths while gossiping. She tapped out a quick text to Gil: *I'll be at one of the tables.*

"Let me guess." She turned to the familiar sound of Peck's deep voice. "Stood you up again?"

"I'm afraid so. You know Gil."

"I'm sure he's got a good excuse. Mind if I have lunch with you?"

"Sure, I could use the company."

They stood in line, amused by the latest trends in teenage fashion and how most kids tapped out messages on their smartphones, never bothering to speak an actual sentence.

"You sure you don't want to eat with the faculty?"

"No, this is great. I love being with the students. Keeps me young."

Keri picked out a chef's salad when they reached the food stand, some iceberg lettuce with a chopped egg and some bacon bits on top. It came with a side of salmon-colored Thousand Island dressing. Some things never change.

Peck snatched up a hamburger, slopped on some onions and ketchup, and tailed behind Keri as she made her way to the far corner of the cafeteria, where there were still a few open tables. She'd always had a soft spot for Peck. Like Gil, his baseball career had been cut short. But unlike Gil, who had planned for a future outside of baseball, Peck had never considered that he wouldn't always be playing ball. Peck had eked out enough credits at ASU to get a degree in psychology but in that field you needed to go for a doctorate. His undergraduate degree was essentially useless if he wanted to be a serious counselor.

Gil had managed to get him on at Prairie, mostly because Gil was desperate for a good assistant coach and Peck was willing to take the job with a meager salary. Peck taught physical education his first three years and morphed into an armchair psychologist to friends.

"I'm worried about Gil," Keri confided. Peck raised his bushy eyebrows.

"Anything in particular?"

"All the stress about this lawsuit." Keri shook her head. "He's never faced anything like this."

"I guess the stress is getting to him a little," Peck said. "Like a few days ago, I caught him pitching balls against the backstop like the world was coming to an end. Nearly tore the leather off those balls. Tell you what, that man can throw. If I could pitch like that, I certainly wouldn't be here."

"He was throwing baseballs? Against a backstop?"

"Yeah, really throwing them."

"And you didn't think that was strange?"

Peck slid his coffee cup back and forth. "Yes and no. Like you said, he's under a lot of stress. Better those baseballs than you. A man's got to work off steam somehow."

"So has Gil been working off a lot of steam lately? His middle-age tire is suddenly gone. He looks like a Roman statue. He never liked working out before. Is he trying to impress someone?" She regretted the question immediately. She'd never suspected Gil of infidelity, and she didn't want to imply as much to Peck.

"You're not complaining, I mean, about his body?"

"Not at all, just a little concerned. I know what it takes to look like that. If he's not working out three hours a day, then the only way . . . "

"No, Gil's not popping pills if that's what you think."

"Forget I said anything. I know Gil better than anyone. You're right. That's not Gil. But he is stressed out about the lawsuit," Keri said. "I was waiting until after the fair to bring it up. He can't deal with anything else right now."

"Okay then, let's talk about how you are feeling," said Peck.

"Changing the subject on me. Playing Dr. Psych again?"

"Just being a good friend. If Gil's too busy to ask, I certainly can. Tell me about your life. Alicia's away at school, and it's got to be hard with her away. You spend twenty years dedicated to the kid, then all of the sudden she's gone and you have all this free time. Thought of what's ahead? Go back to school, pick up an advanced degree, do some travel?"

"You forget. I still have Austin."

"Fair enough, but after that? I mean most women look to something else when the kids leave. You went to college. Don't you want a career?"

"I used to, but Alicia changed all that."

"But now she's gone."

"I don't know. I can work that all out when Austin is finished with high school. For now, I enjoy my volunteer work."

"But wait. You said before you had Alicia you had a career planned. If that's what you want, why not go for it?"

"I'm not sure. When you're young, you think lots of things."

"But Alicia wasn't planned."

She didn't know whether she should reach over and slap him across the face or just stand up and walk out. But she knew his brashness. He was going to work her over until he felt he'd uncovered every part of her soul. "Not exactly. Did Gil tell you?"

"I did the math."

"Probing, aren't you? You're not going to give up until I tell you. If you think I was abused or rebelling from my parents, it wasn't anything like that."

"Really? That's where I think you are wrong. Everybody runs from something."

"Not me. I was a normal college kid coming from a normal family, if there is such a thing. Probably drank a little too much and slept through a few too many classes . . . and did a few things during spring break that hopefully my kids will never hear about."

"And that's why you exercise two hours a day, sporting a leaner figure than any girl here? You can't tell me there's nothing behind all that." Peck held up both hands. "Not jumping to any conclusions, but sounds like you're being defensive."

"Look, I don't have any skeletons in my closet. I exercise for the fun of it."

"Don't regret giving up your youth?"

"Come on, Peck. You're not still talking about Alicia."

"No, but since you brought it up, here's what I think: You were loving college, being a normal, fun-loving coed, but then Gil came along, and you had a night of passion and got pregnant. And that was the end of your carefree life. You had to grow up and be responsible, and your running is your attempt to recapture what you gave up."

"You know, Peck, I think you're about the only person who could get away with a mouth like that. I don't know how Gil puts up with you."

Peck shrugged. "What did your parents think?"

Keri slapped down her fork and a boy with freckles and a mouth full of silver braces shot them a glance. "You don't give up, do you?"

"That's what friends are for."

"Okay, if you really want to know what happened, Mom cried and Dad was upset, but they came around, especially after they met Gil. Nothing like how Gil's father reacted. Anyway, over time, they saw it was the best thing that ever happened. Mom is very close to Alicia, and Gil is a great father. Sometimes things just seem to work out for the best, even if we do slip up."

"I can't argue with that. Tonight might work out for some lucky baseball players. With the baseball strike, all kinds of retired players are being called back. And tonight the fans get to vote on the player they want to be part of the team."

"I know. Austin's been talking about it for days. He's refusing to come to the fair tonight so he can watch."

Peck's eyebrows lifted. "It could be an interesting evening."

10

IT WAS NEARLY three o'clock by the time Gil rushed into the gymnasium, weaving his way around the empty tables in search of Keri. He'd be a little late for warm-ups with the team, but he needed to apologize for missing his date. What he was going to tell her? Gil found Keri on a ladder tacking up letters on the back wall. The place looked impressive. She always poured herself into the job of decorating for the science fair.

"Sorry I'm late," Gil called out.

"You're more than late," she said curtly, wanting him to know she was not pleased. "You sure you have time for this—for us? I mean, you are a very busy man from what I hear," she sniped. "But don't worry, Peck covered for you. He took me to lunch."

Gil knew it was never good when Peck and Keri talked because he would tell her everything. There were simply no secrets with Peck when it came to Keri.

Keri descended the ladder, gave her husband a whimsical look and then a hug.

"What am I going to do with you?" she asked rhetorically. "I've got to talk to Peck to find out what's going on with *my* husband." She lifted her arms up and rested them on his shoulders, feeling the tenseness of his muscles. She squeezed them, moving her hands up his sloping neck.

"You're awfully tight," she said as she squeezed his deltoids. "You okay? Anything you want to unload from the shoulders?"

He hesitated just for an instant. "That's what I wanted to talk to you about. I missed our lunch date because I went to see a doctor—like you've been asking me."

"And?" She kept her iron clasp. "Now you really have me worried."

"That's what I was afraid of. Don't worry about me. It was nothing, just a routine checkup."

"And they gave you a clean bill of health? Did you ask them about your sudden weight gain?"

"The doctor didn't seem too concerned. He said to take it easy, lay off the weights for a bit and stuff like that. Look, I'm late for practice. Can we talk about this tonight?"

"Of course. Practice. But we're going to talk tonight, no matter what time you get home."

She let her arms fall and stepped back.

"Deal," he said, scanning the alternating white and black tablecloths. "And I love the decorations."

Gil spun around and with long strides headed for the locker room. He stuffed his hand in his coat pocket, searching for his phone and any messages from Peck. Then he tried the other pocket, finally shoving his hands into both of his jeans pockets.

He'd left it with Dr. Chavez on the exam table.

11

THE GYMNASIUM BUZZED with excitement. Groups of students were intentionally distanced from their parents, speculating on whose idea was best and who would take home first prize, including the $2,500 scholarship. Some of the students were occupied with more interesting discussions, like what they would be doing after the night's festivities. Text messages were flying through the air, with students' eyes fixated on their smartphones, not wanting to be left out.

Gil snatched up the final tallies from the judges' table and bounded to the podium, erected on a set of risers.

"Okay, let's get this show rolling. Welcome, everyone, students, all the parents who helped their students, and of course, this year's judges." Gil introduced the panel—scientists and engineers ranging from an aircraft engine designer to a nuclear physicist from a local government energy department.

"We have a busy night, so let's jump right in. As you all know from the colorful decorations put up by my wife, Keri, this year's theme is opposites. I wanted the students to learn that almost everything in nature is driven by opposites. In fact, you cannot generate power without them. So my challenge to you was to find some opposites in the natural world and demonstrate how you can use those opposing forces to create power. And, I have to admit, you all came up with some pretty creative ways."

Gil slipped the microphone from its holder and began winding his way through the tables of exhibits. "Did I say everything in nature uses opposites to create power? Some of you look skeptical. Now, if you don't believe me, pick any pair of opposites and I'll show you: hot and cold; fast and slow; hard and soft." Gil paused and held his finger to his ear. "Let's hear a few more."

That was all it took. "Wet and dry," one said. "Heavy and light," came another. Then, a high-pitched voice screamed out, "Heaven and Hell." The audience erupted in laughter and the freckled-faced boy buried his head in his mother's lap.

"Yes, that too is an opposite, I suppose, but as a physics teacher, I am here to teach about the world around us. What I want the students to understand is that the harnessing of opposites drives our modern world, even though the principles have been in use for a long time.

"Take, for example, Kelly's example of the waterwheel. It's all about taking advantage of the law of gravity using high and low. Flowing water falls into the buckets of the wheel, causing the wheel to turn as the water moves to a lower elevation. These contraptions were used all over America to grind grain or run machines. Even a small stream has the ability to generate tremendous power."

A small commotion stirred through the audience and Gil paused, squinting in the bright lights. More than half his students were busy hacking away at their phones. "Okay, guys, a lot of work has gone into tonight's activities. Let's put away the phones before I have your parents come get them." The phones slipped into pockets and purses, but the hushed rumble of voices didn't cease.

"So with that, let's get down to business. The envelope please."

Gil held out his hand and a petite freshman, wearing a lime-green sundress, popped out of her chair and bounded up to the podium with her ponytail bobbing with each step.

"Thanks, Tina," he said.

She slipped back into her chair while Gil broke the seal.

"Taking third place—and landing a five hundred dollar scholarship to his school of choice—is Tommy Krishna with his project that he calls 'Opposites Attract.' Tommy, why don't you come up here and explain?"

A lanky Indian boy half-skipped to the front of the room and grabbed the microphone, and, out of breath, began speaking so fast it was hard to follow.

"Okay, my idea is really simple. I use a magnet to generate electricity. The magnet has two ends with opposite poles that attract each other, creating a magnetic field between them. Just move a wire through this magnetic field and you get electricity." As he spoke he shuffled over to his exhibit and quickly grasped a long magnet in the shape of a Snickers bar. He then took a copper wire that was coiled about an empty roll of toilet paper. The wire coil formed an electrical circuit that included a small lightbulb. As Tommy slid the magnet back and forth within the tube, the light flickered, causing a few *ahhhs* to float up from the audience, followed by polite applause.

Gil stepped forward. "Great presentation, Tommy. How about a round of applause for Tommy?"

"I think we are ready for the next winner."

"This year's runner-up, which comes with a one thousand dollar college scholarship, is Jonathan for his demonstration of 'Fast and Slow.' Jonathan, please come up and explain how we can fly."

The large boy lumbered to the front of the gymnasium. He fumbled through his explanation of how the faster moving air over the curved airplane wing forced it to rise. Gil thanked him and sorted through his papers, looking for the envelope containing the next award.

Before Gil could resume, the sound of heavy metal music interrupted the stilled silence, causing heads to readjust and find the culprit who forgot to turn off his ringer.

Peck, slumped down in the second to last row, head bowed into his folded arms, jerked awake and spastically fumbled in search of his phone. He yanked it out of his front pocket, looked at who was calling, then jumped out of his chair and bolted for the back of the gymnasium, nearly knocking over the table displaying the water wheel project.

Amid the laughter Gil could still hear Peck's bellowing hello. "Yes, sir. Of course he's here. Let me get him."

Peck held up the phone, wildly waving his arms. Then he began waltzing past the tables waving his cell phone as if he were encouraging a rock band to perform an encore. Gil paused in a useless attempt to stop the childish antics of his assistant coach. Peck handed Gil his phone, put his hand over Gil's microphone, and leaned over toward Gil's ear.

"Sorry about this, Gil, but it's Ratcliff."

A TV reporter covering the science fair moved forward, followed by his cameraman and two assistants.

News about the mysterious over-forty man firing pitches at over 100 miles an hour had buzzed around the Rockies organization. One of the station's sports reporters was tipped off to the identity of the man behind the myth. That was the real reason the news team was at the science fair with a full crew. They wanted to be there live when the offer came in.

Gil could see heads swiveling between him and the camera, and the sounds of hushed whispers. He noticed Keri out of the corner of his eye, pushing her arms forward, leaning forward to hear what this was all about.

He pried Peck's hand off the microphone. "Just a minute, folks. Looks like one of our sponsors is going to chip in a little bit extra for an honorable mention award. Aren't they, Mr. Peck? If you'll excuse me for just a minute, Mr. Peck will give the award and I will be right back."

Gil slid the phone from Peck's hand and replaced it with the microphone. "Good luck, MC."

"Wait," Peck said. "I need a little bit more to go on."

"It's her lemon project—where she turns a lemon into a battery to make electricity. Rich and poor, you know, for electrons."

The gym door had barely closed when Gil answered, followed by the camera crew.

"This is Gil," he said.

"How bad do you want to play for the Rockies?"

Gil paused, wondering if this is really what he wanted. This was his chance . . . finally. "Who wouldn't?"

"Good, because we want to make you a Colorado Rockie. What do you say, Gil?"

"But I thought the fans were voting, and tonight you were announcing the winner. I can't keep my students off their phones."

"Yes, all true, but there are plenty of other open spots on our roster, and one of them is perfect for you."

Gil squeezed his eyes tight and tried to gather his thoughts. "You guys are *serious*?"

This had once been his dream, and the dream of nearly every boy in America—one he'd given up on two decades ago. Now this freak of nature had put it within his grasp. He felt like he was in college again, when Keri used to lie in his lap, and together he'd tell her about his dreams of making it big.

Keri. He still hadn't told her. Gil noticed the camera lens zoomed directly at him, the microphone poised. It was live television. He didn't have a choice. Ratcliff needed an answer.

Then there were his kids to consider. Austin would be ecstatic. He was oblivious to protocol. But Alicia would realize his faux pas. He paused and breathed out deeply.

"Of course, I'm ready to go," Gil said. "But can you give me just a few minutes? I'm right in the middle of announcing the winner of our science fair."

The line went silent. Gil could only imagine what Ratcliff was thinking. *The Rockies are giving him an offer to play with them, and Gil wants to think about it.*

"Sure, sure, but make it quick. We've got to move out tomorrow morning."

Peck breathed heavily into the microphone as he nervously paced back and forth. The audience seemed to share the awkwardness.

"You know, it's really hard to get mad at Gil," he blurted into the microphone. Several in the audience began clapping. "Alright, I'll let you in on the secret. Or maybe it's not a secret. Gil tried out for the Rockies. The reason why Gil had to step out on us is because—" he paused, "This is going to be Gil's last science fair with us." A few began clapping, and Peck held up his hand. "No, wait. Let's all give him a standing ovation when he returns."

Before the listeners could react, Gil emerged from the shadows into the bright lights of the gymnasium. Keri had both hands over her mouth, her eyes wide open. But nobody noticed.

One clap started, then another, then the whole crowd erupted in applause. He half-sprinted past the exhibits and snatched up the microphone.

Gil wanted to get eye contact with Keri, but he could feel his chest swelling and he needed to keep his composure.

A few in the audience started chanting *Rockies, Rockies, Rockies...*

"Sorry for the interruption folks," Gil called out. "Some pressing personal business."

The crowd laughed and the chants started again . . . *Rockies.*

"Sorry, everyone, but this isn't Coors Field. We're here today for the kids and the science fair, so let's forget about baseball for the moment and continue to honor these great kids."

The crowd hushed. Peck turned red and rubbed his face. Keri, in disbelief, quickly strode out of the gymnasium.

Gil gestured Peck with his hand. "Take over for me, would you?"

"Sure, go ahead. Looks like you have some explaining to do," Peck said softly as Gil handed over the microphone.

"You didn't help matters any," Gil said in a surly tone to his assistant. "Tambry's steam engine is the winner—for hot and cold. And don't forget to announce that my father's church is sponsoring the cash award."

"Okay, folks, I'm going to take it from here. Gil is, understandably, distracted."

Everyone laughed and pointed as Gil exited the gym, winding his way through the science projects in an attempt to reach the back of the room so that he could explain himself. If he was lucky, he could make it to the parking lot and intercept Keri before she left.

Once he reached the hallway he took off at a full sprint, his leather shoes sliding on the polished floors. Although the days were getting longer, the sun had now set, leaving the parking lot dark except for a few safety lights. Gil quickly scanned the rows of parked cars, frantically searching for Keri's SUV. He caught a glimpse of Keri's taillights and heard tires screeching.

Gil reached into his front pocket for his cell phone. The one he fished out was Peck's; his was still at the doctor's office. He pressed the "on" button, hoping Keri would take his call.

Suddenly, a voice sounded from behind Gil.

"I've been trying to find you."

Gil turned to find his father, breathing heavily from scampering across the parking lot. "What in heaven's name went on in there? Is that really true, about an offer from the Rockies?"

Gil sighed. He didn't have time to explain this, and even if he did, his father wouldn't believe it.

"Well, out with it," his father insisted.

"I'm not sure I can explain it. For some reason, I just started pitching fast—really fast."

"How fast is really fast?"

"Like over a hundred fast." Gil explained the events of the last week while his father intently listened with eyes as wide as saucers.

"This can only be a sign from God that you are forgiven for your past indiscretions," Pastor Ron said when Gil was finished. "This is your second chance to pitch for God. You've got to accept. You need to call them back right now and accept."

He didn't want to go there with his father.

"I need Keri's blessing, and she's really upset right now. Besides, I'm not sure I want to give up my life. I love my job."

"No, you've got to call back and accept the offer. The hand of God is in this. Can't you see? This is not Keri's decision; it's a calling from God. She won't ruin this one again."

Pastor Ron reached out and slipped the phone from Gil's grasp then tapped the screen twice.

"Go ahead, son. Make the call. The secret is out and everyone knows the Rockies are waiting to hear from you." In his most authoritative voice he urged Gil, "Make the call, son."

Gil stared at the phone. Pastor Ron had Ratcliff's number already illuminated on the display screen. "Call him," he insisted.

Gil looked up to the starlit sky, closed his eyes, and pressed the button.

12

ALL THE LIGHTS in the house were off, even the kitchen light, which Keri always kept on when Gil came home late.

He headed straight for the bedroom, feeling his way down the darkened hallway. The kids' doors were shut, and so was his. Keri never closed their bedroom door, and Gil paused before turning the handle. What was he going to say? She'd given him the chance to come clean when she'd raised the issue of the lawsuit, another little detail he'd kept hidden. Now this. There was nothing he could do but face the firing squad.

The streetlight slipping through the window curtain afforded just enough light to make out a lumpy figure beneath the down comforter. Gil made his way to the bed and gently sat on the edge of the mattress. In the dim light he could see the covers tucked underneath Keri's chin. Her eyes were closed, but the shadows only left to his imagination how swollen they would be after hours of crying.

"I'm sorry, Keri," he whispered.

Her still figure didn't stir. She couldn't possibly be asleep. This wasn't a case of giving him the silent treatment. The youthful days of game playing, like withholding sex as a weapon when she was angry, were long over. No, she was genuinely hurt—beyond words.

"I don't have any excuses, I should have told you. I'm sorry. Please talk to me."

He stood over her, afraid to touch her for fear it could make things worse.

Gil heard the rustling of the sheets and Keri's nearly hoarse voice. "I'm scared," he thought he heard her say. Not angry, not upset, not disappointed. *Scared.*

He crouched next to her face. It was hot and wet, dripping with sweat. He pulled down the covers, noticing her wrinkled skirt intertwined between her legs. She was mourning.

"Did you say that you were scared?"

Keri's eyes opened. "What if I ever lost you, Gil? You can't leave me alone." He could feel her slim frame shaking under the covers.

"What, like going to prison?"

His attempted humor failed. "Knock it off, Gil. You know what I'm talking about. I knew something weird was going on with you. You don't just lose your tire and put on a chest like that. Everyone has been talking. People say you're taking steroids, or drugs, or something . . . Do you have a girlfriend Gil? Do you?"

He rubbed his finger under her eye, wiping a fresh tear.

"What kind of nonsense is this?" He studied her eyes. "Keri, come on. Why would you think something like that? There are no drugs and no girlfriend. Peck made me try out, I swear. He told me we were going to see a lawyer about the lawsuit but took me to the Rockies tryout. He knows somebody there. I don't know why I went along with it, but I did. And now they want me. Can you believe it? They want *me* as a big league pitcher!"

"You're forty-four, Gil. No normal man can pitch at your age. If anyone knows your body it's me, and suddenly, you're not normal. Every muscle is rock hard, like you're some kind of cartoon superhero. Things like this just don't happen by chance. There is something medically going on with you."

He leaned over and kissed her cheek. "I'm fine, just a jerk for not telling you."

She scooted up, twisted her body, and instantly his face was burning with the slap of her hand. "Yes, you are. Now tell me what on God's planet is going on. And why am I always the last to find out? Mr. Chatterbox to everyone but his own wife!"

Gil rubbed his stinging skin and breathed deeply. He focused his gaze on the whites of her eyes.

"The truth is that I was going to tell you, but Peck ruined it. I wanted to surprise you." He stopped and shook his head. Her eyes had turned away. "Okay, the truth." He gently put his hand underneath her chin and turned her head. "The truth is that I was afraid to tell you."

"Afraid? Gil Gilbert afraid of confiding in me?"

Gil dropped his head. "I just thought you wouldn't want me to pitch." He regretted saying this as soon as the phrase left his lips. He knew it was a lie.

"And why in the world would I try to stop you?"

Gil kept his eyes lowered. He couldn't look at her. "Before, when I had the chance and you were pregnant ..."

"That's a lie and you know it. I begged you to keep playing." She bolted upright and pushed herself away from him. "I told you I'd have gone to Egypt with you if that's what it took."

Gil bit his lip. "I'm sorry." He paused. "I didn't play before because I was afraid I wouldn't make it."

"Stop it. You have never been afraid of baseball. You are the definition of confidence. You'd have played in a heartbeat if it weren't for your father. That's the real issue that you've never dealt with. Your whole life you've cowered to him, been his little boy. You didn't play because you couldn't stand up to him. You were his little poster boy for the cause of God. But then the golden child gets his girlfriend pregnant, and the mighty man of God says your baseball career is over. You couldn't stand up to him. That's why you didn't play."

But *she* had stood up to the pastor, although it took her a year to take him on. She'd told him that even if he couldn't accept her as his daughter-in-law, she would still consider him family but that she could never forgive him for insisting that Gil give up his dream just because he didn't fit the Christian mold.

Gil momentarily cupped his hands over his ears.

"You need to hear this," she continued. "He said you were like Esau when he sold his birthright. He was the one that told you to do the honorable thing, to give his wife stability, a steady income, a secure job."

Gil closed his eyes, squeezed them tight. "I'm sorry you have a loser husband."

She put her arm around him. "How can you say that, Gil? Yes, you need to stand up to your father, but look at all you've accomplished. You're always voted the favorite teacher, and your coaching record can't be touched."

"And that's another issue. During the fair, I realized how much I like my life. I'm not sure I can just walk away from all I have worked for. I mean I really love those kids. I finally get my big break, right out of the blue, and now I am waffling. Maybe I don't want to quit my job. Maybe I could be perfectly fulfilled without ever throwing a pitch in Coors Field."

"Well, as long as your health is okay, I think you should play. I'm just embarrassed I didn't know. You were on television tonight, and I didn't know anything about it. All I heard was something about a miracle man in his forties with a triple-digit fastball."

"No, this whole thing is wrong. I'm sorry. I am going to call back and turn down the offer."

"Are you crazy? I think you should play, if for no other reason than to spite your father."

"That's what else I needed to tell you. My father is now all for it, and he insists, saying that my new arm is a calling from God."

She grunted. "Well, I still think you should play, but for heaven's sake, play for yourself, and not because you are afraid of your father, or God for that matter. You should follow your dream just because it is your dream."

"Maybe, but I'm really not so sure it is my dream anymore. I will look like an idiot out there with all those kids," Gil said.

"That's even more of a reason," Keri chided. "You've got to face your fears."

Keri paused. "Gil, just how fast are you throwing?"

"Fast."

"How fast, Gil?"

"How about over a hundred-and-five fast?"

Her eyes widened. "How's that even possible?"

"I don't know," said Gil. "That's the scary part. I'm throwing fast, a lot faster, and with more control than I did when I was in my twenties. Heck, starters in the majors aren't even throwing that hard."

He told Keri about his medical appointment and how the Rockies' doctor found nothing unusual and certainly no drugs.

"I'm clean. They couldn't find anything wrong."

She clenched her hands about his bicep. "How do you explain this?"

"I can't. I guess it's my calling from God."

She tightened her grip. "Not funny. Well then, I can't see any reason why you shouldn't go for it. But if you ever keep anything from me again, I swear I'll leave you. That was so insulting."

"I promise." He leaned forward and kissed her.

"So tell me how all this is going to happen."

"The team leaves tomorrow for Arizona. Shortened spring training, then a delayed start of the regular season."

"Tomorrow? That's impossible. Who will teach your class and coach the team?"

"Figured I could send out an e-mail tonight. It's not like it's a secret."

"Do you know when you are coming home?"

Gil shrugged. "Good question. I have no idea. How many clean pair of underwear do you think I have?"

"Are you asking me to stay up all night and do your laundry?"

Gil smiled. "No, go back to bed. I got myself into this mess, and I don't expect you to clean up for me."

Keri swung her legs onto the floor and began to unbutton her blouse. "If I'm going to be up all night, I might as well get comfortable. What else are you going to need to pack?"

13

GIL HAD NEVER been to Centennial airport, the exclusive choice for the elite of Denver's business community. As he pulled his Ford into the parking lot, he noticed the inferiority of his vehicle, the dent in the front fender and the rust over the rear wheels. He saw all the cars neatly arrayed before him: BMW, Lexus, Porsche, Range Rover. He found an empty spot, grabbed his duffle bag out of the dusty truck bed and slung it over his shoulder. He felt his large muscles tighten as the bulges from the extra clothing Keri had packed dug into his side. He wondered what surprises she had tucked in it—maybe her famous chocolate chip cookies or his favorite sour candies.

The sliding glass doors whizzed open as Gil approached the terminal. "Howdy there, partner," an attendant in tight-fitting jeans and a faded T-shirt said. "Plane's waiting. Most of the other players are already on board."

The man held out his hand and Gil politely shook it. "All I can say is: Don't change when you get all famous. Remember us little guys. We're the ones that buy the tickets way up where it's hard to breathe."

"You sure you have the right guy?"

"Fastball at close to a hundred and ten? Yes, you're the man, the pitcher to beat. Picked up my opening day tickets last night because I knew you were going to win. And I don't care about this strike stuff. You are going to be pitching for the Rockies." He plucked two brightly colored tickets from his back pocket. "I'm not supposed to ask for autographs, but . . . "

Gil slipped off his duffle bag. "No problem. But I have one question: What makes you think I'll be starting opening day?"

"Ratcliff won't have a choice. Everyone in Colorado is going to demand to see what kind of punch that arm of yours is packing."

"Like I tell my players, one practice at a time. Let's see if I can survive spring training before there's any talk about the regular season."

The man hefted up Gil's luggage. "Fair enough. Wouldn't want to jinx you. Now let's get you on that plane. Breakfast is waiting. Just walk right on up. No lines, no security screening. Welcome to the big time."

Before Gil had taken his first bite of his croissant, he could feel the vibrations beneath his feet as the plane rumbled down the runway. With an upward burst, the shaking stopped and everything was smooth as the jet shot skyward. He felt queasy and looked around for a paper bag, just in case. He hoped it was motion sickness, but it was more likely the knots in his stomach churning and turning.

He flipped open the shade and peered outside, hoping for a distraction. Beneath him he watched the brown, barren landscape slowly begin to fade. There was no turning back now. He'd made the leap, the first major decision he'd ever made without calculating the consequences.

He looked east, shading his eyes with his hand as he tried to find his home. They were too high to make out any specifics, but the familiar winding roads and cul-de-sacs made it easy to locate his subdivision.

Austin would be getting ready for school. Keri, who'd sent Austin to bed at midnight, had woken their son well before his alarm clock so he could congratulate his father. They'd called Alicia as well. Gil could still feel Austin's hands clenched about his shoulders as he pulled himself up from his bed and shook the sleep from his eyes.

"It's awesome, Dad! I got a million texts last night. I can't wait to go to school. What did Alicia say? This is like the coolest thing ever, to have your dad pitching for the Rockies. Think you can get us all tickets?" He paused. "But wait, Dad. I thought you were too old and stuff. Are you really going to pitch? But you were on TV. It's got to be true."

Out of the corner of his eye, Gil watched for Keri's reaction. Austin turned to her, leaning on his elbow. The cowlick on his left side forced a mop of brown hair straight up.

Gil could see the moisture in Keri's eyes, but she held it together. She always held it together for the kids.

"It's true. I'll call you when I get to Arizona to let you know what training camp is like."

"I wish I could come watch you. Can't you get me out of school?"

"I'll tell you what. The first home game I start, I'll make sure you are on the front row. Deal?"

"Cool. Well, good luck."

As Gil watched the buildings shrink, the sickness returned. He rubbed his whiskers. At least baseball players didn't need to shave. Yet Gil knew he would. They made him look older, and that was the last thing he needed.

* * *

Salt River Fields at Talking Stick was the first major league baseball spring training facility to be built on Indian land. Shared by the Rockies and the Diamondbacks, the eleven-thousand-seat stadium complex had twelve practice fields and office buildings housing major and minor league clubhouses, as well as the training facilities. It was state of the art: 30,000 square feet of weight training equipment and cardio machines, a locker room with mahogany benches and marble showers, along with their own kitchen and a crew of chefs, ready to blend a player's favorite fruit or vegetable smoothie.

Spring ball had become big business in Arizona. This was baseball's informal preseason. Eastern teams joined the Grapefruit League while those in the West were part of the Cactus League. Thirty games in thirty days—but not this year. With the condensed schedule, spring training was shortened to ten games. The first would be in just four days. While the star players didn't always play, the managers knew they needed at least a few starters on the field to keep the fans coming. So the games were a mishmash of legitimate players with a mixture of promising minor leaguers. With the strike, management's hopes were to create a new lineup of stars.

The problem faced by Connor and his new pitching crew was that pitchers and catchers needed the most time together, learning pitches, giving signals, and building endurance. Most usually showed up in mid-to-late February, and games started in March. With only ten games before the regular season, Connor was sweating bullets. The other problem was that the teams agreed to let film crews follow them through the season. While the press had always been welcome, opening practices, team meetings, and players' private time were unchartered territory. There was already a lot of buzz about the middle-aged schoolteacher with a rocket arm.

As he trotted onto the dark green grass, Gil ignored the cameras, keeping his eyes fixed on the players on the practice field. Some were running bases, practicing their footing as they rounded the bags. He'd learned most of their names from the short plane ride to Phoenix, then the team meeting later that morning. There was Biondi, with his goatee and penguin waddle, Slider, the arrogant third baseman who'd chosen to cross the picket lines, and Timber Johnson, the oversized catcher.

As he reached the practice pitching mounds, he heard someone shout, "Wait a minute. Isn't that Mr. High School Teacher?"

Connor, amid his ragtag pitching crew, turned and observed his newest celebrity trotting onto the field.

"Hey, Slider, over here," Connor shouted, while motioning Gil over with his hand.

"The kids at school call me Gil."

"Hey, everybody. Take a break. I think we're all here now. Since we're all new, let's make the proper introductions. I want you to meet our newest addition, Gil Gilbert."

"I go by Gil."

"I'm Melendez," said a man with a two-day-old beard on a well-chiseled face as he stepped forward and held out his hand. "We'll try to hold off on the old man jokes. If you don't mind, we all want to see you throw a few balls."

Gil turned to Connor.

"They saw the show last night," Connor said. "The guys think the clock was rigged. They don't think you can throw that fast," Connor said with a grin, winking at Gil.

Gil slipped off his cap, wiped his hairline, and slid it back on. "That's why I'm here, to prove myself. Let's go."

The pitching staff greeted Gil warmly, each stepping forward and shaking his hand while Gil sized them up. As DeJesus offered his hand, Gil thought him more akin to a middleweight boxer than a pitcher. His dark Cuban skin accentuated his well-developed shoulders and arms. He was the complete opposite of Tajima, with barely a muscle on his bicep, and his insistence of remaining in the shade kept his skin fair.

Gil wanted to tell them that he wasn't some sort of strange creature; he was just like one of them, one of the boys. Humility was always the best way to break the ice.

"I haven't pitched competitively since college, so I don't want to hear any snickers behind my back when I throw it over the backstop, and my wife made sure I took I my vitamins this morning, so nobody needs to worry about carting me off to the emergency room. And, yes, I have a daughter that is probably as old as some of you, and don't bother to ask: She's off limits."

A man with an enormous frame lumbered across the field, his catcher's mask teetering on his head, just above his ears.

"Timber Johnson," he said, holding out his beefy hand. "Pleasure to meet you."

"Timber?"

"When I was born I was thick as an old sycamore tree, so Dad called me Timber. But everybody calls me Preacher. Got that from Dad, too. He's a real preacher, not like me who just likes to think I'm one."

"Preacher, I like it. My father's a minister. We can do a lot of pontificating this year." Gil snatched the ball out of Preacher's glove and headed to the mound. "Let's get this started."

A complete warm-up could take as much as a half an hour. After about fifteen minutes his muscles were loose, so Gil strode up the small hill of dirt and kicked his foot back and forth alongside the rubber. He'd had a routine in college. Pitchers need a routine, just like basketball players at the free throw line.

Always, do things the same. It blocks everything else out. For Gil, it was tapping the ball to the inside of his glove three times. He'd started it in little league, kept it in college, and now picked it up again. *"One, two, three strikes you're out,"* he chanted to himself as he repeatedly pressed the ball into his webbing.

He wriggled his right foot into the freshly dug trench and nestled it against the hard rubber. He again adjusted his cap, clenching the tip of the bill between his right thumb and index finger, then let it slip free and fall into his glove, where he found the familiar feel of leather and stitches.

Gil gripped the ball along the seams and tossed the ball at Preacher, who was still standing up. He was just playing catch; there was no need to be a hero and pull out his arm.

After a few minutes, Preacher crouched down, pulled his mask over his face, and waved. "Okay, time to bring on the heat. Give me what you've got."

It was a mild day, barely over seventy degrees, but Gil felt a drip down his forehead and onto his eyebrow. He flicked it away. He sensed the gaze of his teammates. His heart raced. He shook his head and took a deep breath. All was still. Eyes from the other pitchers fixed on him and the speed clock behind the backstop. Connor folded his arms across his chest, clenched his jaw and stared with the intensity of a perched eagle looking for prey.

Gil came up out of his stance. He could feel the glares. He again wiped his brow, found the grip on the laces and held up his glove to hide the pitch. Gil positioned his fingers over the seams and cradled the ball with his thumb. He'd start with a four-seam fastball, an easy pitch to control, but also an easy one to hit. *Pitching is like golf. Swing a golf club nice and easy and you send the golf ball sailing toward the green. Take a big cut, and you'll duff it.* Gil told his high school players to think of the ball as an egg, one that needed to be handled softly. The grip between the ball and his palm felt right; *maximize backspin, minimize friction,* he reminded himself.

His mechanics worked out. Gil fired a fastball right at Preacher's chest. Preacher's glove exploded with a leathery *pop*.

The large catcher stood and studied his glove, rolling the ball over and over. "Holy crap," Preacher said. He looked over his shoulder at the clock. *104.* "Nobody's going to hit that," Preacher mumbled to himself.

Tajima removed his cap and scratched his head. "I swear that pitch rose. I know that's impossible, but I swear I saw it. Fans are going to think he can make his four-finger rise."

The Japanese pitcher was right. No one—at least no one he'd ever heard of—could make a ball thrown overhand actually rise.

"What else you got?" Preacher said, trying not to look too enamored.

Gil lifted his cap and wiped his face with his sleeve. "Used to have a decent curveball and a slider on the days it decided to cooperate."

"Definitely going to need some good breaking pitches to complement that fastball. Bring it!"

"Let's see your curve first," Connor called out.

The curveball was the perfect complement to a really fast fastball. If thrown correctly, the ball would come in high, and just as it reached home plate it would suddenly dive toward the dirt, as much as two feet, causing most batters to swing over the ball. When it isn't thrown with enough spin—or speed—a curveball will "hang" over home plate without falling, making an easy mark for hitters. Gil had taught lots of high school pitchers how to throw a good curveball. "Grip the ball like you were shaking someone's hand," he'd say.

Gil let the ball fly. It didn't have quite enough spin, but its sheer speed created enough friction to make it dive into the dirt a foot before reaching Preacher's mitt.

"Not bad. Let's see your slider."

Gil hated throwing sliders, mostly because of his inconsistency in getting the right combination of spin and speed. In college, his slider often didn't *slide,* coming in straight instead, and batters creamed it.

Keeping his wrist loose, he threw it hard, like it was his fastball. Preacher dipped his glove to snatch it up before it crashed to the ground. "Nice movement. Got anything else? Knuckle, splitter, change-up?"

"Not for this old-timer. I like to keep things simple. I always tell my players that two good pitches are better than a handful of mediocre ones."

"A lot to be said for that," Connor said, "but for you, we'll work on some others."

Gil's focus was so intent that he failed to notice that the rest of the team had stopped their drills, both outfielders and infielders, and had closed in on the pitching mound. They were all standing behind him, arms folded, shaking their heads at what they had just witnessed. Even his breaking balls were clocking in the nineties.

Ratcliff, watching from the stands, shimmied off his seat and trotted over to the fully-assembled team. Slider was feverishly kicking at the dirt. "I can see that we're not going to get much done until we get this over with."

Slider snatched up a stray bat. "Come on, give me your biggest and baddest fastball."

Nobody came to Gil's rescue. Preacher reached down and snatched up his mask. With a batter up, he'd need the protection.

Slider took two practice swings. "Okay, give me what you got."

Ratcliff raised both hands and began waving like a football referee calling the end of a play. "If we are going to do this right, let's take the fight out of this sandbox and onto a real field. Come on everybody. Back to the field, and Slider I want you wearing a helmet. The last thing I need is for you to get hit in the head and I get slapped with a lawsuit."

Gil lagged behind as he followed the eager players to the main field, where the preseason games were played. Practices were open to the public, and with news of Gil's arrival, a large crowd of fans spotted the stands. As the players huddled around second base, some of the fans hopped down the stands to get a better view.

Preacher came up beside him. "So here is the plan: First one high and tight. Fast as you can throw it. Really brush him back, let him know you mean business. The rest, all sliders. He can't hit low and into him. You are both righties, and he can't hit your slider when it's zipping down to his ankles. Trust me, I know. Got it?"

"I think so, but it doesn't seem like such a good idea to try taking down your best batter on my first day of practice."

"Yes it does. You'll see why none of us can stand him. They'll all be thanking you. And, if you don't let him know who's boss, he might just hit that fastball of yours, no matter how fast you throw it."

Gil took a few more warm-up throws then waited for Slider to step in the batter's box.

"Give me all you got, Teacher. Don't hold nothing back. I don't want to hear any excuses when I crank this baby over the centerfield fence."

A few cameras popped out in the stands—incognito sports writers who now smelled a story. The filming crew set up just off of third base.

Gil kicked at the rubber, readied his glove, and gripped all four seams. Preacher crouched himself behind the plate and wiggled his index finger to Gil's right, signaling he wanted Gil's pitch to go inside.

"Come on, you afraid?" Slider wouldn't shut his mouth.

Preacher's right, Gil thought. He hurled at Slider's left shoulder, causing Slider to jump backward, clear out of the box. Preacher's glove thwapped.

Slider took two steps toward Gil. "So that's how it's going to be between you and me? Cut the crap and put one over the plate before I shove this piece of lumber down your throat, unless you'd like it up your ass instead."

Slider made his way back to the plate and steadied his helmet. He took a few swings slicing the air with his solid arms. "Just put it over the plate. Over the plate. On the dope, aren't you, old man?" he taunted.

Preacher set up, low and tight next to Slider's knees. Gil nodded. The moment the ball left his hand, Gil knew he had a winner. The ball whizzed straight toward the middle of the plate, but its rapid rotation made it dive toward Slider's ankles just as it came within reach of Slider's bat.

"Strike one," Ratcliff called out.

"Got lucky with one pitch. Come on, throw me something else. I want to see that fastball. None of this slider crap."

"A slider for a Slider," Biondi said, moving toward his position at first base. "It's got a nice ring to it."

Preacher signaled for the same pitch. Gil hurled the ball. It followed the same path, and Slider once again missed.

"Strike two," Ratcliff called. "Throw him a fastball, right over the middle. I want to see whether he can hit it when he knows what's coming."

Gil could hear shouters clapping in the stands. He took the ball in his hand, rolled it in his glove and located the four seams. Gil reared back, reaching as far as his arm could go, then shot the ball forward with all he had.

Slider took a full swing, but the ball was in Preacher's mitt before he even got the bat around. The clock read 107.

"Damn! What was that?" Slider said.

"That was our ticket to the post-season," Preacher said, standing and holding up the ball. "I think there is smoke coming off it. Fastest pitch I ever saw."

Slider yanked off this helmet and flung it to the dirt. He meaningfully strode up to the mound and shoved his bat into Gil's face. "Don't you go making fools of us. If you are on the juice, I want to know it. Right here and now. We don't need any of that crap on this team. You can come clean now, and we'll just forget all this happened."

Connor ran to the mound and slapped down the bat. Ratcliff took a step then stopped. He'd let his pitching coach handle this one. "He's clean, Slider. We checked."

"I'm not buying it," Slider said. "No human can throw that fast. This guy is a demon. He's got a new drug you can't detect."

"No drugs," Gil said.

14

GIL WAITED UNTIL the door to his room clapped shut before he ripped out the large envelope from his duffle bag. It was his contract. He wanted to call Peck, to discuss its terms with a former player, but he remembered his promise to Keri.

His hands were shaking as he ran his finger along the seal, tearing a big chunk of the tan colored paper as he did. Gil didn't know why he was so nervous. He knew he would take anything they offered. But something in Ratcliff's voice when he handed him the offer made him cautious.

"Glad to have you on board, Gil," Ratcliff had said. "You are going to be a critical part of our success. And Lord knows we need it. This is going to be one crazy year. You understand that the strike could settle any day. And, if it does, we can't guarantee your position. But, if you end up playing all season and do a good job, next year we'll consider you for a permanent position."

Gil started reading the first paragraph, something about Gil desiring to play baseball for the Rockies and the Rockies desiring to engage Gil's services as a player. The document was loaded with legal jargon.

I should call Keri, he told himself. *I promised. No, I should call a lawyer*. Almost all players used agents, not only to argue for better terms, but to sort through all the confusing contractual clauses. But agents took a cut of the deal, and giving up a percentage of what was sounding to be like a meager offer didn't sound attractive.

He collapsed on the bed and fumbled on the nightstand for the phone. He dialed his cell and waited for an answer.

"Well, it's official," he said when Keri answered. "I have a contract."

"And, what does it say?" she eagerly asked. "Are you a millionaire?"

"We're going to find out together.

"What, Gil, you really haven't read it yet?"

"Not past the first sentence. I figured we could read it together."

"You're making progress. Okay, so go ahead."

As Gil labored through the language, loaded legalese, Keri didn't speak a word, but he could hear her breathing.

"They are screwing us, Gil," she finally interrupted. "How much, Gil? What's the number?"

"A hundred and fifty thousand?"

"That's it?" she said, exasperated. "That's next to nothing. They're going to plaster you all over TV, make you pitch a whole season, and then dump you when the real players come back."

"I am a real player," Gil said sheepishly. "And one hundred and fifty grand is three times what I make now; and I only make that much because I coach *and* teach. Remember, I'm a replacement player. I don't really have a choice."

"That's a tenth of what the pitchers who have an ERA over six make. And what is the crap about only giving you five thousand a month and holding the rest until you finish the season?"

"ERA? I didn't know you knew what that even meant."

"Give me some credit, Gil. You know how many of your Friday afternoon games I've watched over the years?"

"But they did give me an incentive, and I really do think they are running low on cash, what with the strike and all."

"Until you show up and fill the stands," Keri huffed. "I say turn it down and look for another team. Read it to me again. What incentives are they giving you?"

He reread the contract, speaking slowly and letting Keri absorb their future. When he'd finished, she spoke. "Okay, now what was that about drug tests and moral turpitude? That worries me more than anything."

"Moral turpitude is no big deal. I'm sure every contract has this. The owners require this so if the player does something really bad, like statutory rape, they can cancel the contract."

"So why don't more get canceled, with all the off-field antics, I mean?"

"Because if a player can win games, a few flings on the side isn't going to get him fired."

"Are you worried about the lawsuit?"

In the suddenness of what had transpired in only a few days, Gil had completely forgotten about his own legal problems. He'd made no attempts to settle the case. Even worse, he refused to contact a lawyer, assuming the school district would defend him. The pretrial conference, a meeting where the judge scheduled discovery and a trial date, was rapidly approaching. Normally, nobody other than the lawyers showed up for these meetings, but if Gil signed a contract with a major league team, that could all change. Lots of people would be interested.

"I'm hoping that all goes away. I didn't do anything."

"You know that it won't. With this, it will only get worse."

"That just means the Rockies have an easy out if they want to get rid of me."

"And what about these drug tests? You told me you were cleared."

"After the steroid scandal, every player has to consent to this. They want to check my urine once a week, and make me take a blood test once a month. That's what our world has come to, unfortunately."

"You also said there was also something about being healthy?"

"That's got to be standard language. If you are too sick to play, the team doesn't want to pay you to sit on the bench. It's all just lawyer stuff. They are just covering their bases."

The line momentarily went silent. "Promise me one thing."

"What's that?"

"You promise?"

"Sure."

"Well, actually two things—that you won't get mad at me, and that you will go see another doctor."

"How many doctors do you want me to see? Between you and the Rockies, when am I going to have time for baseball?"

"You promised."

"Can't we count my physical from the Rockies' doctor?"

"No, I found my own."

"Keri."

"You promised."

"Yeah, but—"

"No yeah buts."

"Let's not get hung up on this. I want to talk about my contract. Is all this really worth a hundred and fifty thousand dollars?"

"Alright, if they are going to gamble on you, let's raise the stakes a bit. Don't change anything, but just add a few more incentives."

"Like?"

"If the strike doesn't end and you have a twenty-game season then a two-hundred-thousand dollar bonus, and throw in another hundred if you take the Cy Young Award. And let's talk playoffs. I think a cool two-fifty if you win the first round, another five hundred for the League Championship Series, and a million for the World Series."

"Are you serious? I don't think they will go for it. They know they've got me. I've quit my job, and they have me hostage here in Arizona. It's take it or leave it."

"I am dead serious. If the Rockies make it, it will only be because of your arm. And you can't tell me they won't have the cash to pay."

"You really think I'm going to win, don't you?"

"I have always believed in you, Gil. I thought you could go pro out of college, but now I can see why I wasn't so excited about it. It's funny how life has a way of working things out. You stay home, raise a great family, have a great career, then when you least expect it, your dream comes true."

"You're just trying to butter me up so I will ask for more money."

"That too. But I do think you are going to take baseball by storm and be the hottest thing since the Golden Boy."

"You know about Mantle?"

"I told you I know my baseball."

15

"SO WHEN ARE we going to start him?" Ratcliff asked Connor. "First game of the preseason is tomorrow, we're only two weeks away from the season opener, and we are still in the dark as to whether he's any good."

"He's so green, I just can't see putting him in yet. If this were a normal year, we wouldn't even be having this conversation. He'd spend the entire year in the minors."

"You're forgetting that everyone is green, except for the ones that are already over the hill."

"True. Maybe we'll try him a few innings this week."

"The front office is putting pressure on me to give him the nod. Full start, not just an inning here and there. He's already got an incredible fan base. Twenty thousand followers on Twitter, and he isn't even tweeting. If we put him on the mound, all these seats are going to fill up. And isn't that what it's all about anyway?"

"Did he sign the contract?"

"Last night. Gil did some more negotiating. Worked out an 'eat and kill' deal. The more he kills, the more he eats."

"So he's got to win to get paid. I like that. But what if we don't start him?"

"That's the issue. We don't want to be accused of breaching the contract by not giving him the chance to win. Plus, the front office wants him to play. Speed will sell tickets, even if he can't win. Fans will show up just to see him crank out a hundred-and-seven-mile-per-hour fastball."

"Damn circus is what it's going to be. It's like the old home run race between Sosa and McGwire, and you know how that ended up."

"Exactly what the front office wants. You ask a hundred baseball fans, and they could never tell you how the season ended up for Cubs or the Cards, but they could tell you how many home runs they hit."

"And what steroids they were on."

"That's not going to be the case with Gil. We'll make him like Tebow, clean-cut, puts God and family first, but then God gives him this ungodly arm, right out of the blue, and he has no choice but to use it. For the glory of God, right? We can come up with some kind of prayer chant for him. He'll whip the crowd into a frenzy."

Connor raised his eyebrows. "I'm not sure that's what we want. No team owner wanted Tebow because the fans booed whenever he sat on the sidelines. If a guy can't win, the fans won't stick around forever, no matter what his charm, or his arm."

"Let's just hope he really is clean."

"We'll give him the standard drug tests that the league requires. Not sure what else we can do. Dr. Chavez couldn't find anything. Just keep poking him, running the tests and keeping a medical log. And, his contract gives us permission to release the results to the press. No secrets here. If he's clean, we'll tell everyone. But even the controversy itself will sell tickets. It's been a long time since Coors Field was packed. I sort of miss the ringing in my ears."

"I thought we had Chavez run some additional tests, just to make sure."

"We did, even though the rules don't require it."

"And the results come back when?"

"Two or three days."

"You're not thinking about opening day?"

"Not a chance. You know how ticked off Melendez would

be? He's going to be our ace this year, and we can't afford to do anything to screw him up in the head. His wife's a real mental case. He'll never hear the end of it if he isn't king this season."

"Alright, if he's clean we'll start him for the third regular season game with the Cards. We'll see how he throws on the road. Why don't we get him some playing time tomorrow against the Mariners, and if he doesn't make fools out of all of us, he may get one more start before the season opens. Plenty of time to see his stuff and get the word out."

16

GIL THREW OPEN his hotel room door, presented himself in the mirror, and slipped out his contact lenses. He rubbed his whiskers and studied his face. His cheekbones were more pronounced. The conditioning drills were beginning to show, wringing the last ounces of fat off his already lean physique. The practices were more demanding than he imagined, much more intense than what he put his own players through.

Weight training during a high school season was almost nonexistent, but professional ball required him to pump the iron at least twice a week. Cardio drills were daily, with only Sunday being spared.

Exhausted, he yearned for his bed. Gil sprawled out, closed his eyes, and focused on his breathing. Keri taught him to meditate years ago to reduce the stress of coaching. Freeing his mind for just a few minutes each day brought a new perspective to life. In recent weeks, these silent moments took on a new meaning—a daily log of how much more laborious it was to breathe.

Sliding his phone off the counter, Gil fell back onto the firm mattress and dialed home, waiting for Keri's face to appear on the screen. Keri preferred just talking, but Gil hated talking to the ceiling. The screen illuminated with the familiar bookshelf situated in his home office, and Keri, wearing a sweatsuit and baseball cap, warmly greeted him.

"Like my outfit?" she said.

"Take the dog for a walk?

"No, just haven't gotten around to showering. We have unexpected company."

Another face slipped onto the screen, a younger version of Keri, but with no wrinkles and dyed blonde hair.

"Alicia, what are you doing home?"

"Mom will tell you. Got to finish unpacking." Her face flitted away as fast as it entered.

"She quit school?" Gil asked.

"She wants to take a leave, just for a quarter. Boy trouble."

"With Zach? What happened? He didn't do anything to her."

"Oh no, other than putting pressure on her to get married. She wants to talk to you about it alone, so I won't steal her thunder."

"But why come home from school?"

"Gil, you should know your daughter by now. She can't be pressured. She wants to have some time alone to think through where her life is going. You know how she is; she has to talk everything through. She got that from your genes."

"And I'm not there to be her sounding board."

"You'll be home soon enough. That's one of the reasons she came home. She needs some fatherly advice and with your new job, she wouldn't be able to see you. Now she can come to all your games."

"But she hates baseball."

"Not anymore. Not with such a famous father. And that reminds me—Austin is really upset."

"I am?" came a high-pitched voice.

Gil watched as his son's face appeared next to Keri's.

"Hi, Austin. What's up?"

"English class," Keri reminded her son.

"Oh yeah, Dad. You know how we are going over tall tales: Paul Bunyan, Johnny Appleseed, Jack and the Beanstalk, and that kind of stuff? Anyway, Cole said you were nothing but a tall tale. I told him to shut up, and he said you were a fake, that you were taking drugs and when the real players came back you'd be out on the street without a job. I punched him, but then one of his friends jumped on me. Half the class piled on before Mr. Stinson could call security."

Keri rubbed her fingers through his hair. Gil could see a red welt on his cheek. "Why don't you finish your homework?"

"I already did it."

"Then find something else to do," Keri huffed.

"So you want me to leave? I'm not stupid."

"Your father and I have a few things we need to discuss." She pushed him away and closed the door.

"I don't have a good feeling about any of this," Gil said. "Alicia needs me, Austin's now throwing punches, and my body is feeling hammered."

"It gets worse. The camera crew showed up today. They film everything, wander into our bedroom, you name it."

"Austin's black eye?"

"Yep. And you know Austin. He can't stop himself. He gave me a play-by-play of his little skirmish at school. You know it's going to be on national television."

Gil stroked his chin. "This is all too much. Are you sure we should be doing this? I mean, look at what it did to the Kardashians. And what about my health?"

"If it helps, I found a specialist. Maybe we're worried about nothing. I think we will all feel better if we have an expert look at you."

Gil paused, but didn't put up a fight. "When?"

"They'll fit you in as soon as you are back in town. You're quite the celebrity these days. Just let me know your schedule."

"We can talk tomorrow. Are you still coming?"

"We wouldn't miss it for the world."

17

IN A NORMAL spring training game between the Rockies and the Seattle Mariners, finding a good seat was not a problem. But not when the Rockies announced that Gil was going to be on the mound. As Gil poked his head out of the dugout, a third of the seats were already filled. In the dazzling sunlight, he lowered his cap and trotted to the bullpen for warm-ups. Cameras were everywhere—in the team room, in the dugout, on the field, with the fans. It was crazy.

Not everyone was cheering. The fluorescent, hand-painted signs were impossible to dismiss: *Go home scabs*, read one billboard. *Gil's a fake*, read another. Gil wondered where his family was sitting and what they were thinking.

The game proceeded to the fourth inning when Ratcliff nodded to Connor, who gave the sign to the bullpen. Gil was up.

"Go get 'em, Gil," Slider yelled, whipping a ball to Biondi on first base. Slider punched his glove in the direction of the press box, waving for their attention. "You don't want to miss this," he yelled. Gil kept his focus on the green blades of grass as he plodded through the outfield.

"They're going to clobber him," Slider said to Manzi as he eased his way over to the shortstop. "Man, can I tell you how much I don't like that guy? Gil Gilbert. What a stupid name. My bet is that Ratcliff yanks him before he gets two outs. They'll have batted the lineup by then."

By the time Gil made his way to the mound and kicked a few sprays of dirt from in front of the rubber, he could hear the shutters clicking. He tried not to look up, but to focus his gaze on the catcher's mitt. The tosses were soft, just enough to loosen his shoulder. The heat wouldn't come until he was facing a batter. His chest felt a little tight. He threw one a little harder, wondering if this was going to be a repeat of when he'd frozen on his first day of tryouts.

Before the umpire called for the first batter, Connor took off for the mound. "Okay, here's the deal: We're taking a big chance on you, and you've got to deliver. Just remember that baseball isn't about throwing fast. Pitchers get us outs. That's what we need—outs. So don't try to be some hotshot and throw your arm out on the first pitch. This is preseason ball and a chance for you to see what it's like with some real hitters. Get your rhythm down and everything will be okay. Got it?"

"Got it," he said, feeling like he was in the shoes of one of his own high school players. The game never changed, even at the professional level. The speeches were the same; egos on the field. That's why he loved baseball.

He felt Connor's bony arm reach over his shoulder. He could smell the tobacco on his breath as Connor pulled Gil's ear down. "But this is business too. Show business, I hate to admit it. When you're warmed up, give it a good hurl. Lord knows we could use some excitement around here. You throw over a hundred and the press is going to start to buzz. Over one-ten and I'm buying rounds for the whole team. You throw like we all know that you can, and that will make all of our lives a whole lot easier. Got it?"

Gil smiled. "Of course."

Gil couldn't help but scan the bleachers while waiting for the first batter to enter the box. Clearly, more than two-thirds of the dark green seats were filled—nearly 8,000 spectators. He found his family, all standing and wildly clapping.

Preacher sat quietly in his stance, waiting for Gil to settle himself. But the calmness of his catcher didn't stop the butterflies.

The leadoff batter for the Mariners was their first baseman,

Cory Spangler. Gil had studied their lineup. Spangler had led his team with a .311 average—before his knee surgery. The Mariners released him, figuring he'd never be much good in the field again because he couldn't run. But he could hit the ball and would likely cream the inexperienced mediocrities playing *strike* ball.

Gil let out a deep breath and waited for Preacher, who signaled for a fastball down the middle. The sweat was beading up on Gil's upper lip, and he wiped it with his forearm, sliding his arm across his face like a little kid wiping smeared catsup from his lips. Rules prevent pitchers from touching their face with their hands, but not their forearms.

"Hey batter-batter, hey batter-batter." It was Slider, acting like they were playing a little league game. Gil couldn't believe it. Nothing like this ever happened in the majors. What was Slider thinking?

Gil nodded, tapped the ball three times, silently chanting to himself, and took a full windup. He felt awkward, tight and tense, but there was no turning back. Spangler jumped on the pitch, a little too eager and pulled it foul. Gil looked at the clock, a measly eighty-seven.

When Preacher called for another fastball high and inside, Gil waved him off. Instead, he threw it outside, making sure Spangler couldn't put wood on it. The ball tailed so far left that Preacher, sprawling out, couldn't reach it. The ball sailed all the way to the backstop. The clock measured just eighty-four.

Preacher didn't wait for the next pitch. He slipped off his mask and hand-delivered the new ball he'd taken from the umpire.

"What's going on?"

"I was going to ask you the same thing. The speed isn't there today. I just don't want to let anyone down."

"You can't be afraid; *be a major league pitcher*. Nobody can intimidate you. Hear me? The batters will smell you all the way to centerfield. You can throw faster than anyone on this planet, now get to work."

His father's last words popped into his mind, about God giving him a second chance to redeem himself, so he could be God's emissary. That's who he couldn't let down. But he knew that he couldn't pitch for God back then, and he couldn't now.

He remembered the evening he'd gotten Keri pregnant. After two decades of reflection, he wouldn't change that, not when that union had given them Alicia. Keri was right. He needed to pitch for himself, not for what his father wanted him to be.

Preacher headed back down the mound, paused and returned. "And one more thing—

Remember the first time you threw to Slider?"

"Yeah, I threw it right at him."

"So do it again. Get him off of the plate. It's your plate, not his. You want to win at this game, you've got to dominate. "

Gil wiped his face again and nodded.

Preacher sat in his crouch, not bothering to flash any signals. Gil wanted to look over to the dugout for some kind of assurance from Connor, but that almost seemed like tattling. So, he tapped the ball three times, took his windup, and aimed for Spangler's left shoulder.

How the pitch didn't hit Spangler, Gil never knew. In a flash, Spangler was sprawled out on the ground in a puff of dust. Preacher had managed to get some leather on the ball, but it squirted past him and crushed into the fence. Gil peeked at the Mariner's dugout, wondering if the bench was going to empty. It would have except that the batboy started shouting and pointing at the clock.

In blazing lights it read: 109.

"Brilliant!" came Slider's voice from behind.

The umpire rushed the mound. He poked his finger hard into Gil's chest.

"If you ever try that crap again while I'm on the field, you're out. Got it?"

Slider spoke something inaudible into his glove. Gil turned and glared.

The crowd was silent, their eyes still glued to the three shining digits on the scoreboard. It was history in the making, and they all knew it.

Preacher didn't wait for any kind of celebration. He set up, inside, right next to Spangler, signaling to the leadoff batter what would happen if he tried to crowd the plate. Then he motioned for a fastball right down the middle of the plate. Spangler backed off, even only a few inches, enough to let everyone know he was scared, as scared as a little leaguer. The momentum of a leather baseball with that much speed could do some serious damage to human flesh and bones.

Gil took his time, letting the crowd refocus while Spangler stood at attention. Gil was no longer thinking about pitching, just playing the game. The speed gun flashed 107, a dead-centered strike. He followed it up with two more. Spangler struck out, looking shaken. The entire crowd was now on its feet.

When Gil reached down for his rosin bag, he caught sight of a familiar-looking bald head adorned with oversized, discounted sunglasses, popping up and down as the man sought Gil's attention. Gil squinted. Peck was sitting next to Austin wearing a cutoff Prairie Ridge T-shirt, and the tops of his pale white shoulders were a bright red. Gil tossed the bag onto the turf and nodded. Peck signed back, lifting his thumb to the sky while his other hand held a foot-long hotdog hanging out of what looked like an entire loaf of bread. Gil shook his head.

You don't get many friends like that, Gil thought. It was only a few weeks ago when he'd wanted to kill Peck, first for bringing him to the Rockies' training facility, then for announcing to the whole school that he was going to be the Rockies' newest pitcher, even before he'd discussed it with Keri.

He wondered what she was thinking at this very moment. He knew he was being televised, as were they. Yes, this was just a preseason game, but everyone in the nation now knew about his incredibly fast fastball, and now the media melee had started. Commentators even started speculating that maybe there could be a season with replacement players, fueling the animosity between the replacements and the regulars.

Ratcliff kept him in for another inning. Two players managed to get wood on the ball, a slow grounder to Slider and a pop-up to Trudeau at second, but that was all. That was enough to let the sporting world know the nuclear arsenal now in the Rockies' lineup.

"Rest your shoulder. You've earned the right to a start before the season begins," Ratcliff said.

"We got lucky with this one," Connor said when Gil sat.

"Yep," Ratcliff said. "Two weeks ago we thought our careers were over. Now, this could be our best season."

"At least in terms of ticket sales."

"No, I think he's going to be more than just a fascination. Look at how all the other players are stepping up. Did you see that throw from Gonzalez from center?"

"Except for Slider. He hates Gil."

"Of course," Connor said. "Slider hates everyone."

18

KERI WAS WAITING when the Rockies' chartered plane landed at Centennial airport, enough time for a day off before the grueling regular season. Alicia was standing by her mother's side in the front lobby. They both came rushing toward him when the door opened. It had only been two weeks, but that was enough time for him to forget the little sway in Keri's hips, accentuated by her petite waist. He slung his arms around her and pulled her tight. She kissed him.

"Glad the hometown hero isn't too cool to remember his wife."

He smelled the sweetness of her hair. "Not this boy."

His lips were still wet with her kiss when he noticed the camera only a few feet away.

"You'll get used to it," Keri said. "Just make sure you don't come out in your boxers for breakfast like Austin did this morning."

Gil took her hand and slipped past the film crew, scooping her into the waiting car where they rushed off to the medical plaza where Dr. Donald Doty kept his office. Keri had selected a cardiologist when Gil complained of a sore chest.

Dr. Doty ran Gil through all the standard tests: treadmill, blood pressure, ECG. After two hours, Dr. Doty was finished, but declined to give an opinion. He'd study the data and consult with Dr. Cherrie Kempski, the internist that Gil would see on his next trip back to Denver.

Keri gave Gil ten minutes to shower and change while they picked up Austin. Peck arrived, having just finished practice, wanting to hear the news. When he learned they were going to dinner, Peck invited himself along, then insisted that they drop by the school so that he could pick up a few things he'd left behind when he scampered out of practice.

The front parking lot of Prairie Ridge High was full, and cars were parked along the street.

"Basketball tournament tonight?" Gil said turning to Peck.

"Something like that," Peck said. "Keri, can you just drop us off in front?" He then asked Gil to accompany him. "I need some help carrying a few things."

"Sure, but I don't know where you are going to put them." With five people crowded into their SUV, and Gil's gear stuffed in the back, they were at capacity.

"We'll find room, trust me," Peck said, throwing the door open and stumbling out.

"This can't be a basketball tournament," Gil said, studying the sea of vehicles. "Our team stinks this year. You know, I don't think I've ever seen so many cars, not overflowing onto the street like this."

Peck didn't stop to answer but tugged the front metal doors open. "Come on, we've got to hurry."

As soon as Gil entered, thousands of voices yelled, "Surprise!"

"You left before they could all say a proper goodbye," Peck said. "So this is our little way of sending you off."

With this, they all clapped their hands and snapped photos. Gil's face broke into his patented smile, and he shook his head. "I really don't know what to say, and that says a lot for me."

"That's true," a boy close to the front row shouted, "Mr. Gil loves to talk."

"Well, all I can say is, *thank you*. I didn't really know how much I would miss everyone at Prairie Ridge until I went away." As he was speaking, he felt Keri nuzzle up to his side. He put his arm around her. "Just ask Keri. That first night I was really homesick and wondered if I'd made a horrible decision. You've all really gone overboard with this. I can't believe you all came out just to wish me well."

"This is nothing," Peck said. "I need everyone to proceed—very slowly—to the gym. We've got barbeque, salads, and all kinds of desserts. Help yourself. And while you're eating, we'll let Gil answer a few questions about what it's like to be with the Rockies."

A microphone mounted on a chrome stand was perched at mid-court, ready for Gil to face the questions fired from the bleachers. He waited for plates to be heaped with American comfort food. As he stood to face the friendly faces, Gil still felt like he was their baseball coach at a pep rally. Gil snatched the microphone and moved toward the stands, catching sight of the all-to-familiar film crew. "Okay, so I guess it's that time. Anything you want to know about the Rockies?"

"Mr. Gil, what's it like to pitch in a real pro game?" The question came from one of the cheerleaders.

Gil rubbed his chin. "Well, that's hard to say. I still haven't pitched in a real game, but I'll tell you next week when I start against the Cards."

The students erupted, jumping up and down on the wooden bleachers.

His shortstop, Wilson, raised his hand. "Coach, what I want to know is what is Slider really like? I mean the press makes him out to be this real jerk, but I kind of think it's all for show."

"Yes . . . Slider. Let's just say we're still getting used to each other."

Gil answered a dozen more questions then said it was his turn to eat and their time to talk.

When Gil left Keri for a quick trip to the bathroom, a small, balding man approached.

"Mr. Gilbert," the man said. "I think we need to talk, in private." He was carrying a manila folder.

"Why should I talk to you?" Gil said.

"Sorry, I don't think I properly introduced myself. I'm Randall Kite, Shaila's father, and I have some information to share with you. I tried contacting you through Shaila's attorney, but you're a hard man to reach."

"I've been a little busy," Gil said.

"Yes, I see you've signed a nice contract with the Rockies. All the more reason we should talk before these get out," he said, holding up the folder.

The door to the chemistry room was ajar, and Kite pushed it open. "It won't take long."

Gil didn't want to cause a scene. His legal problems with Shaila had so far gone unnoticed.

"You've got one minute," Gil said, stepping inside.

Kite slipped on a pair of bifocals, his hands trembling. "Nobody has seen these yet, but if you refuse to settle and the case goes to trial, my lawyer tells me these photos will be made public, and they certainly will be used as evidence. The jury, and everyone else, will see them."

Gil plucked the folder from Kite's hands. He could feel the blood pulsing through his temples. "I didn't do anything wrong, and you know it." Kite stepped back, and Gil flipped the file open. Gil blinked twice, hoping this wasn't real.

The photo on the top of the pile showed a group of girls, most wearing shorts and white T-shirts emblazed with the Prairie Ridge logo. But a few had their shirts flung over their shoulders, with their shoulders bare except for their brightly colored sports bras—showing off for the boys. The picture captured one of the cheerleaders in the process of pulling her shirt above her head, and just behind her was the unmistakable image of Gil, his eyes as wide as saucers, his mouth hanging open. Gil lifted off the top photo. All the same cheerleaders were in the next photo, but one of them was now clutching the side of her face, while another had her mouth wide open observing the injured girl.

"It's Photoshopped," he said when he regained his composure, knowing he hadn't been gawking as the picture implied.

"No, they are real. We've got witnesses lined up to testify. Any expert can tell you these photos have not been doctored."

Gil tossed the pictures onto the closest desk. "That's not what happened. Look, I'm not afraid of these. I've got to go."

"Shaila's asking for five hundred thousand to make this go away. Otherwise, these will be front-page news. You know I could show these to your little reality show friends right now."

"Shaila's asking?" Gil said, lunging forward. "No, you're the greedy piss ant who is trying to blackmail me. It was an accident, pure and simple. If anything, it was your daughter's fault. She's the one that ran onto the field when Bushman was batting. Did she tell you that? Did she say how she was flailing her arms, bouncing down the baseline asking for a chance to bat? Ever been to a baseball practice? Players hit balls really hard, and they go all over the place. That's life. Look, I'm sorry this happened to Shaila, and I'm glad she's okay now. You have your apology, now why don't you drop this little lawsuit of yours and we'll both get on with life."

"I need money, not just an apology."

"It's not what you think," Gil said. "I'm not paying you a dime."

19

KERI WIPED HER forehead with the back of her hand, trying not to smear flour on her face. Alicia handed her a towel and grabbed the beaters, plunging them into the raw cookie dough.

"You spoil, Austin. You know that, right?" Alicia said.

"Of course, he's my baby, the last to leave the nest."

"Not anymore."

Keri scooped up some of the stray ingredients from the counter and said, "Do you have something to tell me?"

"This morning, I made my decision final. I'm breaking off my relationship with Conklin and coming home."

"For how long?"

"At least until the baseball season is over."

Keri's face fell.

"I thought you were struggling with boy problems and finishing your education. Have you been talking to your father? You've never liked baseball."

"We had a good talk last night."

"And?"

"He had some good ideas. I mean, you know how he is, always kidding around and never being serious. But this time he really listened to me. He wanted to know more about Conklin and his MBA plans and what I thought about picking up and moving halfway across the country when we weren't even married."

"And your career."

"Of course he asked me about that. You know how Dad thinks we all need a PhD."

"So what made you decide to come home?"

"I asked Dad how he knew it was right when he asked you to marry him."

Keri held her breath. She'd never told either of her children the truth about her pregnancy, but she always wondered if Alicia knew. The math told the truth.

"It wasn't at all what I expected," Alicia said. "He just said you two were so in love you couldn't pry yourselves apart."

Keri smiled. That much was true, at least when they were in their twenties.

"Dad told me that I should take my time and get it right. 'Unless your heart says jump, just keep hiking up the mountain,' he said. Eventually, I would get to the top and then I'd be ready. When I thought about it, that all made sense. I remember hiking Mt. Bierstadt with Dad when I was little. When we got to the summit, it felt like I could just hold out my arms and jump, and that I'd really be flying. It's that really special feeling you get in your stomach when you're peering over the edge of the cliff. When I think about spending my life with Conklin, I realized I just didn't feel that way. Yes, he could provide for me, but I wasn't about ready to fly. That's when I knew I had my answer."

Keri scooped out some dough.

"But you know what my heart also told me?" Alicia said.

"What?"

"I had this gut feeling that I needed to be with Dad this summer . . . it's hard to explain."

Just then, the doorbell rang.

Keri opened the door and was greeted by an oversized envelope centered on the doormat. She returned to the kitchen and opened it. The contents were thick and stiff. On top was a handwritten letter. Beneath it was a photo of Gil, his eyes wide open, gawking at a high school girl taking her shirt off. Keri curled it back only to be greeted by another picture of Shaila holding her head while a crowd of cheerleaders in sports bras huddled about her. Keri's hands were shaking.

20

TENSIONS WERE MOUNTING between the striking players and their replacements. At first, the strike games were a novelty. Now that it was clear that MLB would proceed without its stars, baseball fans and player sympathizers turned ominous. There were attacks on players showing up at stadiums and even threats on their families.

The Rockies had dropped their first two regular season games to the Cards. DeJesus and Melendez had respectable outings, but the team was far from jelling. Starting the season with two losses chilled the team's initial optimism. As with the first two encounters with the Cards, the players showed up at the gates on team buses, unloading together and quickly being escorted by security guards making a protective line. As Gil stepped off the bus, he was pelted by an egg.

"How's that for a fastball, you stinkin' scab," the fan yelled.

"Don't worry about it," Ratcliff said, when they entered the locker room. "You're here to do a job. Just focus on that. Half these people yelling and screaming would kill to trade places with you."

As Gil entered the field he kept his eyes from wandering in the stands. He wanted no distractions. He had warmed up in the bullpen and was ready for his debut. His day had finally arrived. He tapped the ball in his mitt three times, and let the first pitch go. It clocked over a hundred, but it was high and outside. Preacher called for a fastball in the middle of the strike zone. This time, Gil hit one hundred and nine, but it was low, almost in the dirt.

That didn't matter. He'd already made history. Nobody had ever thrown that fast. Cards fans began clapping.

Gil remained wild, and when he walked the leadoff batter, Preacher made his first trip to the mound.

"I've got lots of velocity, but I've lost my control."

"You're playing like a robot," Preacher said.

"A robot?" Gil said. "Just trying to be serious."

Preacher shook his head. "What made you a successful high school teacher?"

"I've never really thought about it. I'd like to think it's because my students like me."

Preacher reached up and put his arm around Gil's shoulder. "Now we're getting somewhere. Gil, that's exactly right. People like you. You're warm, personable, fun to be around. Now, the secret to pitching is to pitch your personality."

"Pitch my personality?"

"That's right."

"Kind of like, just be myself."

"No, more than that. Pitch like you're in front of your class explaining some scientific principle. Imagine the students in your class, how you're trying to connect with them, to keep their attention while also helping them to understand a difficult topic. Give your pitches some personality, some feeling, like a concert pianist playing a concerto. You're a musician. You should understand that."

Gil nodded. "I can do that."

Preacher called for a fastball, low and inside. Gil kept his routine, but put a little rhythm into his ball tapping. His windup had a little beat to it, and he let go with a smile. The ball slammed into Preacher's glove at a whopping one hundred and ten. The replay made it look like the batter swung a full minute after the ball passed home plate. Following Preacher's lead, Gil whipped over two more strikes and registered his first major league strikeout. He popped up the next batter, followed by another strikeout to end the inning.

Nearly every pitcher has a way to exit the field, by lowering his cap and avoiding any fan interaction. In spring ball, Gil had done the same, figuring this would keep his focus. But that wasn't his personality, and not what Preacher had just admonished him. He couldn't keep from smiling and letting everyone know he was having the time of his life. So he tilted up the brim of his cap, flashed his gleaming teeth and sparkling eyes, not caring who was snapping photos. It felt good to be Gil, pitching his personality.

Both teams remained scoreless through the second inning. Slider got the first hit in the top of the third inning. He looped the ball over the first baseman's head and into shallow right field. Most players would have taken the single, and the first base coach assumed that's what Slider was going to do. But Slider ignored the coach and rounded first base at full speed. He lowered his head, churned his muscular legs, and took off.

The Cards' right fielder casually scooped up the ball then jumped to action at the sight of Slider, chugging to second like an out-of-control train. He wound up and threw the ball so hard that he lost his balance and landed on his hands and knees. The throw was dead on, but Slider did one of his famous head slides and slipped underneath the tag. He hopped up, spat out some dirt and called himself safe, sweeping his arms in a flowing motion.

Gil watched Ratcliff's jaw muscles tighten. NFL players could get away with antics like that, but it was taboo in baseball. The owners refused to let their sport turn into the pro-wrestling circuit.

The crowd booed, prompting Slider to flex his bicep. While Gil understood that Slider was showing off his tattoo, his yin and yang, it looked more like he was flipping off the Cards' fans.

Ratcliff signaled Manzi to get into the batter's box, hoping this would take the spotlight off of his problematic shortstop. The crowd kept up their racket, turning their hatred of Slider to that of Manzi, who most felt should be out of baseball after his sex scandal while he played for Chicago.

Manzi took two strikes, ignoring the taunting fans. He fought off a few pitches until the count was full. Then he lined one into right center. The ball took one bounce and leapt over the wall, a ground-rule double.

The crowd watched in silence as Slider rounded third. That he was going to score was already concluded when the umpire signaled Manzi to stop at second, declaring a ground rule double. Slider was going to make a statement. Everyone sensed it, like a basketball crowd waiting to see how LeBron James would dunk the ball on a fast break.

Slider kept up his trot toward home plate, and when he was halfway there, he shortened his stride, increased his speed, then did a cartwheel, followed by a backflip, landing perfectly on the white pentagon-shaped plate. He held up both hands like a gymnast who'd just nailed the perfect landing.

All sorts of garbage, bottles, popcorn containers, even half-eaten corndogs were hurled onto the field.

The umpire was in Slider's face, his mask thrown to the dirt. "Who do you think you are? This is baseball, not some Cirque du Soleil act. This is your final warning, Slider. One more misstep, and I'm tossing you."

Slider didn't move, keeping his feet planted on the plate. "Says who?"

"Don't go there, Slider. We all know you think you're above the law, and that the rules don't apply to you. But try me, and you'll find out."

Slider poked the umpire in the chest pad. "I don't think I'm above the rules. I'm just different and that's why your rules can't reach me."

The umpire threw up his hand, his thumb extended. He'd tossed Slider from the game. The crowd erupted. Ratcliff bolted onto the infield. The umpire braced himself.

But Ratcliff didn't rip into the official. He planted himself right in front of Slider. "You shoved an umpire. You can't do that."

"This little bad boy of yours doesn't want to play by the rules," the umpire said. "Says he is different. Well, he's different now. He isn't playing."

Slider started for the dugout, but Ratcliff pulled him back. "I'm not done with you. I haven't even started. What do you think you're doing with all this Hollywood crap? This isn't All-Star Wrestling. We don't act like this in baseball."

"I do," Slider yelled back.

"We have rules for a reason, and we all keep them. We keep the game pure. Baseball is about sameness. That's what's made us great, and that's what will keep us that way. So just stop with all your crap. Okay?"

"What if I don't want baseball to be the same?" Slider said. "What if I think it's boring the way it is? That's why I'm different."

"The rules are to protect baseball against players exactly like you. The game has to be the same. That's it. Period. Get out of here."

Slider stomped off then turned around. "Baseball pure? What about all these replacement players? What about Gil?"

Gil retired the side in both the fourth and fifth innings. The energetic Cards fans were silenced, and more began to applaud each time Gil whipped over a fastball. At the end of each inning, Gil focused on another section of the stands, intentionally trying to zero in on one of the Cards' fans. On the third row, just to the left of the dugout, he found what he was looking for—a middle-school-aged boy, donned in a Cards cap, standing in the aisle with his camera raised. The boy reminded him of Austin, skipping school so he could see the game. Gil paused, increased the curve of his smile, and lifted his glove.

"I got him! I got him!" the boy yelled to his father, scurrying back to his seat.

In the dugout, Gil took his seat next to DeJesus, who was still licking his wounds from the previous day's loss. "I was going to ask you," Gil said, taking a paper cup from the batboy. "Do you think you could show me how to throw your cutter? Mine stinks."

DeJesus kept his eyes focused on the field. "I don't see why. Seem to be doing fine with that ungodly fastball. Putting me and Melendez to shame—we're both winless. Besides, you're the coach. You should know how to throw it."

Gil swung around and lifted up DeJesus's cap. "You're the Cutting Cuban. Who else is going to show me how?"

DeJesus pushed him away. "Go get Castro to show you."

"What does Castro know about baseball? Come on, you're the best. Imagine what I could do with your cutter."

"Then where would that leave me? You'd be the one pitching for freedom."

"Not true," Gil said, spinning back around. "Preacher says I have to pitch my personality. Like this." Gil smiled until the corners of his mouth nearly reached his ears.

DeJesus finally turned and arched back when he saw the whimsical look on Gil's face. "Pitching your personality. Sounds like Preacher. Tell me one thing, Gil."

"Sure," Gil said, the corners of his mouth falling.

"Why do you have to be so damn likeable? Can't I just hate you for a while?"

"Sounds fine with me," Gil said. "As long as you can get Melendez to like me. My family got season tickets right next to his wife."

DeJesus laughed and shook his head. "Slider's going to ride you hard when he sees that one. Don't worry about Melendez. He's an old softie. He's just pissed at you like I am because it's not fair you come out of the middle of nowhere and take the baseball world by storm, when we've busted our guts our whole life to get where we are, even if we are a bunch of replacements."

Ratcliff pulled Gil in the ninth inning. Tajima was pitching well and Ratcliff was worried that Gil would overdo his arm in his first outing. Thanks to Slider, the Rockies were holding on to a one-run lead. Tajima, his tall, lanky frame, gave him the appearance of a basketball player on the mound. But his sidearm throw was nearly impossible to hit. Ratcliff looked down when Tajima gave up a single with the first batter. But then Tajima managed a double play and the bases were clear. He popped up the last batter, and the Rockies had their first win of the season. But their new golden boy overshadowed the win. In eight innings, Gil had shut out the Cards, giving up two walks, striking out nine, and averaging 108 miles per hour on his fastball.

Gil hustled out onto the field with the rest of the players as they lined up and congratulated each other. He saw Keri, still clapping, and jogged over to greet his family.

"Great game," she said from the front row, leaning over the railing. He gave her a quick kiss.

"Yeah, you were awesome," Austin said.

Gil ruffled his hair, feeling his goosebumps. Gil turned, signed a few programs and turned for the dugout.

* * *

The press insisted that Ratcliff cough up his two most colorful players: Slider and Gil.

The two players sat at a table in the pressroom, microphones placed in front of each one like they were witnesses at a government investigation. Gil studied the sportswriters, trying to guess what they were going to ask him. He could handle the inevitable drug questions. He just hoped they didn't know about the lawsuit.

"Tell us what Timber Johnson told you to settle you down in the first inning." The question came from a female ESPN reporter with some sporty turquoise glasses.

"Preacher? Just some good old-fashioned advice—to pitch like my personality."

She scribbled something on her notepad and sat down.

"Slider, what did Ratcliff tell you after you were ejected?" asked another reporter.

"Just the opposite," Slider said without hesitation. "He told me to play without personality. This guy can show off by throwing hard, but I can't express myself by sliding hard—or not sliding at all. I don't like those rules. We're trying to do the same thing, just in different ways. Just like baseball is always done. It lets some poor schmuck who's down on his luck come and forget about life for a while. I'm that artist that does that and no rule should tell me that I can't."

"Gil, this one is for you." It was a seasoned reporter wearing a linen sports coat. "Your fastball. How so fast? Doctors, physical therapists, and even physics professors say you can't throw that fast. It's not humanly possible. What gives with your bionic arm?"

Gil smiled and looked him straight in the eyes. "That's what they told Roger Bannister when he tried to break the four-minute mile. Now we have marathoners doing it for twenty-six miles. Do you think they are all on drugs?"

The room erupted in laughter.

"I wasn't implying you are on drugs," the man said, still standing.

"Perhaps not you, but everyone else is. So let's get the record straight. I'm not doing drugs. Never have, never will. I won't even let me wife buy my supplements—even though she says now that I'm getting older, I should be taking a calcium pill." The reporters laughed again. "But I am being serious. I have nothing to hide."

21

THE MOMENT THEY entered the lobby, the attendant arose from her chair to greet them. "No need to check in, Mr. Gilbert," she said. "We've got everything waiting. We know you have a busy day."

She led them down a hall to an examining room. Keri, Alicia, and Pastor Ron followed. Dr. Cherrie Kempski was all business. She wasn't at all what Gil had expected—thin, wiry, well past retirement, but still running marathons. Gil fidgeted as he sat on the exam table while Keri, Alicia, and his father sat on three plastic chairs in the corner.

"I'm not sure why you're so adamant about putting Gil through this," Pastor Ron told Keri. "God is blessing him with this talent. Nothing is wrong with him. It's another distraction he doesn't need."

Keri pursed her lips. She'd learned long ago she could never win an argument with her stubborn father-in-law.

"Ready?" Dr. Kempski said, her arms folded.

Gil nodded.

"How many strikes did you throw last game?"

"I'm not sure."

"Baloney. Every pitcher knows his own stats."

"Okay, I threw about sixty pitches, and I think about forty-one were strikes. But that's just my best guess, because I really don't know my numbers."

"Yeah, right. It was exactly forty-one, and that's about how many times I'm going to poke you with a needle today. I hope you're not pitching soon, because I'm going to draw about a pint of blood. We're going to keep the lab about as busy as your bullpen when DeJesus is pitching."

"I like you," Keri said, her legs crossed while she sat in the lone chair tucked in the corner of the office. "You talk faster than Gil."

"Strip down, except for your undies, and put this on," she said, tossing him a light blue drape. "Then go ahead and sit on the table."

The family excused themselves. Gil obeyed, and a minute later Dr. Kempski was listening with her stethoscope while she poked and prodded. He breathed deeply, coughed and complained when she smacked his knee to check his reflexes. Then she put on the blood pressure cuff, measured his pulse, and studied his pupils. Then she asked questions about his diet, how many times he visited the bathroom, any difficulty in breathing and how many hours he slept.

"Fit as a fiddle," she said, pulling off her gloves, "at least on the outside. You're middle-aged, but have the body of a twenty-year-old." She drew the front of his gown shut like a pair of curtains and invited the visitors back into the room.

"Nicest chest I've ever seen, and believe me, I've seen a lot. Keri must be a happy woman."

"It's not his outsides that I'm worried about."

"I've got the first test back from Dr. Doty. Let's see what we have."

"Did you notice Gil's right shoulder is a little bit bigger?" Keri said.

"What?" Gil said.

"Of all people, I should know."

"I wish I knew what size it was six months ago, but we'll just have to use this as a baseline. It's not unusual for a person to have uneven muscles, especially associated with their dominant arm."

Dr. Kempski slid her clipboard on the desk and tapped out

a few keystrokes on the keyboard. She ran her finger down the monitor, studying the test results provided by Dr. Doty. After a couple of minutes, she looked up from the screen.

"Gil, your initial numbers are all out of whack. Your proteins, white blood cell count, enzymes—they're all over the board. The problem is that I don't know what any of this means.

"What is more problematic is that your muscle and bone tissues appear to be excessively dense. We're going to have to dig a lot deeper, Gil. I'm going to have my assistant take about twenty vials of blood. I'm ordering every test imaginable. From allergies to cancer, I'm running it. Oh, and I need to check your skeletal structure. I can't figure out how the bones in your arm are handling the stress produced when launching a hundred-and-ten-mile-an-hour fastball. I'll need you to run over and get an MRI."

Gil shifted his gaze, searching for a clock. Doctors' offices never seemed to have any.

"I'll send all the results to the Mayo in Rochester. They've got a good doctor there, a clinical virologist, who has asked to see it. There's no evidence of cancer anywhere, but the growth of your tissues is concerning. We'll take the blood tests every week for the foreseeable future. I've already set an appointment for you to see Dr. Kusha at the Mayo. By then, we should have enough data to make some predictions."

"Predictions?" Gil said. "No diagnosis? And blood every week? I can't keep losing that much juice and still keep pitching. And what about when I'm on the road?"

"I've already spoken to Dr. Kusha. Medical science hasn't advanced far enough to tell us what all these chemical variations mean, other than we know the data is troubling. We'll just need to track it and look for trends. That should tell us something. If I were to tell you anything else right now, it would be pure speculation. Is there some mutation in your DNA that is causing this? Or is one of your organs malfunctioning? Could it just be a dysfunctional thyroid? We don't know, and I'm certainly not qualified to give an opinion. That's why you're going to the Mayo—no exceptions."

"I agree," Keri said with a scowl.

Gil shrugged. "I'm not arguing against it."

"And," Dr. Kempski continued, "I'm going to give you a stronger steroid. I think you've got some inflammation in your chest. It should take it down, loosen up your muscles, help you breathe a little better."

"Are you sure?" Gil said. "I can't take steroids."

"It's either that or . . . "

"What?" Keri asked.

Dr. Kempski looked at Alicia.

"You can tell us," Keri said.

"I'll put you to bed."

"No baseball?" Pastor Ron interrupted.

"Let's run the tests and stick with the steroids for now."

22

OPENING DAY IN Denver was a time-honored tradition, at least for the relatively few years that the Rockies had been a chartered professional team. Businesses emptied, kids skipped school, and the bars on Blake Street filled. Game day turned out to be perfect, in the mid-sixties with a slight breeze.

Opening day tickets usually sold out. But this year with the strike, there wasn't much hope of that—not until Gil Gilbert came along. Sports commentators and writers were all over him, constantly calling, showing video clips of his lightning-speed fastball, having fun with speculating on how an *old man,* a simple high school coach, was breaking one of baseball's most coveted records.

The Gilberts showed up two hours early. Keri finally relented after Austin nearly drove them crazy asking when they could leave. Peck called in sick and found the Gilberts already seated. He took Austin to the concession stands and bought him a slice of pizza and a drink.

In the locker room, Gil was lacing his shoes—for the third time. Out of the corner of his eye, he studied the other players, watching their routines, wanting to make sure he looked like he knew what he was doing.

Ratcliff entered toting his clipboard, and called for a team meeting. He stood in the center of the locker room, resting his shoe on the wooden bench. The players circled around their coach. Following tradition, he spoke to each player in turn, starting with the down-and-out player he'd just obtained from the Cubs.

"Manzi, this is payback time. The Cubs threw you into the flames and the best way to make them hurt is by driving in some runs. Are you up to showing what your bat can do?"

The new shortstop nodded.

"You young guys, Gonzalez, Slider, we're going to need to count on you both if we're going to get anywhere this season."

Slider looked away and rolled his eyes. Gonzalez, the center fielder energetically said, "You can count on me for a hundred and ten percent."

"And you veterans—Preacher, Biondi—you're the heart of this team, and we're going to lean on you for your leadership. Let's show this team what we can do this year." Preacher nodded while Biondi smoothed his goatee.

"Trudeau, you got your head in the game?" The second baseman winked.

"Alright. Juarez, we all know your knee is shot, but that shouldn't stop your bat. And Boclin, you've had four years in the majors. It's time to make a name for yourself. Let's see what you can do."

Both men nodded.

"And Gil, you've brought new life to our team. Take your lead from Preacher and stay tough. Rockies, we're going to win this one."

Before Gil went to the mound, he wandered over to where the players' families were sitting. He waved at Keri, Austin, and Alicia. Peck gave him his usual thumbs-up sign.

"It's going to be a great season together," Peck said. Melendez's wife gave him a sour look. "Don't worry, we'll get along famously. I like chick stuff. You know, the *Twilight* series, Nicolas Sparks."

A dozen kids scampered down the aisle, holding out any piece of memorabilia for Gil to sign. He took a marker from a freckled-face boy and signed his glove. He put his signature to a cap, a program and even a bare hand.

"Okay, I've got to go pitch," he said with his familiar smile, his teeth gleaming. "Wish me luck."

As Gil approached the mound, he noticed Slider standing on third base, hands on his hips. "Why do you bother with those people?"

"It's good for the game," Gil said.

"No, I'm good for the game. I leave my signature on the field, not on some piece of paper."

Gil shook his head.

After warm-ups, the two teams lined up on the baselines, removing their caps for the national anthem, which was sung by a local country singer. The roar of a fighter jet from Buckley Air Force Base rang in their ears, followed by the booming and crackling of a wall of fireworks that shot up from behind the left field bleachers. The mayor of Denver threw out the first pitch then shook hands with a group of returning soldiers and a few disabled fans—all a calculated marketing effort to make everyone feel good, like this was the most charitable way to spend their afternoon.

The loudspeakers began to blast the latest top-forty music while the giant LCD screen streamed highlights from last year's lackluster season. Beer guys began scaling the stands. "Ice cold beer! Get your ice cold beer!" Dinger, the Rockies' mascot, ran down the left field line while live cameras tried to capture little tykes attempting to touch their mascot.

Season ticket holders lugged armloads of concessions, from hotdogs to ice cream, to their second places of residence. The serious fans, with headphones tucked over their ears, listened to radio commentary while they adjusted their seat cushions and applied sun block.

The twenties crowd danced to the music. Even though the dog days of summer were months away, those caring about fashion already donned their short shorts, revealing white legs protected by six months of winter. Already, hundreds of fans sported recently purchased Rockies jerseys, purple with bold white letters: GILBERT and the number 8.

Gil trotted to the mound, powdered his hand with chalk and took up the baseball. By the time he'd kicked the dirt clean in front of the rubber, the entire stadium was on their feet. Gil warmed up slowly, making sure he didn't pull any muscles. When his shoulder felt fluid, he let his first fastball rip.

The scoreboard normally didn't post the speed of the pitches during warm-ups, but this year would be different. These fans came to see speed, and the front office wasn't about to disappoint. When Preacher's glove popped, the bright lights read *111*.

Biondi pointed to it, as if anyone needed to be shown. Then he casually tossed a grounder to Trudeau and waited for its return. In the outfield, Gonzalez stood gazing with hands on hips then continued throwing pop-ups to Juarez and Boclin.

The Chicago Cubs had taken second place in their division and managed to get a wild card spot in the playoffs, but floundered in the NLCS. Their manager had sworn an oath that this season they would win it all. And the owner pulled out his checkbook to prove it. The team loaded up on talent, and when those players went on strike, the Cubs filled its shopping bag with expensive replacement players, many from the vaunted baseball leagues in Japan, South Korea, and the Dominican Republic. The club even enticed, with big pay, some Triple-A minor league stars to break ranks with the baseball union.

The Cubs put up their third baseman as leadoff batter. As he swung his bat, Gil found himself hopping on his toes. He was bursting with energy and refused to let the moment pass unappreciated. Gil looked around the rim of the stadium, then let his gaze lower, hoping he had time to nod at every fan. *This is life, just where I want to be*, he told himself. He was going to pitch like he loved being here.

Preacher called for a fastball, and Gil delivered. His first pitch flashed *112* on the clock. The batter's swing was so far behind the pitch, it looked staged. The crowd, all on their feet, went wild. Even from the mound, the noise was deafening. Gil clenched the ball in his fist. This was for real. He was living his dream. Preacher signed for two more fastballs, and Gil again put the heat on his pitches. Two more swings and he retired his first batter.

Gil couldn't help but to look above the Rockies' dugout. Austin had jumped into Peck's arms, who himself had sprung to life, swinging Austin around in the aisle.

Next was the Cubs' slugger. Most managers stacked the

lineup so that the power hitter was number four in the lineup, known as the cleanup hitter. But the Cubs' manager was trying a new strategy. He wanted to get the firepower going right out of the gate, not later in the lineup. The batter was a large, muscular player who had hit forty-seven homers in the Cuban League the previous season. The scouting report indicated that the slugger could crunch curveballs, and if he got even part of the bat on a slider, he'd rip it down the left field line. He could hit a fastball, but most often struck out swinging at them.

Gil watched as Preacher signaled for a slider, low and inside. Gil shook his head, waiting for Preacher to signal for another fastball. Preacher repeated the signal, and Gil wondered why he wanted a slider. He finally relented. As soon as he released the pitch, he gritted his teeth. He couldn't control his slider like his fastball, and the spin was all wrong. The batter took a shortened swing and hit it sharply foul, right in front of the Cubs' dugout.

He's ahead of the pitch, Gil told himself. The scouting report was right. Unless I get more heat on my next throw, he's going to nail it.

But Preacher called for another slider, the same pitch. Gil signaled "no." He wanted a fastball, and he wasn't going to back down. Preacher again signaled for the slider. Gil shook him off and started his windup anyway.

The release felt good, enough velocity to be well over 110. Gil heard the crack of the bat even before he came up out of his follow-through. It was a sickening sound. The ball shot out of the infield on a straight line. It never dipped but headed 530 feet straight into deep center. The deafening roar of the crowd instantly stopped. Gil could hear his own breathing.

Preacher sat in his crouch while the base runner lapped the bases. He watched as the umpire threw Gil another ball. Then Preacher waited. Gil stared, anticipating Preacher's signals. None came. Gil waited another minute, but Preacher refused to signal for the pitch. He needed to throw again, to spark the crowd to life. He felt naked, with all eyes upon him, wondering if all the hype was for nothing.

After an awkward moment, Gil walked down the mound toward home plate. Preacher stood, kept on his mask and waited for Gil to reach him.

"Who in the hell do you think you are?" Preacher shouted, his mask hiding his lips from the cameras.

Gil looked away, venturing his eyes toward the crowd of stunned fans. Nobody was standing, the mobile phones were packed away, and the cheering had stopped.

"I gave you a signal for a reason. I called for a slider."

"Sorry," Gil finally said, still looking away. "The scouting report—"

"You listen to me. That's your scouting report. I hope you've learned your lesson."

Gil tried to turn his head, but Preacher was so close there wasn't room to move.

"I can't tell you how pissed I am right now," Preacher continued. "I'm the only one sticking up for you, and this is what you do to me? Think you're hot stuff because you can throw fast? That's not going to get you anywhere. They are going to camp on your fastball and knock it out every time. I don't care how hard you throw, these guys are pros. They'll hit the shit out of you if you put it down the gosh darn middle. From now on, you listen to me. Got it?"

Preacher turned and clomped away from Gil.

"Preacher," Gil said when he was halfway to the mound. Preacher looked up and walked to Gil.

"What?"

Gil's smile shot back on his face. "I thought you didn't cuss."

"What in the hell are you talking about? We are in the middle of opening day and you're asking me about cussing? I do cuss, just don't take the Lord's name in vain, but you pull this crap one more time, and I certainly will."

Shaking his head, Preacher took his place behind the plate and put on his mask but remained standing. He held his right arm straight out to the side, calling for a pitchout.

Gil's mouth opened and his jaw dropped. The call didn't make sense. There was nobody on base. Gil's first thought was to look over at Connor to see what he signaled, but that was no use. So, Gil wound up and threw the pitch three feet outside. Several fans began to boo the call.

Preacher stepped in front of the plate and yelled, "Okay, now we understand each other. Let's play ball!"

Gil's smile was back and he struck out the side with a combination of breaking balls and heaters.

The Rockies' thin lineup couldn't produce any runs. Slider walked twice and Juarez hit to the warning track three times, but with no base runners he failed to drive in any runs. Ratcliff let Gil go all nine innings, hoping his team could tie it in the bottom of the ninth, saving his relief pitcher, Tajima, for any extra innings. There were no extra innings, and the Rockies lost one to nothing.

Heads hung low in the locker room. DeJesus approached Gil. "Like I said, one bad pitch. That's all it takes."

Ratcliff was furious. He threw down his cap and kicked it. Biondi nervously scratched his goatee while Slider plucked at the stitching on his pants.

"We are two and a stinking five. It's disgraceful. Our pitcher gives up just one run, and we still can't win."

They endured the rest of his tirade then hit the showers.

Gil was one of the last to leave the locker room, mostly to avoid the media.

"Gil, you gotta learn to face the music, so go on," his pitching coach, Connor said. "You did well today; nothin' to be ashamed of. The team let you down. Keep it positive, and you'll be alright."

He did. Reporters swarmed as he left the dressing room.

"You must be feeling angry about the team's play. You strike out nine guys and give up just two hits and you lose. How does that make you feel?"

Gil thought for a moment of the pep talks he'd given his school's team after a tough defeat.

"The great thing about this game," he said, "is we get to try again tomorrow, and then the next day and the next. Improving is as important as winning, and, believe me, this team's gonna improve."

23

THE NEXT DAY Gil's pickup truck rambled up to Denver's Children's Hospital. Melendez had warned him about these events. "Yeah, it's great to be involved in the community, to give back, but not like this."

When Gil asked what he meant, Melendez explained that growing up in East LA, he knew what it meant to need charity, and a ten-minute visit from some baseball player or celebrity wasn't going to get you a place to live or help get your father off drugs or buy you a bullet-proof jacket.

For Gil the entertainer, any visit to someone needing a boost was something worthwhile. If he could brighten a little girl's day, it was worth a few hours of his time. At least that's what he thought.

As soon as he entered the reception area, Eugenia, the Rockies' community involvement planner, jumped up and pranced over to Gil, grabbing his hand. "Oh, thanks for coming, Gil. This is going to mean so much to these children. They need your smile, to give them hope. You have no idea how much this means to them." With that, she pulled Gil past the reception desk and down a long hallway.

Moments later, Gil found himself walking through a set of doors with a sign marked "Oncology" above the doorframe. Eugenia, still tugging Gil along, turned sharply left and into Room 103, where the occupant was secluded behind a drawn curtain. Slider, arms folded, was standing and tapping his foot. Eugenia dropped Gil's hand and put her fingers to her lips, then spoke softly. "I found him. Are you ready?"

"Been here for nearly fifteen minutes," Slider said. "What do you think?"

Eugenia brushed past him, parted the curtain and peeked inside. "Oh, it's perfect," she said, looking back at the two players. "There is this little eight-year-old boy in here. He has brain cancer, or maybe stomach cancer, oh I can't remember, but that doesn't really matter. He loves you, Gil, and you too, Slider. I'll get a photo with you on both sides of the bed, with your arms around him. His father left the family a year ago, so you two are his new godparents. Gil, you can tell him that you'll pitch a no-hitter just for him. And, Slider, you can show him how you do one of your famous headfirst slides. *Sliding for the cure.* Oh, I love it."

She threw the curtain open and barged inside, fumbling with her clipboard. "Tommy, is that right? And you must be Tommy's mom," she said to the woman standing beside the bed.

The bald boy with the shiny white head was propped up by two fluffy pillows. A half-dozen tubes wound their way from his pale body to a pole carrying an assortment of fluid-filled bags. Slider plopped himself on the edge of the bed and rested his head on his elbow.

"I'm not sure it's okay to sit there," Eugenia said.

Slider waved her off. "Oh, he'll be fine. Let him see his Slider."

The boy's eyes lit up. "Slider, Gil. It's really you. I didn't think you'd come."

Eugenia, being less than subtle, reached for a camera from her bag. *Great photo op,* she thought. *The front office will love it.*

Gil glanced at Slider, then up to Eugenia.

"Tell you what," Slider said. "I'm going to show you how I set up for one of my world famous slides. It's all about body position. Say third base is over there by the TV. I get my body moving forward then throw my arms forward like this."

Slider flung his arms forward and lay over Tommy's lap, blocking Eugenia's lens.

The boy giggled then coughed. "That's awesome," he said after he regained his composure.

Slider leaned over and whispered, "When I was your age, I didn't have a dad either. It stinks, doesn't it?"

Tommy cupped his hand over Slider's ear and spoke so that nobody could hear.

"I'll never tell a soul," Slider whispered back.

Eugenia bustled her way to the back corner and snatched up an acoustic guitar, wiping off a streak of dust. "Okay, we have another surprise. Tommy, can you tell us your favorite song? Gil is going to sing it for you."

Gil looked at her. "I am?"

"Oh, I forgot to tell you. I heard you can play anything." She slipped a cracked-leather shoulder strap over his head.

Gil slid the pick out of the strings and strummed the guitar. "Well that doesn't sound too good," he said, reaching for the tuning pegs. "Pick your song," he said, tossing up the pick.

"Can you play *Lady Antebellum*?"

Gil raised his eyebrows. "You like country? Or you just have a crush on that cute little lead singer?"

"I wish I could sing like them," Tommy said.

"I hate that country crap," Slider said, still sprawled out on the bed. "Can't we watch TV or something? Let's see if I'm on *SportsCenter*."

"Ignore him," Gil said. "He doesn't have any kids of his own. Someday he'll understand."

The boy coughed out a faint laugh. "Think you can sing one of their songs?"

"I can try, but my voice isn't as good as theirs. What's the song?"

"*Learning to Fly*. I like the part about wings and flying. When my insides really start hurting, I dream about flying. I hope I get wings someday."

"Like an angel's wings?" Gil said. The boy nodded, and Gil could almost feel Eugenia's scowl. "You can't have them until you get a lot older than me." He strummed a chord then began the tune.

The boy leaned his head on Gil's shoulder.

"You know, we're a lot alike," Tommy said when Gil finished. "We both have a disease that nobody understands. My mom says it's God's way of letting me go to the other side more quickly."

Gil rubbed his hand over the boy's hairless head. "I wouldn't worry about that. Everyone has to die someday. Don't worry about getting your wings now."

"But when?" Tommy asked. "I don't want to wait. I need them now."

"Nobody knows. That's what makes life so special."

"We have a busy day," Eugenia interrupted, tugging Slider off the bed.

The players wished Tommy and his mother well and slipped into the hallway. Eugenia stayed behind, finishing her paperwork, having Tommy's mother sign the legal waivers.

"I hate stuff like this," Slider said.

"Visiting little kids?" Gil said.

"Yeah, I hate kids. No, of course not. I'm not totally evil, but forcing me to go to crap like this then staging the whole thing. I don't do stuff like that." A nurse slipped beside them and Slider lowered his voice. "It's bull crap, just bull crap."

"Well you came, didn't you?"

"Only because I'm in the doghouse for sticking my finger in the ump's chest. I can't afford any more fines."

"But you do like kids?"

"Yeah, as long as they aren't snot-nosed."

Gil frowned.

"Just kidding. Lighten up. That was really cool, how you sang that song for him."

"Nicely orchestrated by Eugenia."

"I have an idea," Slider said. "I'm done with all this little boy cancer stuff. It's so cliché. If you want to make a difference without all the publicity, go visit somebody that nobody cares about, somebody the world has left behind."

"Am I really hearing you right? Is this the same Slider who spit in a kid's glove last year when he held it out for an autograph?"

"The world doesn't understand me. No matter how bad you have it, somebody's life is worse. Come on."

Before Gil could object, he was on Slider's heels, out a side door and into the parking lot. At a jog, Slider went about four blocks until they came to a single-story red brick building. Gil, still toting Eugenia's old guitar, held it in front of him to keep it from bouncing on his hip. "An old-folks home. Nice idea," Gil said as they approached the door. "Think anyone will even know who we are?"

Slider stopped. "Mr. Gil, everyone knows Slider. Don't you forget that. Just watch."

The front entry looked more like funeral parlor than a convalescence center. Slider nodded his cap to a lady wearing a white uniform and kept walking.

"Wait, you need to sign in," she said.

"Hi, how are you?" Gil said.

"Fine, and who are you here to see?"

"His friend," Gil said, pointing to Slider.

"And who is he?"

"Him?" Gil looked at Slider. "I thought you two knew each other."

"Never seen him here before. I hope you're not coming to see your mother. Just get out of jail or something?"

Gil burst out, "You really don't know him?"

"No, he looks like some king of hoodlum.

"Watch any baseball?" Gil said.

"Not the Rockies if that's what you mean," she said, pointing at Slider's cap. "Why should I emotionally invest myself in a team that always loses? And this year is even worse, with all those replacement players and stuff."

"Know any of their players?" Slider said, stepping forward and slipping off his glasses.

"Just from what I heard about them—from that reality show, you know. They have some hot-shot pitcher."

"That's enough," Slider said, slipping past her. "Consider myself checked in. I've got to make a visit."

Slider randomly picked a room halfway down the main hall. He didn't knock, but pushed the door open. The only light came from a window with half-drawn shades. Gil's eyes adjusted quickly. The room wasn't much different from Tommy's hospital room they'd just come from—a small bed, neatly made up, with a single nightstand. A television set was mounted to the wall, but was silent. Sitting in a lone chair was a white-haired woman, staring at nothing. No crochet, no book, just blankly looking at the wall, with her arms resting in her lap. Gil wondered if they'd made a huge mistake.

She raised her eyes, and when she saw the two men, her countenance lightened. "Well hello," she said. "I'd ask you to come in, but it looks like you already helped yourself." The two men paused, and the woman said, "Don't be shy now. I'd invite you to sit on my couch, but I don't have one, so the bed will have to do."

Slider looked at Gil and plopped himself down, like a little boy trying to see how high he could bounce. His body weight created a loud pop. Gil bit his lip.

"I'll bet that old bed has never had its springs rocked like that before," the woman said. "It's about time."

"I like you," Gil said, holding out his hand. "I'm Gil and this here is Slider."

She waved him off. "I know you two. Rockies players. And, the only two decent players on the team, if I may say. You look kind of funny holding that silly guitar."

Gil held it up. "This? Long story."

Before he could continue, the white-dressed attendant barged in. "I'm sorry, Melvelene. I'll get them to leave."

"No need," she said, waving her off. "A couple of old friends."

Slider furrowed his brow at the woman, and she stormed out.

"Melvelene. I've never heard that name," Gil said. "It's pretty."

"I thought you were going to say *old-fashioned*," she said.

"She is spunky, isn't she?" said Slider.

"My father liked it, and he ruled the house, so that's why he named me *Melvelene*."

"So you know about baseball?" Gil said.

"Great sport for when they lock you up in a place like this and forget about you. You can kill a half a day with just one game." Gil looked at Slider. "Oh come off it, you two. I'm kidding. I'm not one of those people who sit in here waiting to die. I love baseball. One-eleven, fastest clocked pitch ever. But I watch the Rockies because I like to watch you, Slider, all those muscles bulging in your uniform, those cartwheels; oh, I wish I was twenty years younger."

"Just twenty?" Slider said.

"I'm only forty-four, and don't you tell a soul I'm any older." She tugged on Gil's arm. "Come here to sing me a song?"

"Sure," Gil said. "We do stuff this like all the time, don't we, Slider?"

"Liar," she said. "But I'm glad you came. Heaven knows we could use some excitement around here. You don't know any of the songs we used to listen to, so I'll spare you. But I do want to feel Slider's bicep. I'm single, you know, so I can flirt all I want. My husband died over a decade ago."

Slider nodded at Gil. He'd one-upped him. "Don't need a beat-up guitar for that," he said, flexing his arm.

They talked for nearly another hour until Gil realized they were going to be late for practice, and Slider said he didn't care, except that if he was late one more time, he'd get a ten thousand dollar fine. They said their goodbyes and headed back to the hospital to find their vehicles.

"Tell me, Slider," Gil said when they reached his truck, "what did you tell that little boy?"

"The kid is going to die. I entertained him, just like Eugenia wanted."

"Come on, Slider. "

"Don't *Slider* me. You didn't tell Melvelene anything about how you flunked out of baseball, and it's just some freak of nature, your so-called medical condition, that got the attention of the Rockies. You know she wanted to hear about it."

The barb stung. Slider was an enigma. One moment he was letting a widow feel his muscle, and the next he was tearing you to pieces.

"Maybe."

"You're funny, Gil. You love to talk, but you never say anything with substance."

"I don't need the world to know about my insides."

"Then that makes two of us. Let's leave it at that."

Gil opened his door.

"Hey, you left your guitar," Slider said.

"I know," Gil said. "So I'll have an excuse to go back."

24

GIL DID HIS normal rounds before the game, signing a teenager's bright green cast and sitting on the handle of a paraplegic's wheelchair while he presented a baseball. Slider chased down a ground ball in front of them. He snatched up the ball and made a motion to throw the ball to a crowd of kids who'd rushed to the infield in the hopes of getting a souvenir. In unison, they held up their hands, some their gloves.

"Just kidding," Slider said, then whipped the ball to Biondi at first.

Gil shook his head, took another ball out of his mitt and tossed it to the disappointed fans. In five seconds, Slider had managed to undo all of yesterday's good.

"I told you, Gil," he shouted from third base, "I'm not their role model. Never been, never will."

Gil wandered over. "You could be."

Gil fully expected the Yankees players to be sizing him up, watching him warm up, calculating how they would react to his pitches. But they were intentionally ignoring him, the reality show celebrity who had no business playing professional baseball. They were joking around, slapping backs, ignoring

Gil, like they were completely oblivious that this guy could put to shame any of their pitchers, replacements or not. Every few minutes, one of them would turn and spit some chew onto the dirt, wipe his face, then turn back around.

Preacher too was zeroed in on the Yankees' dugout, glancing over after throwing the ball back to the pitcher's mound. And he surprised Gil when he called for three straight fastballs to the leadoff hitter. Three strikes and the first batter went down swinging. Preacher had Gil pitch fastballs the entire first inning, and Gil responded by striking out the side. The roar of the crowd was deafening.

When the Rockies came to bat, Slider led off with a walk, once again bringing the crowd to its feet. After the next three batters left him on first base, the crowd calmed down. They'd seen this before.

Both teams remained scoreless into the third inning, when Preacher called for an inside fastball. Preacher set up almost behind the batter's box. Either the batter leaned forward, or Gil left it too far inside. Either way, it hit the Yankees player in the forearm with a sickening crack. The trainer came out, pressed his arm in several places then led him off the field and into the dugout. Gil stepped forward to apologize, but Preacher waved him off.

"You don't apologize when it wasn't intentional. Stuff like that happens in baseball," he said when he got to the mound. "Shake it off and don't let it get to you."

The next batter hit into a double play. Gil followed this by a strikeout, and the Rockies were up to bat.

Gil came to the plate after Gonzalez popped out. He had barely finished adjusting his helmet when the pitcher finished his windup and hurled his first pitch straight at Gil.

The fastball struck Gil in the left forearm. Connor bolted out of the dugout.

"Is it broken?" was the first thing Connor said, rubbing his finger over the bruise.

"I don't think so, but it hurt like you wouldn't believe."

"Can you still pitch?"

"No problem. My throwing arm's fine."

Gil trotted down to first base, and Slider took the batter's box. So far this season, base runners were a rarity, and with Slider at the plate, there was a real chance Gil could advance to third base, if not score altogether.

"Why don't you try that again?" Slider called out to the Yankees' pitcher. "Then let's see what I can do to your face."

The umpire readied himself, and the pitcher threw right at Slider's head. Slider hit the dirt, and the ball flew past the catcher. Gil almost walked to second base. The umpire shouted a warning while Slider brushed the red dirt off his white pants.

"Got me dirty," Slider said while taking a practice swing, "and you don't want to see me play dirty."

The Yankees' pitcher threw three more sliders, all tailing inside. Slider nonchalantly tossed his bat and began his walk to first. Nothing seemed out of the ordinary until Slider was halfway to the base, when he suddenly took a left turn and bolted toward the pitcher's mound.

Slider charged the pitcher, grabbing his arm, wrenching out his shoulder. In a flash, the entire Yankees team piled out from the dugout and onto Slider, swinging fists and kicking cleats. The Rockies charged the mound too, pulling, pushing and punching Yankees.

The officials had to call security to clear the players. When Slider got up from the dirt, blood was pouring out of his nose, and his eye was red. And, he had a giant smile. The pitcher was escorted off, with the trainer supporting his wounded arm.

Gil stood on second base, hands cupped to his mouth, shouting at the players. He wanted to join the melee, but thought of the example that would send his high school kids. Gil hated fighting.

Play resumed, and at the bottom of the sixth, both teams were still scoreless. Gil could sense his throwing arm tightening— and his blood pressure rising. The Rockies needed to score, and nobody was stepping up. Gil put on his batter's helmet and yanked out his bat.

Gil took his stance, squatting low and leaning over the plate. If he couldn't put wood on the ball, he was ready to get hit again. He must get on base.

On the first pitch, Gil punched his bat. It was an ugly sort of half-swing, half-bunt. But it was enough to loop the ball over the first baseman's head. His adrenaline flowing, he glared into the Yankees' dugout and pumped his fist as he stood on first base.

"That's what we need," Ratcliff shouted to his players. "Get some fire in you like Slider. Yeah, he's in a whole boatload of trouble, but at least he's passionate. If you have no passion then get off my team. I want to see some kind of fire in the belly. A passionless person is useless. Yes, Slider gets tossed, gets into trouble, but at least he plays out of his heart."

Boclin took to the batter's box, swung his hips like he was dancing to a Brazilian hip hop song, and slugged out a base hit, advancing Gil to second. Manzi then loaded the bases. It was up to Juarez to deliver some runs. Favoring his good knee, he advanced to the batter's box and tagged a line drive into the corner in left field, clearing the bases and putting the Rockies up three to zero. The roar through the stadium was deafening. Banners waved and fans jumped on their seats. They realized that their ragtag team might be going somewhere.

Ratcliff kept Gil in for all nine innings. He finalized his decision when, in the top of the eighth inning, Gil kept his fastball above the century mark. Preacher managed to homer in the top of the ninth and the Rockies won, four-zip.

As the umpire belted out the last called strike, the entire Rockies organization sprinted to the mound to shake Gil's hand. Security guards, waving their batons, blockaded the aisles to prevent the onrush of spectators from bolting onto the field.

"It's only April, and we're all a bunch of misfits," Gil said as he shook Preacher's hand, "but it sure feels good." They walked side by side to the dugout, savoring the cheers of the lingering crowd.

Preacher poked Gil with his elbow, nodding to the darkest corner of the dugout. In the shadows, Slider, dressed in street clothes, pulled his cap over his eyes.

"You stole his show," Preacher said. "And the reason we got all those hits was probably because Slider took out their pitcher."

Gil leaned over the railing. "Hey, Slider. I owe you one."

Slider flicked the brim of his cap, raising it a quarter inch. The whiteness of his eyes glowed in the dimming light. "Sure do."

Gil raised his finger. "Wait. I've got an idea. This one's for you."

He sprinted back onto the infield, and in full stride, raised his arms, flung himself into the air and managed an awkward looking cartwheel, nearly landing on top of one of the grounds crew who was busy raking the baseline from third to second.

As soon as he caught his balance, Gil wheezed then coughed. He tried not to put his hand to his face, but habit overtook him. He whipped his head around, hoping that no cameras were focused on him, but he knew that was impossible. He breathed out deeply, and when he did, he noticed that his chest hurt. Yes, it was usually tight, but not like this. He quickly rubbed his breastbone, then began a slow jog to the dugout. Slider pumped his fist, pointed to Gil, then slunk back into the locker room.

25

COLORADO SCHOOLS LET out for summer the first week of June, and Austin and his grandfather had already planned out their summer. Attending all of the home games was a given, but Austin also had plans to go on the road. After all, Peck would be flying to see them. Keri put her foot down, and Austin threatened to run away, although Keri and Alicia both knew he'd end up at Peck's place if he ever skipped out.

Gil came up with a compromise: The family would go on one road trip each month while Austin was out of school. But when it was time to hit the books, home games would have to suffice. When Pastor Ron heard about it, he offered to take Austin to an additional away game each month.

That didn't end the matter. Home games were not just games for Peck—not something where you showed up halfway into the second inning and left before traffic got too bad—but an all-out event. He made his appearance when the gates opened at ten in the morning and stayed until the last fan left and security escorted him out. Austin was determined to go with him. Peck offered to drive them all, but three hours in a ballpark were plenty for Keri and Alicia. At least for today, Austin won, but only because grandpa agreed to be an escort. After breakfast,

Austin filled his backpack and waited for Peck's honk.

The Rockies had meshed and now had a winning record of twenty-eight and twenty-four, only five games behind the divisional leaders, the Diamondbacks. Today, DeJesus was on the mound, but Gil still had to attend team meetings and pre-game practice. He left thirty minutes before Peck pulled his battered pickup into the driveway and rapped on his horn.

The families of the Rockies' players had jelled more than the team. Bunched together in three rows, nobody cared about assigned seats. They plopped themselves down wherever suited them. Peck strategically positioned himself right in the center. Pastor Ron and his grandson took the seats closer to the field, away from the constant focus of the reality show cameras.

At first, Keri worried that this big oaf would offend the women, and she'd be the one stuck asking him to find a seat elsewhere in the stadium. But there was a hidden side to Peck that nobody, not even Gil, knew existed. The first game he sat with them, he pulled out his tablet and went to his Pinterest site. He still wore his sleeveless shirts, and by this point in the season, his oversized shoulders were a dark brown with thousands of black freckles. He managed a two-day shadow on his face, and constantly rubbed balm on his chapped lips.

"I can't stand my curtains," he said after DeJesus struck out a batter in the first inning. "Haven't changed them since I bought the house."

Rosie DeJesus stopped her clapping. From the row behind, she peeked over his shoulder. "I love those," she said, pointing at some satin panel curtains.

The cameraman moved closer. Peck, the replacement baseball coach for the Prairie Ridge High School baseball team, had become a star on the weekly show.

"I agree they are cute," Peck said, "but I'm going to start with the kitchen. Maybe some blinds would be better."

"I love my kitchen blinds," Trista, Melendez's wife, said. She reached over and took Peck's tablet. "Here, I'll show you what I just got."

Trista tapped the screen a few times. "No way, she's got extensions."

Peck snatched his tablet back, noting the model on the

curtain advertisement. "Everyone has extensions these days. Fake boobs used to be a big deal, but now it's all about the hair. They're getting better, but I can still spot them a mile away—that, and an actress with an eating disorder."

"What about me?" Rosie said, drawing her fingers through her silky black hair. "Is mine fake or real?"

"Real," Peck said without even looking up. "I noticed your hair the first day I sat here. Love the full body, really healthy."

Alicia leaned over and whispered to her mother, "Sometimes I swear Peck's gay, but Dad says no way. He really likes women. I can't believe he can't stay married."

"Look at how he keeps himself," Keri said. "His beefy arms are always hanging out, usually sunburned, and he's got hair all over him. He's kind of like a scary truck driver."

Trista stole the computer back, and Peck nonchalantly waved her off. "Keep it for a bit. I'm hungry." Peck waved down the concessionaire and paid for two hot dogs and a bottle of beer. "Can I get a glass for the drink?" he said, handing over a twenty-dollar bill. "Anyone else want something? I've got some carrots and broccoli in my cooler if you're on a diet."

Keri usually took him up on the fresh foods, especially by the fifth inning, when her stomach began to gurgle. Peck reached into his bag and pulled out a plastic bag and handed them to Keri. "How many miles did you run this morning? Got to keep that body fueled up."

"Just six," she said, smiling for the camera.

Peck snatched back his bag of vegetables. "You need to put some meat on those bones." He tore off half of his hot dog and shoved it toward her face. "Open up if you don't want to be sorry."

She reluctantly pried open her mouth and let the soft white bread slip in.

"Anyone here have Botox?" Rosie asked, watching Trista sorting through one of her searches.

"If I knew, I wouldn't say," Peck said, picking off a few more inches of his bun and gently resting it on his tongue as if it were the Eucharist. He poured his beer into the glass and took a small sip, then licked his lips and shook his head. "The only thing I'll say is that with your high cheekbones, Rosie, you should never let a surgeon touch you."

"You're such a dainty eater," Alicia said.

Peck tore off another bite, licking the catsup from the end. "Hey, Trista, let me see that," Peck said. "I want to look up Herhold's stats against lefties. And how are the Mets doing?"

"Winning four to two," Austin said from his perch two rows below. "If DeJesus gets the win today and the Mets score stays the same, we'll be eight games behind the best team in the National League. Not bad, but the Rockies have got to do better if they're going to have a run at the pennant."

DeJesus was struggling in the fourth inning. Two batters were on base, and he was behind in the count. Rosie kept flipping through her magazine, yelling out for her husband to settle down and get the guy out.

"Rosie, I wanted to ask you something about your husband," Peck said. "Why's he always got that scowl, like he wants to beat you up?"

"Because he does," she said. Rosie explained how her husband's father was one of the boat people who made his escape from Cuba. DeJesus's mother was expecting a baby, and she had insisted that they flee to America where the baby could have a better life. The inflatable raft was crowded, and his father had to straddle the edge. Either from exhaustion, drunkenness, or possibly suicide, DeJesus's father disappeared from the raft the first night in the water. His mother always told a heroic story of how the boat was so crowded, her husband's leg had to float in the ocean, and that almost certainly he was pulled under by a shark. The story became the driving force in DeJesus's life.

"My husband grew up poor, mostly in the projects or on the streets," Rosie said. "When he got to be a teenager, he had a choice. He could retreat and become a recluse, probably a druggie. Or, he could go balls to the walls, let his anger at God come out in his baseball. So that's why he's a crazy thrower. He says he likes to throw at God. And that's why he pitches out of anger, hoping someday his people will be free from their dictator."

"Makes sense to me," Peck said. "I'd do the same thing."

"So, Keri, what's Gil's story?" Rosie asked. "He's like this mystery man. We don't know anything about him except he's this really popular science teacher and he coached high school ball."

"Nothing like your husband. I mean he wasn't abused growing up." She paused, waiting to see if her father-in-law was paying attention. When Pastor Ron kept up his discussion with Austin, she continued, "Gil had a normal childhood. He liked his job, and he loves his family. I think the best way to describe Gil is how Preacher put it. Gil told me that Preacher wanted Gil to pitch his personality. That's so much like Gil. He's always been the happy-go-lucky guy, like a kid who never grew up. Kind of a fun innocence about him."

"That I can vouch for," Peck said. "I think that's why the kids like him so much. Ever seen him without a smile?"

"But Keri, what's his real story?" This time it was Melendez. "My husband likes him too, but he can't figure him out. I mean he comes out of nowhere and takes the baseball world by storm. Why didn't he play before? That's all we really want to know."

Keri shook her head then turned from the direct shot of the camera lens. The comment surprised her. They'd become what she thought to be good friends; they'd even been over to the Melendez home for dinner, but maybe that was just a fishing expedition. "I don't know. All I can say is that pitching professionally is something he's always wanted to do. He's always had this dream, and then one day he wakes up and he's got the arm to make it happen. I couldn't tell him no."

"So you didn't want him to pitch?"

Pastor Ron spun around and cupped his hand to his ear. Alicia looked at her mother, waiting for her answer.

"I was afraid he'd look foolish, then regret he'd ever tried. You know he had to give up a job he loved. I wasn't sure if it would be worth that. But I knew he would regret it if he didn't give it a try. He wanted to go pro after college, but that didn't work out. This time, I knew I had to let him do it."

The wives were looking at each other.

"I know everyone thinks he's doing drugs, like he's pulling a Lance Armstrong, but he's not. I've read the articles. That's just not Gil. He understands you have to pay a price for everything. Believe me, I'm having every doctor I can think of looking at him."

"God is smiling on him," Pastor Ron finally said in a gruff voice. "This is His will, for Gil to spread God's word. He'll be fine."

Austin tugged on his grandfather's sleeve and pointed to the runner on second base.

"I'd be worried," Trista Melendez said.

Alicia grabbed Keri's hand. "We both are. Mom, tell her about the Mayo."

Keri paused, leaned forward, and put her lips to Trista's ear. "Okay, but you can't tell anyone. If the press finds out, it would devastate Gil. When the Rockies go to Minnesota next week, Gil will be seeing another specialist. He's a clinical virologist and came highly recommended. We're hoping he can give us some answers."

"I dropped out of school to be with him," Alicia said. "I don't know what I'd do if anything ever happened to him."

"I'm sorry if my husband said anything," Trista finally said. "He's worked so hard, and I think in a moment of weakness said something he shouldn't have. Please let us know what you find out at the Mayo."

26

GIL HAD HEARD about Mecca trips to the Mayo Clinic, but he had no idea what to expect when he rolled into Rochester, Minnesota. Keri had flown out to meet him. Gil could feel his stomach grumbling as he waited for the clinical virologist to attend to him. Nearly every doctor wanted him to come fasting, and he was getting accustomed to going without food, but it never got any easier.

Dr. Babak Kusha's bifocals rested on his oversized nose. Gil was glad to see his dark wavy hair was graying around the ears. He was nothing like Dr. Kempski. He took a seat, crossed his legs and introduced himself.

"I have all the test data from Dr. Kempski. Do you want the extended play or the condensed version?"

Gil didn't stop to think, looking at Keri and then grabbing her hand. "Condensed version. Just tell me what I'm facing."

"It's a mixed bag," the physician said. "It's something we've never seen before, but medical science has advanced so fast just in the last decade that, with time and money, we could tear apart your DNA to see what is causing your muscle and bone mass to explode."

"So you don't know what is happening to me?"

"From the weekly blood, urine, skeletal, and muscle data that Dr. Kempski was kind enough to send us, it appears that both your bone and muscle density are increasing at an alarming rate. But your neuromuscular system is also adapting to these changes. So not only are you getting stronger at a time when your body should be weakening, your fast-speed muscle fibers have the uncanny ability to deal with these changes. That explains why you can throw so fast, without tearing your arm apart or shattering your bone.

"What is not so clear is your chemical makeup. We can't understand your protein levels, and, like I said, we really need to dig deep into your DNA to see why your blood makeup is far from normal."

"Okay, that all makes sense. So do I need to worry about anything?"

"Yes, you do." Dr. Kusha's eyes narrowed and he leaned forward. "The problem is that all of your muscles appear to be on this runaway train. What is the most concerning is your chest and back muscles as well as your skeletal structure. There is a reason why breathing is becoming more difficult. The growth is happening internally as well. It's like you are one giant black hole that is going to implode. Eventually, and I'm only saying this is a possibility, if the current trend continues, it could either suffocate you or compress your heart to the point of failure. The same could happen to your kidneys as well as your other internal organs. For all I know, it could close off your major vessels. This is serious stuff, Gil."

"But right now my heart is fine? I'm not going to keel over if I pitch this week?"

"I can't say for sure. Anyone can die any time."

"I understand, but you can't see any immediate risk of serious damage to my body if I keep pitching?"

"It appears that the disease is progressive, and every pitch counts."

Gil folded his arms. Doctors never gave straight answers.

"Is there something you can give me? Some medicine to help stop the progression?"

"Of course, medical science usually has some kind of drugs to mask your symptoms. If you want something benign, just take some anti-inflammatory, maybe ibuprofen, but I doubt those will help for long. Steroids may provide temporary relief, as well as a muscle relaxant."

"Right, but I can't pitch with those, and the league's drug policy forbids them anyway. I'd never pass a urine test."

"If you want the truth, Gil, you shouldn't be pitching at all."

Gil's eyes widened. "What?"

"You heard me right."

"So now you're saying that if I keep going, it could be fatal."

"We don't know that for sure, but it is a real possibility. We need to find some way to arrest its progress."

"Okay, so let me ask you this: If these so-called trends continue, how long for me?"

Dr. Kusha hit a key and pulled up a colored graph. "We plotted the density data for your bones and major muscle groups, and if the disease progresses just as it is now, which is simply an assumption, it could be sometime next season. That is assuming you keep pitching and attend spring training next year. I can show you all of our assumptions."

"Alright, so what if I completely stop in the off season? What would your graph look like? Or if Ratcliff went on a six-man rotation? Is there a chance it will just stop on its own?"

"Of course, anything could happen. But I think the better question is what happens if you stop throwing right now, which I would strongly recommend, but it is your life."

Gil shook his head. "No, I've got to keep going. Can't you do anything for me?"

"Like I said, if we had enough time and money we could tear apart your DNA to see what is causing your system to go haywire. I'm just not sure we have enough time."

"Money's no problem. I can get you money," Gil promised.

"I understand. You're fortunate. But the research could take years, maybe even decades. Look at how many millions of dollars and years it's taken us to understand AIDS."

"Okay, then what other options? There's got to be something we can do."

Dr. Kusha stood and slipped his pen in his shirt pocket. "We don't know because we have only tested your body while you have been pitching. Probably my best recommendation is for you to take a month off and see what happens."

Gil lifted his cap and combed his fingers through his hair. "I need some time to think about it."

"That's fine. You two talk it over, but please seriously consider what I've told you. I'd like to send you home with a heart rate monitor. You wear it at night, then upload the data in the morning to our website. That way, I can make sure your heart is still beating properly."

"No problem," Gil said. "And I'm sure you'll tell me when it stops beating."

27

IT HAD BEEN a month since Gil abandoned Eugenia's scratched-up, out-of-tune guitar in the old folks' home. Leaving the guitar was his excuse to return.

The front desk of the nursing home warmly welcomed their hero. Gil found Melvelene in her chair, fiddling with the remote control. The volume was blaring the shrill voice of some talk show host touting the newest way to lose weight and feel great. She sharply slapped the handheld device onto the chair. "Piece of crap!" she yelled.

"I completely agree."

Her head snapped up. "Well, look who the cat dragged in. Been wondering when you'd be by to pick up your fiddle."

"Guitar," Gil corrected. "Have you been doing okay?"

"Great, actually. I've been enjoying watching you. Network television, even ESPN, when I can get it. They won't pipe it into our rooms—too darn cheap. We have to watch it in the lunchroom, but Ernie and me are the only ones who like it, so we have to fight to keep it on. We tell them Slider's going to get into a fight."

"Slider, huh?"

"You know a lot of people don't like him, but I do. Baseball needs a little irreverence every now and then. Gets kind of boring sitting for three hours. Need the bench to clear every once in a while to generate a little excitement. You know I rate his slides. Zero to ten, kind of like *Dancing with the Stars*, but for baseball. His best was when you played Detroit and he sailed right over the catcher—that is until the catcher stood up and threw Slider into a tailspin. That was a ten."

"He's certainly an enigma."

"You've heard the other rumor?"

"About Slider?"

"Yeah, and that Dave Matthews song. Some say he's like the Babe, calling his own home runs."

"You know Dave Matthews?"

"I do now. *The Space Between*. Some sportswriter said they played that song during the seventh-inning stretch, and Slider told you guys he was going to send the ball in the space between left and center. And he did."

Gil grinned and shook his head. "It was something like that."

"By the way, congratulations on dropping below one on your ERA."

Gil could feel the blood rushing to his face. "So tell me, what were you like in your twenties? I take you as kind of a rebel."

"Nobody was a rebel in the late fifties. I'm just a big talker. My life really isn't that exciting."

"No?"

"I was like all the other girls my age. Got married really young, had a few kids, and worked hard to raise them. We lived in a small town in Southern California; my husband was the foreman at an almond farm, and I drove a school bus."

"School bus. Really?"

"And I saved every dime. Used it to put a down payment on a second home that we rented out for twenty years. Rode the real estate boom, then sold it and moved here to be with my daughter. That's what pays the bills here."

"You're not living with your daughter."

Melvelene shrugged. "Used to, but she moved me here a few months ago. My memory is going, and she's got a little girl with Down's syndrome. I was more than she could deal with. So we use my life's savings to pay for this great beach resort. Like it?"

Gil sprang up and drew upon the curtains with a *swoosh*. "Yeah, the parking lot has this nice shimmer of turquoise to it, doesn't it?"

"My daughter doesn't know it yet, but I withdrew most of my money and put it down on a cruise. I'm going to get her a nanny, and then we're both sailing for a week in the calm waters of the Caribbean. She needs a little break."

"Just you two?"

"My husband died fifteen years ago, and my son's overseas in the Army. We worked so hard all of our lives, it's time for a little celebration. He's got a month leave, and I'm going to surprise him too."

"I think it's a great idea. Wish I could come."

"You've got more important things. Got to get those Rockies to the Series before I die. You're on the mound tonight, aren't you?"

Gil glanced at his watch. "Yeah. Connor wants me there a little early. I should be going."

"Did I tell you how much I love Slider's slides? I said that before, didn't I? I'm sorry. My daughter is right. I am losing my marbles. Can you forgive me?"

Gil turned for the door. "You're still sharp as a knife. I think you're the only one who knows my ERA."

"You're kind, but it's not true. Are you taking your guitar?"

He shuffled to the dark corner and snatched it, sliding his hand over the peeling shellac, then returning it to its former resting place. "Naw, I think I'll leave it for when I come back. You okay with that?"

"Perfect. I'm not going anywhere."

Gil had just reached the door when Melvelene shouted out, "Wait, I forgot to ask you: What did Slider tell the Detroit catcher after he did the flip? My eyes are getting bad. I can't read the papers anymore."

That Melvelene yearned for him to stay was obvious.

"He told him if he tried anything like that again, he'd kick out his teeth, with his mask on."

Gil cracked open the door.

"Wait, I heard you made the All-Star team. You'll be pitching in San Francisco."

"That's right."

"Well don't let anyone put a ball in the Bay. I have a piece of news for you," she said with lowered eyes, trying to keep her new friend from leaving.

Gil stepped toward her. "Good news?"

"Only if cancer is good news." Her words hung in the air. A joke with no humor.

Gil spun around. "You're not kidding me?"

"Wish I was. It's cancer, and the doctor said six months if I'm lucky."

Gil stooped and put his arm around her. "I'm so sorry."

"No, don't be sorry. That just means I've got six months to squeeze in everything I've always wanted to do."

"The cruise?"

"For sure. Cindi wanted to cancel it, but I said no way. I don't care if I die on that ship. We're going to make our last memories together."

28

THE SEASON HAD a way of wearing down the players. They were hounded to keep up their stamina, and the strength coach was constantly herding them into the weight room every time they were back in town.

Some guys, like Slider and Gonzalez, loved the weight room. They loved bulking up, showing off their physiques. The old-timers, like Preacher and Biondi, hated it. Preacher's knees were shot from decades of squatting behind the plate. Occasionally, he'd do a few sets of bench and curls—*gentlemen lifting*, Slider called it. You could smoke a cigar and put up the barbell at the same time.

Pumping iron was show-off time for Slider, the strongest player on the team. Gil watched in amazement as Slider slid four twenty-kilo plates on each side of the barbell, causing the solid steel bar to bend. Gil slipped behind him, offering to give him a spot when his muscles reached failure. Slider assured Gil he wasn't needed. With little effort, Slider cranked out six reps and re-racked the weights with a loud slamming sound. He jumped up and clapped his hands, sending off a cloud of white chalk.

"Your turn," he said to Gil, lightly punching him in the shoulder. "How much should I take off?"

"I'm fine," Gil said, rubbing the spot where Slider had struck him. "Shoulder's a little sore." Dr. Kusha's warning was enough for Gil to shy away from lifting any weights.

Gil slipped over to where Trudeau and Boclin were doing some leg extensions. Briscoe, the Rockies trainer, noticed Gil's lack of participation and made his way over.

"Gil, I haven't seen you hitting the weights in a long time. If your shoulder is sore, let's do some squats. You've got three days off. Need to keep those legs strong."

"Yeah, sure." Gil strained to come up with an excuse. Dr. Kusha's warning had him scared. He was afraid to bend down and pick up his own shoes. Every morning he was sending his heartbeat data to the Mayo, wondering what secrets his body was giving away. His breathing was still labored, especially when he pitched. He was certain Dr. Kusha was going to demand he stop pitching.

Gil sauntered over to the squat rack and bent over while he tugged on one of the weights. Suddenly, he pinched his nose. "Be right back," he said in a nasal voice. "Bloody nose."

The training room was the perfect place to hide until weight lifting was over. Gil dimmed the lights, then slid onto one of the padded tables and perched his hands behind his head. His eyelids felt heavy, and he let gravity pull them closed.

Gil's catnap was interrupted when the door sprang open. Slider, a backpack slung on his shoulder, silently crept in. Gil remained motionless, observing as Slider plunged his hand into the front pocket and slipped out a syringe. The needle was within an inch of Slider's vein when Gil revealed his presence.

"What in heaven's name are you doing?"

Startled, Slider let the syringe slip from his fingers, sending it clattering on the floor.

"I should be asking you the same thing. Afraid those weights are going to bulk you up a little too much? Whatever you're on, it's ten times worse than what I'm doing."

"You don't know what you're talking about, Slider. You have no idea what my life is like."

"I know enough to know that you're afraid to lift. Lifting is supposed to be good for you, build you up and make you strong. But not for Gil. He doesn't use gravity to build his muscles. He doesn't think the laws of nature apply to him. He's found an artificial way to make himself a hero."

"This body is for real."

"I'm not buying it. Nobody pitches like that. Everyone wanted to be like me until you got here. Tell me what kind of crap you're on."

"Spinach," Gil said.

"Real cute," Slider said, fishing for his needle. "I'll tell you what. You keep my secret, and I'll keep yours. That way, we'll both get along just fine."

"Why can't we be friends?"

"Friends? I don't do friends, not even with you. I don't trust anyone. You trust someone, and they'll always stab you in the back. And you're no exception."

"You can't go through life like that."

"No? Then why did you start this campaign to be an All-Star?"

"Come on," Gil said.

"It's not right, man. I was supposed to be the only Rockies player, and now you're starting ahead of me. Mr. Likeable gets the fans to vote him in as a starter, and you've never completed a season. They're a bunch of idiots. All they care about is seeing you pitch fast—that doesn't make a good player. Melendez was right—you don't deserve it."

"So that's what this is all about?" Gil insisted.

"I think we're done with this conversation."

Toting a handful of tissue, Gil made his way back into the weight room. He found Preacher slouching on a chest press bench, resting his chin on his hands, deep in thought.

"This bit about opposites ..." Preacher said when he saw Gil, straightening himself.

With Gil's popularity came an analysis of every facet of his life, including his former life as a science teacher. "It's funny, you do something that you think nobody cares about, this little science fair of mine, and all of the sudden it's the most important thing in the world."

"Don't shortchange yourself. What you did, it was really good. You've really got me thinking."

"About?"

"This idea came to me today when I was watching Gonzalez doing his reps, pumping this barbell up and down off his chest. I should have been one of your students. I came up with a great idea for your science fair—weight lifting."

Preacher lay back and slipped himself under the barbell. "Look, you have this pair of opposites: up and down. And you have the law of gravity to make objects heavy or light. While the aim of lifting is to get the weight to the top of the repetition, you're not supposed to stay there. That's because the real reason for wrestling against the law of gravity is to make your muscles grow. You have to keep moving the weight in a cycle between up and down to generate power. You can't stop at the top and think you've made it."

Gil nodded. "When do you want to go back to high school? Tell you what. If I'm teaching school again next year, I'll let you enter my science fair. 'The Preacher Who Fights Gravity to Gain Power.' You'll be the exhibit. My kids would love it."

"Wait," Preacher said, "you missed the point. That's not what hit me. I'm not talking physical power, Gil. I'm talking about an inner power. You, me, everyone, we've got to use the unfairness of life, the heaviness we all face, to generate more power. But if we quit trying and give up, that will never happen."

Gil nodded, still thinking of Slider. "It's what you do with your power that's important. You really should have been a minister. You're nothing like my father."

Preacher shrugged his massive shoulders. "I have something else for you." Preacher dug a folded piece of paper out of his pocket. "You're going to need this; it's my scouting report for every All-Star you might face next week. Since I can't be there to call the pitches, this is as good as I can do. Good luck."

29

GIL COULDN'T GET Melvelene off his mind. This would be her last season to ever see a game, so Gil got her tickets. She could come with her daughter. It was nearly ninety degrees at game time, but Melvelene still had a blanket draped over her lap. Her daughter, Cindi, pushed her wheelchair along the concourse, followed by two Rockies staff, who hefted the steel contraption down two sets of stairs to where the Rockies' families had their season tickets, then gently lifted her out and sat her in Alicia's assigned seat. A TV film crew followed. Pastor Ron introduced himself and guided them along, making sure they didn't bang her legs, and insisting that he rearrange her blanket. Austin was sent off to buy some hot dogs and drinks.

Melvelene waved her hand. "I'll bet you're wondering why I'm cuddled in a blanket when it's ninety degrees outside. Kind of like a pig in a blanket. That's what cancer does to you. Just hope you don't get it. Anyway, I'm the new cheerleading talent—discovered by Gil and Slider."

When Gil saw the film crew, he understood. *Another publicity stunt.* Gil avoided venturing over, hoping he could greet Melvelene after the game. But ten minutes before the national anthem, Eugenia popped out of the dugout, took Gil by the elbow, and shepherded him over to where the players' families were sitting.

"We've got to do a photo shoot with Marlene before the game."

"Melvelene," Gil corrected her. A cameraman was already following them across the infield. Security opened the gate and parted the dozen children who flocked down the stairs for an autograph.

When he reached Melvelene, he bent over and hugged her. "I'm glad you came. Sorry about all the fanfare."

She squeezed his hand, and he could feel the sagging flesh on her bony fingers. They were cold and clammy. "Wouldn't miss it for the world," she graciously replied.

Gil barely reached the turf when he saw the film clips blazing on the large screen, and the announcer blared out a blurb about how Melvelene, recently diagnosed with cancer, was the special guest of the Rockies. Pastor Ron seized the moment, asking the fans to keep Melvelene in their prayers, to pray for a miracle. *Two peas in a pod*, Gil thought. *One does PR for God and the other for the Rockies.*

Gil's first pitch was a fastball, in the low nineties. The crowd sensed something was wrong, and so did the batter. He kept his feet planted in the batter's box and adjusted his helmet, his eyes daring Gil to throw another fastball with no heat on it. Gil felt his magic slipping.

Preacher called for a curveball. Gil obeyed, tapping the ball in his glove, but the joy of living the dream faded. He tried blocking out the Mayo Clinic diagnoses and the exploitative media coverage and PR. *"Nothin' pure about this . . . all a big phony show,"* he thought. Gil couldn't get much movement on his breaking balls, and his control was off. He breathed out deeply when his slider crashed into the ground, six inches in front of the plate. If the pitch had been a strike, it would have been crushed out of the park.

Gil watched as Preacher called for a repeat of the same pitch. Gil wiped the sweat off his forehead. He had no confidence he could place the pitch. His mind wandered to his father's antics. He'd tried to exploit Melvelene, just like he'd tried to control his life. He could be dying, for heaven's sake, and his father could care less, only whether his son's sacrifice might be God's way to save a few more souls. This time the pitch was a strike, but it had little movement. He heard the crack of the bat, then saw Gonzalez backpedalling in center field. The ball struck the wall, a stand-up double.

The stadium went silent. Not since the first of the season had Gil floundered in the first inning, but this was a sharply hit ball, and Gil was rattled. He was throwing like a worn-out pitcher in the eighth inning. Why did his father have so much control of his life? Gil knew that if he'd stood up to his father twenty years ago, none of this would be happening. He'd have already finished his baseball career. There'd be no need for this silliness. The next batter took his position, and Preacher called for a low fastball. Gil mustered up his courage, but the ball had no steam. The only good news is that the pitch was low enough that the batter sent it sky high and down the right field line.

Juarez locked on the trajectory, but hesitated. Then he jogged leisurely, as if he were hoping the ball would hook foul. It didn't. The ball was fair by three feet and trickled into the right field corner. Juarez picked up his pace, but not by much. By the time he threw the ball into the infield, the batter was on third and one run had scored. Juarez took off his glove and massaged his knee. When Briscoe started running on the field with his trainer's medical kit, Juarez called him off and shoved his mitt back on.

Two runs scored before Preacher made his way to the mound. He kept on his facemask, hiding any words of reprimand from the cameras.

"Not flying today, are you?"

"Let's not talk science right now, okay? I don't have time for religious theory. I need to throw the damn ball, that's all."

Gil's mind was a fog. He couldn't remember any of his pitches, only that when he began to walk to the dugout, he'd let three runs score. His vision seemed foggy. Maybe his medical condition was worse than he thought. This had all been a giant mistake. He should quit chasing his nonsensical dream, go home and take it easy like his doctor had asked him. Go home with his tail between his legs. Be a quitter, just like he'd done two decades ago when the first crisis struck. He lowered his cap and collapsed onto the bench. It was empty. He was the only one sitting. All the other players chose to lean against the railing, as if this were the most important playoff game that they couldn't miss. At least they blocked the cameras, Gil thought.

"You're empty, man." Gil looked up. DeJesus was standing in front of him. Yesterday he'd won his sixth game, his best start ever. "No passion in those eyes. You're pitching like a girl. You need to get pissed off like I do. Think about smashing that reporter, putting a ball right between his eyes. Kill him, dismantle him." Gil remembered the rumor about how DeJesus had a catcher's mitt with the face of Castro tattooed on it, but that the league banned him from using it. DeJesus was throwing like a man possessed, and it showed.

Slider turned to adjust his cup. Gil blankly stared past him. "What, you want a little boost? Don't look at me, man. I don't do that kind of crap. I'm not that stupid. The drugbusters are going to be all over your blood like a vampire in one of those chick flicks."

The Rockies failed to score any runs, and Gil headed to the mound with his team down three runs. He could feel the fans' mocking eyes focused on him. He lowered the bill of his cap farther. He flexed his shoulders, raising and lowering them like he always did to loosen his muscles. His chest felt tight, and he remembered Dr. Kusha's warning. Maybe it was a good thing if he was pitching toward his own death. Maybe if he threw harder he could get himself out of his predicament. He could make it all go away. Just throw as hard as he could, progress his illness and leave this world.

Preacher signaled him to start the next inning with a fastball.

Put yourself out of your misery, Gil told himself. He reared back and hefted the ball with every muscle clenched. He hated himself for being in this situation. Life would have been so much better teaching kids how to light a Bunsen burner or to see how much sugar could be dissolved in a beaker of water.

When the crowd clapped for the first time, he knew he had broken the century barrier. He stole a peak at the scoreboard. The speed clock flashed 103. In a rage, he threw and threw. Sweat was dripping from his face and his shirt stuck to his back.

"Easy there, partner." It was Biondi slapping him on the back. "Inning's over. You retired the side. Time for the dugout."

Confused, Gil shook his head and followed his first baseman to their underground hideout.

By the time the game had reached the sixth inning, Gil looked like a racehorse who'd just passed the finish line. Foam covered the edges of his mouth, and his hair was dripping. Ratcliff looked at Connor and both men understood. "Go ahead and hit the showers," Connor said as Gil collapsed onto the bench.

Gil hung his head and stared at his shoelaces. He'd allowed a total of five runs and the Rockies' bats were silent. He wouldn't get a win this game. He was relieved that nobody could see him now. Gil shrunk down and supported his elbows on his knees. Waiting three more innings on a deserted bench would be an eternity.

The crowd restlessly waited while the reliever warmed up.

At the end of the eighth inning, Gil watched as security escorted Melvelene and her daughter up the stairs. He knew her body was spent. He'd wished he'd pitched a better game, if for no other reason than to give her a boost.

He hung his head. *This baseball thing—he'd made the wrong decision. He should have kept his teaching job. After all, he had been happy. None of this was worth it. And now he knew he wasn't Superman. He didn't deserve to be there. I wonder what Melvelene thinks of all this, he thought, as her wheelchair disappeared into the shadows.*

30

IN THEIR YEARS raising Alicia and Austin, Keri and Gil rarely ventured far outside of Colorado, and neither had been to San Francisco. They'd done driving trips to Southern California and Disneyland, but never found a reason to see the city on the Bay.

As they drove past the painted ladies—the vividly colored Victorian homes—Keri pointed and giggled with amazement. Austin had his face smashed against the window, mesmerized by the mass of looming skyscrapers.

"Look at that weird one. It looks like a triangle."

"It's the TransAmerica Building, stupid," Alicia said. "What I want to see is the Golden Gate Bridge."

"Can't see it from here," the driver said. "It's on the other side of those buildings. But I'm yours for the weekend, so whatever you want to see, just give me a jingle and I'll be there."

They stayed at the Four Seasons Hotel, a good fifteen-minute walk from the Giants stadium. As soon as they were settled, Gil wanted to go to the stadium to check things out before the crowds arrived for the home run derby.

After missing her morning workout and being cooped up in a plane, Keri wanted to walk to the ballpark, insisting she needed the exercise. Nobody thought to bring a jacket, not realizing how cold the city was during the foggy summer months. So, three blocks into their journey to the stadium, they stopped in a sports apparel store to buy sweatshirts.

Keri was more enamored with the outside of the stadium than the inside. She circled it twice, amazed at how a ballpark could be surrounded by the San Francisco Bay. She watched as the sailboats came into dock and the runners scampered along the running path, wishing she could join them. Alicia, smelling the irresistible scent of seafood, snuck in line for a cup of chowder and slice of sourdough bread from a street vendor, scattering a dozen pesky pigeons that were mopping up the crumbs left by hundreds of baseball fans already mingling outside the stadium. Even the two dozen protestors with hand-painted signs claiming the All-Stars were nothing more than a bunch of washed-up scabs, couldn't ruin the ambiance. For every picketer, there were two other ticket scalpers waving pairs of tickets, claiming they'd be able to see the fastest pitcher in the world.

"I wonder where the home runs land," Peck said to Austin as he leaned over the metal railing separating them from the murky waters of the Bay.

"I'm not sure, but I wish I could be in one of those boats when they sail over the wall. Slider needs to knock one out."

It was nearly three o'clock by the time Alicia had finished her snack—too late for anymore sightseeing. Keri called the driver to take her and Alicia back to the hotel so they could freshen up. Peck and Austin said they'd stick around while Gil checked in with the other All-Stars.

* * *

The day before the All-Star game, the league sponsored a host of festivities, from speed pitching booths to batting cages. Those who couldn't afford tickets to the actual game often settled for the home run derby, held the evening before the game. Gil wasn't participating, but that didn't stop him from chauffeuring his family on field, where Austin and Alicia shook the hands of the baseball elite and met their families. Alicia spent most of her time picking up toddlers and letting them run their fingers through her hair. None of the players had a child Alicia's age, or even as old as Austin.

Gil was like Ryan Seacrest on New Year's Eve, maneuvering between players, reporters, and fans. The All-Stars were there to have a good time, to relax and enjoy being around baseball's greatest. They all knew that someday, barring some unfortunate accident, or doing something stupid like betting on baseball, they'd all be hall of famers. Cameras were everywhere, and there were so many reporters that Slider could talk all night and never cross paths with Gil.

Sensing the chance of a lifetime, Peck took it upon himself to meet with reporters. He provided an all-American picture of Gil and his family and Gil's life as a high school teacher and coach. For one night, like at the Academy Awards show for actors, controversy was off limits. Reporters focused on the magic of the game, not its darker moments of drug abuse, betting, or sex scandals. His guard down, Gil even let Alicia answer a few questions; they were easy questions, like how much fun she was having spending her summer with her dad and what she thought of his instant fame.

"He's just my dad," she said. "Some people might think that he's just become famous, but he's always been famous to me."

The focus of the evening was supposed to be on the home run kings, the sluggers known for putting it out of the park. Small boats and swimmers in thick neoprene suits filled the waters, waiting for any ball that escaped the park. But most of the cameras couldn't keep from switching to Gil, zooming their lenses to capture him laughing with his fellow athletes, making crazy faces at their children, and demonstrating how Slider performed his slides—while Slider wasn't watching.

Gil wasn't sure what to do when he was introduced to Kenny Chesney, who had a guitar slung around his neck. "What, nobody told you?" the country singer said, shifting the leather strap of his own guitar over his white T-shirt. Before Gil could reply, a six-string was slipped over his shoulder, and a slew of cameras began clicking their shutters.

"Do you know *How Forever Feels*?"

Gil strummed the strings, shifting between the chords of the popular tune. "I can do that," he said with a smile that showed every one of his gleaming white teeth.

"When your season is over," Chesney said, "I'm doing this benefit. We're going to raise a whole bunch of money for multiple sclerosis, and this is my way of asking if you'll join me."

* * *

Having received the most votes for a pitcher, Gil would be starting. The manager for the LA Dodgers was selected to oversee the National League team, and Gil told him he only wanted to throw for two innings. "There's lot of guys here who want playing time, and that's fine with me. My arm needs the break."

On the mound, Gil followed Preacher's meticulous instructions. He remembered the pitches for each of the batters, following his routine of three taps in glove before each pitch. Facing the best batters in the league, Gil gave up a hit in both innings, but no runs scored. But nobody cared about the score; they were here to see speed. Even in the cool, damp air from the moisture lingering over the Pacific Ocean, Gil managed a 109-mile-an-hour fastball. The crowd roared.

No divers would be collecting balls on his watch. As the ringing of the cheers sank in his ears, he still couldn't believe he was here. It was all too surreal. Gil thought of Melvelene and whether she was watching. His father was a different matter. Gil hadn't invited him, and Pastor Ron's face fell when Gil broke the news that he couldn't get him a ticket. Gil knew he should have expressed his disgust over the Melvelene PR stunt, and that was the real reason for not extending an invitation to him to the All-Star game; but he couldn't do it. Gil's stomach churned, and he scanned the cheering crowd to dispel the thought. He was glad to be finished for the evening. If he had to take the mound again, he knew there'd be trouble.

Nestled back in the dugout, Gil enjoyed the rest of the game. The LA manager inserted Slider into the lineup during the seventh inning, where he clobbered a double and shot into second base with his patented slide. The Cleveland center fielder followed Slider, knocking out a homer, as if to ensure that Slider couldn't do a repeat at home base. The National League won seven to six, and Gil spent an hour after the game signing autographs before collecting his family and heading to the hotel.

31

SO FAR, THE details of his lawsuit with Randall Kite's daughter, along with the embarrassing photos, hadn't leaked. Gil had concluded Randall Kite was just bluffing. Shaila's father was an extortionist, trying to swindle him out of money but with no intention of making a scene. How could he be sued for just being a high school coach?

The Gilberts were in a deep sleep when the doorbell jolted Keri awake. She rubbed her eyes, noticed the clock read *five*, and nudged Gil. The ringer buzzed again, accompanied by a pounding on the wooden door.

"Who in the king's name is knocking down our door at this time in the morning?" Keri said.

"Let me get my gun," Gil said groggily.

"You don't own a gun. Do you think our house is on fire?"

That was enough for Gil to throw off the sheets and shake his head. He found some sweat pants draped over the desk chair and slipped them on. He felt his way down the hallway, as he smelled for smoke. The doorbell rang again, and he could hear Alicia stirring in the adjacent room.

Gil didn't bother asking who was intruding on their privacy, but simply threw open the door. He was greeted with a blinding light and the familiar sound of camera lenses clicking. He realized there was a fire, but it wasn't their home burning.

A male reporter wearing a tweed jacket shoved a newspaper into his chest. "Care to comment?" he said with a microphone poked into his nose.

Gil shielded his eyes and tried to focus on the bold font printed on the crumpled paper. "Please, cut the lights."

After his pupils adjusted, he saw the all-too-familiar sight of Caitlyn with her shirt half-lifted over her head, and her fluorescent pink sports bra exposed to the world. And, his ogling eyes were staring right at her. Another picture below captured a half a dozen cheerleaders, all with their shirts pulled up, and Shaila grabbing the side of her face as a baseball ricocheted off her skull. He didn't need to read the headlines to understand the implication.

The blinding lights snapped back on and the reporter repeated his question. Gil rubbed his eyes. "I never talk before my morning coffee." He tossed the paper back and grabbed the brass doorknob. "Now can you please leave me alone?"

That was the first time he'd shooed away any member of the media. He leaned against the door, hoping that somehow he could stay the oncoming tide, and he shoved the door closed. With his adrenaline pumping, it crashed shut, shaking the walls.

Keri was standing in her robe, arms folded. "They know, don't they?"

"The lawsuit? Yeah, they know. Front page news."

"Well, let me see it."

"I threw the paper back at them."

Keri flung her arms down and pushed herself past him. She tightened her robe about her and yanked the door handle.

"They'll get your photo," Gil warned. "You're only going to make it worse."

It was too late. More cameras flashed, but that didn't stop Keri. She forced her way onto the porch, found the first reporter holding a paper and tore it from him. "Give me that!"

Keri once again emerged carrying her prey and shoved Gil out of the way. He listened as she stomped down the hall and slammed the bedroom door shut.

More than twenty years of marriage was enough to know

better than to follow her. Gil flipped on the light in the kitchen and began brewing some coffee. Today he was going to need lots of caffeine. A shot of brandy might be better.

Gil was sitting at the table, blankly staring into his cup when he heard the bedroom door open. He listened as Keri's slippers shuffled down the hall. Her petite figure appeared in the doorway, the paper folded under her arm.

"You knew, didn't you?" she spat out.

"Knew what? About the lawsuit? Of course."

"Don't get smart with me, Gil. You know what I'm talking about. The photos. You knew, didn't you?"

Gil paused, searching for how to respond. He studied her eyes, realizing the hurt that would come if he lied.

"Shaila's lawyer said he had some photos of the accident. Since I didn't do anything wrong, I just figured they doctored the photos."

Keri slammed the paper to the floor. "Doctored!" she screamed. "The *Post* does not doctor."

The heated argument caused Alicia and Austin to venture out of their rooms. Seeing the scattered papers on the floor, Alicia hurried and scooped them up.

"What are you going to do, Gil?" Keri said, her eyes tearing up.

"I need to see my lawyer."

"You have a lawyer? This is news to me."

"It's the school's lawyer."

Gil rubbed his whiskers. He needed a sympathetic ear. He wandered into the front room. By now, Alicia had the paper spread out on the coffee table. Austin was pointing and his mouth hung open.

"Dad, that's Caitlyn hanging out."

Alicia slapped his face. "Watch your language."

"She's wearing a sports bra," Gil said.

"But she's on the front page of the *Post*," Austin said, holding the side of his face. "Everyone's going to see her."

Alicia, kneeling over the wreckage, looked up, her ponytail swaying, and said, "Really Dad?"

"It's not what you think. Girls wear a lot less than that to my class every day, and that's not national news."

"Oh, so you look at them too?" She narrowed her eyes and swatted the paper onto the floor. Without saying a word, she scooted around him and went into the bedroom.

"I can't believe this," Gil mumbled. "Bill Clinton ruins a blue dress and he's a hero, but this—"

Austin shrugged and wandered into the kitchen. "I'm getting some cereal," he said.

Gil sat alone in the front room for close to an hour, pondering his options. He heard the bedroom door squeak on its hinges, and Keri and Alicia emerged. Their eyes were red and swollen. Gil stood up.

"Don't say anything," Keri said. "We're going to sit here and talk this out, but you're going to do the talking."

Before she could continue, the front door flew open.

"Holy crap, you know how many news vans are out there?"

Instantly, Alicia ran to him and threw her arms about his bulky shoulders. "Peck, thanks for coming," she said.

Peck glared over her head at Gil. "Sure, sure. I'm here to help. Have you seen what's on the internet?"

"No," Keri said. "Just the *Post* article so far. What's the damage?"

"That Gil doesn't call his own pitches."

"I don't care about that," Keri said.

"It's not all bad. They did say he was a fantastic high school teacher, and one of the most winning coaches in the state. Lots of good quotes from his students and faculty, including how his science class brings the fun back into learning."

"Don't try to put a good spin on it," Keri said. "Did you catch what they said about his double life, about how he acts good yet he's so bad; about how he's just like all the rest of the sports heroes—nothing but a big lie."

"Didn't catch that," Peck said.

"The drugs?"

"Yeah, I caught that."

Gil reached over and ripped the paper from Keri's hands. He tore it to shreds, letting the papers float to the floor. "Drugs? No, that's not true, and you all know it. I'm not going to take this."

Peck reached over and put his hand on Gil's shoulder. "It's a serious charge, Gil. It's all over the internet, and ESPN is going crazy. They said you're taking steroids, even have a bottle that Dr. Kusha prescribed."

"But how?"

"Who knows? But it's put the baseball world in a frenzy. The players' union is now threatening legal action against the replacement players because of how they are supposedly ruining America's pastime. The drug abuse angle is exactly what they were looking for."

Gil sauntered to the window and parted the curtain, then shook his head. Why all this? He was trying to live his dream, and it seemed like everyone wanted to take it from him. They'd humiliated him and tried to ruin his marriage. He'd lost the respect of his kids.

He couldn't keep living like this. He had to make a decision— in or out. Either he was going to live his dream or he wasn't. If he was, it was going to be on his own terms.

32

GIL STUFFED A pair of clean socks in his duffle bag when he heard the voice of his father in the kitchen. A rustle of papers was followed by a condemnation. "This is all of the Devil!"

He zipped his bag and bounded down the hall to interrupt his father before Pastor Ron let loose on Keri. When their eyes locked, Gil could sense fire and brimstone were about to erupt. "How could you?" Pastor Ron said before Gil could open his mouth.

Pastor Ron picked up the crumpled paper from the table, still riddled with half-filled cereal bowls. Keri pushed her way past Gil. "This time it's your battle," she said on the way to the bedroom.

"I'm asking you to resign," Pastor Ron started. "It's time to put away childish things. You are mocking God. You know, twenty years ago, I had this dream—that you were going to be one of the baseball greats, maybe even a hall of famer. God was smiling on you. But it was for a reason. God chose you to spread his word. When the children of America, the upcoming generation, saw Gil Gilbert praying to God before every game, they would follow. You were called to lead them.

"But you failed God, and you failed me. Having a child out

of wedlock ruined everything. God is good, and he forgave you. Look what you accomplished at Prairie Ridge, and you stayed faithful to your family. So God gave you a second chance at baseball. He gave you that arm. He didn't have to, but he did. And all he wanted from you was to be a good Christian. Was that too much to ask? You're too ashamed to pray anymore, and now I know why. Well, I'm here to ask you to stop the mockery."

Gil placed his arm about his father's shoulder. "I'm going to keep playing."

Pastor Ron's eyes narrowed. "If you do, you'll regret it. You can't make a fool out of God."

His father pushed him aside and stormed out of the room. The side door to the garage slammed shut with a loud bang. Gil looked at his watch. He was late for the ballpark.

33

GIL'S MOBILE PHONE rang. He saw that the call came from Melvelene's daughter, Cindi, so he took it. Cindi said that Melvelene wanted to see him and that it couldn't wait. Her voice had a sense of urgency.

Gil hesitated, wondering if the matter was really that pressing. He had so many things to do, including a visit to his attorney on the way to the game.

"What time would she like me there?"

"Right now would be good," she said. "Melvelene wants to see her favorite baseball player, and she's adamant. The nurse is here too, and she says you should come right over."

He could imagine how forceful Melvelene had stated her request. He would miss his meeting with his lawyer and would probably be late to the ballpark. Still, it was a request he couldn't deny. Whatever his problems, they couldn't possibly compare to what Melvelene must be facing.

He put down the phone and sped over to Cindi's home, where Melvelene was now receiving care. Walking up the cracked sidewalk, he wondered what he should say. What do you tell someone who is having a bout with anxiety, who is apparently struggling with the fear of death? How do you provide any comfort?

He crept up the concrete stairs to the gray clapboard home. The black shutters were cracked and the rain gutters were missing their paint.

It had been less than a week since she'd come to the Rockies game, but Gil noticed a marked change in Melvelene's physical condition. Her step had slowed, her breathing was labored, and her strength was clearly failing. He doubted whether she would ever see Alaska.

"They call me the dough boy," she said, jiggling her belly. "Since you last saw me, I've gained four inches around my waist. I hate this new medication."

Her rotundity did make her look a little odd. Her frame was petite until just a few days ago. "It'll come off, don't worry," she said optimistically.

"Packed for Alaska?" Gil said.

"You bet. Nothing is going to stop me. Wouldn't be a bad thing to die at sea," she kidded.

Melvelene's daughter excused herself so that they could be alone. Gil fidgeted with the sofa's cushion. Melvelene broke the uneasy silence.

"Wasn't Slider great at the All-Star game?"

"Was probably the first game he kept his nose clean."

"I still chuckle when I think of what he did to the Dodgers' second baseman. There was blood flying everywhere."

Melvelene was referring to when Slider had bulldozed the Dodgers player when he rounded second base, then kept going. The stunned Dodgers were paralyzed as Slider rounded third and bolted for home. The shortstop scooped up the ball with his bare hand and whipped it to the catcher. The Dodgers' protector of home plate was even more massive than Preacher, and he steadied himself in front of the plate. If Slider wanted to take him on, he was ready. The catcher squatted, squared his shoulders, and prepared for the collision. The pitcher and first baseman, who'd already positioned themselves behind the catcher, bolstered themselves, forming a three-man defensive wall. The scene looked more like a football lineman with his two linebackers daring the running back to cross the line of scrimmage.

Like a raging bull, Slider was foaming at the mouth, his nostrils as wide as golf balls as he screamed toward the battle.

With no helmet to protect him, Slider, his lip covered with blood, lowered his head and plowed directly into the catcher. The laws of physics were against him. It was like striking a brick wall. The force created by Slider's body jolted the catcher back, but he instantly recoiled and stood firm. Slider kept his legs churning like a running back smelling the goal line.

The umpire called the runner out, but Slider didn't stop. Grunting and straining, he moved the pile slowly backward, forcing the men to backpedal. Slider kept this up until he finally made contact with the white rubber plate. Then he uprighted himself, spat a mouthful of blood onto the dirt, and stared down the shocked fans.

"Broke Slider's nose in two places. Gonzalez yanked it back into place in the locker room. Now he really looks like a hockey player."

Melvelene laughed until her eyes were wet. Gil noticed how her frail frame shook, straining her feeble condition.

"You know I'm not laughing at him, just at what young people do. They'll find a way to survive. Life isn't fun if you don't make it an adventure. But you know all about that."

"I do, but we're not here to talk about me. Tell me your plans for Alaska."

She shook her finger at him. "But we are here to talk about you. What's been eating at you? Your pitching has gone to the dogs."

He finally mustered up the courage. "My father's the problem. It's kind of like we're at war with each other."

"I could have guessed that."

"I'm sorry he used you as his showpiece. He does the same thing to me. I should have known better."

She waved her hand. "No need to apologize. I didn't take it personally. At least you have a father to war with."

"Tell me about yours."

"You sure you want to hear?"

Gil nodded.

Melvelene sighed then started her tale. It all happened one day in Salt Lake City when her grandfather lost his sanity during a domestic dispute. She was still a small child but remembered sitting on the kitchen table while her mother was engaged in a serious discussion with her grandmother. In a rage, her grandfather stormed into the room toting a gun. After some harsh words, he transformed into a crazy gunslinger, waving the gun and spewing out profanities in an unending stream. Then he did the unthinkable—he raised the weapon, leveled it, and shot his own wife point blank in the face, spewing blood and tissue across the room.

The rampage continued. The next victim was Melvelene's father, who tried to stop the madness, only to get cut down with gunfire.

Gil listened intently as she told of how shooting continued as her grandfather wildly shot up through the ceiling in a random attempt to take out anyone unlucky enough to be inside. "He made Swiss cheese out of our home."

Her cynicism wasn't the laughing kind. A sobering chill swept through the room.

Shortly after the funerals, reality struck again when her family was involved in a serious car accident, which took the life of her mother. With fate on her side, Melvelene was thrown free, unharmed.

"I was now completely alone. My grandmother and both parents were gone."

Melevelene then told how she managed to overcome all of that—getting married, having a family of her own. She'd raised two children, scraping and struggling like most everybody else.

By the time she finished her story, she was slumping on the couch—emotionally exhausted. "I haven't dusted off those memories in a long time," she said.

She rested for a few minutes, waiting for her strength to recharge. Gil sat in silence, finally understanding why she'd asked him to come. He was glad he'd come to hear her story. It made his life look easy.

Gil put the pillow down and shifted his weight, getting ready to stand. He struggled to say something consoling. But what could he possibly tell her? Anything he said would sound so feeble, so artificial.

While he mused on his predicament, Melvelene scooted herself up. "Let's talk about your father."

"You see how he is. And when he saw that picture in the

paper, well, now he's demanding I stop pitching."

"Why?"

"I'm 'mocking God.' I'm telling you, I didn't do it," Gil said.

She waved him off. "You did, you didn't, I don't really care. That's not what's important."

"It's not. But wait, I didn't . . . "

"You're a man, and I don't really care if the photo is real or not. What happened, happened. You could have done something a lot worse."

"My father doesn't think so." Gil repeated the history with his father and how Alicia came into their family.

"You've told him about this?"

"I told Keri."

"You should tell your father. Reconcile with him before it's too late."

"I don't think he'll speak with me. I've really hurt him—shattered his world."

"If everyone isn't hurting, God didn't design this world correctly. Let me ask you this: If you had to, would you give up pitching?"

"You mean, just walk away right now? Admit I'm guilty, resign and go back to being a coach? No, I've already made up my mind. This is something I've got to finish."

Melvelene smiled. "Good. You're a fighter. Stick to your guns. It will all work out."

She held up her bony fingers to her mouth and began to cough. It was deep and raspy.

Gil rushed forward and gently lowered her onto the pillow. She faintly whispered her gratitude then closed her eyes. He wondered if she knew that there was a real possibility that he might be joining her soon. She seemed to know everything else about him.

Her coughing continued and the full-time nurse rushed in, glaring at him as if he were a wild beast. She wrapped Melvelene's sweater tight about her chest, making sure every inch of flesh was covered.

Melvelene slowly lifted her eyelids. "I've got to rest now. When do you pitch again?"

"Tomorrow."

Her eyes fell again, and he wasn't sure if she heard him, or if she'd ever see him pitch again.

He'd just turned to leave when he heard her rustle on the couch. "You forgot your guitar," she whispered through closed eyes. "I thought you were going to play for me."

Gil noticed Eugenia's neglected guitar in the corner, brought with Melvelene from the rest home. He walked over and quietly lifted it and slipped the cracked leather strap over his shoulder. He strummed a few chords, then began a song from the Eli Young Band, *Keep on Dreaming*.

"I like that song," she said.

34

GIL WAITED UNTIL Austin was off to school and Alicia ran out for a cup of coffee. Keri was still in her robe, her hair pulled back into a ponytail.

"We need to talk," he said.

She turned her shoulder.

"Keri, I can't. No, we can't keep going on like this. I'm here to apologize. Can we sit down?"

He took her hand and led her to the couch. Then he fished for the remote and shut off the television.

Gil gently took her hands in his and looked deep into her blue eyes. "I'm really sorry for what I've put you through. I know those photos must have humiliated you. I did know about them and should have told you."

"I knew."

"About the photos?"

"Her father sent them over weeks ago."

"Why didn't you tell me?"

"You were pitching so well, and it was your dream. I didn't want anything to distract you."

Gil lowered his head and stared at his heels. "I'm really sorry, Keri, but you have to believe me that they look a lot worse than what really happened. I mean yes, I was watching her take off her shirt, but it was more like, 'What in the heck are you doing?' I wasn't salivating over some teenage girl. I'm not a pedophile."

Keri smiled again. "Yeah, I know. But you should have told me."

Gil nodded. "I know, and that's why I'm here asking for you to forgive me. I've got to get this lawsuit settled and stop all the chatter in the press. The noise it's creating in my head is destroying me."

"What do you think it's going to take?"

"Everything we have, plus everything I'll earn in the next two years."

"That bad?"

"They are down to four hundred thousand, but I'm not paying off a robber."

"I agree."

"I guess that settles it."

"You surprised me yesterday. You stood up to old Pastor Ron."

"Kind of. I didn't want to create a storm in our living room. I'm afraid he's not going to get over it. I know him too well. He's not going to let this go, not until I stop pitching."

"Which you're not going to do."

"Not now. It's how I can stand up to my father. Pitching is not just something to fill my ego. It's a journey I've got to finish. At the end of all this, I'm going to learn something. My father is right about one thing: God put me on this path, and I'm going to throw until I find out what it is. There's only one way I'd stop pitching."

"And that is?"

"If you want me to."

She squeezed his hand. "No, I want to see you on the mound, tomorrow, and the next week, and all the way to the World Series. If there is one person on the planet who has the determination to get them there, that's you."

"You're not worried?"

"I'm scared to death." She leaned over and rested her head on his shoulder. He could feel her bones trembling, and his shoulder felt wet. He sat silently while she wept. Keri eventually raised her head and wiped her eyes. Mascara was smeared on her cheeks.

"There's no way I could live with myself if I tried to stop you. If your heart is telling you to pitch, then you should do it. Your heart will never lead you wrong. And if you don't pitch, something within you will die. Besides, Alicia's a grown woman and Austin's well on his way. If anything happened to you, I'd be fine. You've taught me how to be a fighter."

"You know what's funny?" Gil said. "Remember how crazy we were about each other when we first met?"

"Yeah, you couldn't keep your hands off me."

"It was kind of fun, wasn't it?"

She put her arms around him and nibbled on his ear. "We're alone."

"That's just what I was thinking," Gil said, grabbing her arm.

35

GIL HAD LONG suspected the players' union orchestrated Shaila's father's extortion and the release of the leak of the embarrassing photos to the media.

"Peck, I'm just not sure what to do. This is blackmail. They're ruining my career, my relationship with my wife, and my reputation."

"Gil, sitting and doing nothing ain't gonna work. The Rockies sure as hell won't help. They probably like all the publicity. We've gotta hatch our own scheme; we've gotta fight back."

The two men sat at Gil's kitchen table drinking coffee and discussing scenarios. Finally, it was Peck who came up with the plan.

For a week, while Gil was inundated with baseball, Peck lurked outside of the Kites' home, studying Randall's daily patterns. Shaila, up at five-thirty on weekdays, showed no signs of any injuries resulting from the crack to her skull. She had her driver's license, but Kite insisted she couldn't drive or participate in any of the summer cheerleader workouts. Instead, he drove her to school every morning on his way to work while she quietly watched the girls prepare for the upcoming halftime shows.

The first morning, Peck followed Kite to work, a plastics warehouse across town in Lakewood where he worked until knocking off at three and coming home. Shaila had to bum a ride from another cheerleader, or more often, a football player finishing up in the weight room. The home was covered with shabby, yellow siding and didn't have a garage. Large maple trees, disfigured from the beatings of late spring snowstorms, filled in the front yard, and a driveway led to the side of the house. It was low-cost housing, neglected and rundown.

The woman of the house worked retail. She slept late and worked until closing. Kite was alone with his daughter for dinner, unless she took off with her friends, which was almost every night.

Peck gave Gil the update. If they were going to strike, it would be tomorrow, on garbage day. After finalizing the plan, Gil agreed. He'd need to give the media the slip, but that was becoming much easier. The predictable routine of life meant that the cameras stopped bothering him as he drove downtown. They'd wait at the stadium before their shutters began clicking.

He met Peck a block away and together they waited on the other side of the street for Kite to park his car. Peck knew Kite would roll the large green garbage can into the backyard, and then enter his home through the sliding glass door. Kite was wearing his normal attire: Baggy jeans with a tight-fitting wife-beater T-shirt. He was a small man, barely five-foot eight, and his arms were spindly yet muscular from his daily lifting of plastic sheets at the warehouse. His arms were covered with tattoos from his military stint. A tuft of black hair protruded from beneath his lower lip.

The moment Kite rounded the corner, Gil and Peck slipped out of his truck and snuck up the driveway. They found Kite busily positioning his garbage can against the siding. Peck motioned for Gil to follow. They'd decided Peck would make the first move, making sure Gil's arm wasn't put at risk. Peck was to grab Kite, secure him, then let Gil try to negotiate a settlement. Instead, Peck lowered his shoulder and shot forward, gaining speed and momentum. Just as Kite looked up, Peck hit him, his shoulder driving hard into Kite's chest. The force of the blow instantly toppled Kite onto the grass. Close behind, Gil heard the breath eke out of Kite's mouth and his eyes bulged. Peck didn't wait for his victim to gain his composure, but shoved his forearm underneath Kite's chin and pushed hard against his windpipe. Gil winced and put his hand on Peck's shoulder. The gesture was ignored.

Kite tried to grasp for breath, but ended up convulsing. Peck shook his head. "No, I'm not going to let you breathe until you drop this stupid lawsuit of yours."

In sheer desperation, Kite reached his arms up to grab at Peck's face, but Peck pushed harder. "No man, don't do that. You relax, and I'll let you breathe. Otherwise, you're going to meet your maker. Understand?"

Kite dropped his hands and nodded. Peck loosened his pressure, but still kept his forearm positioned on top of Kite's Adam's apple. Kite sucked in a gulp of air and began coughing. "You're crushing my chest," he gurgled.

Gil crouched, making sure Kite could see him. "I'm afraid Peck's not getting up, not unless you drop that lawsuit of yours."

Kite coughed some more, his eyes shifting between the two figures hovering over him. "If you're going to beat me up, go right ahead. More for the jury to consider. And when I tell the media, your little sham of a baseball career is over."

"Who says I'm going to beat you up?" Peck interjected. "I'm thinking of killing you. That way you can never enjoy the money. Maybe your wife can, but she'll be on vacation in the Bahamas with some young stud, and you'll never be able to open that mouth of yours again." Peck once more pushed down on Kite's throat, waited thirty seconds, and then released it. Kite's face was a bright red.

"Okay, I'll lower the asking price."

"No, drop it or no deal," Gil said, nodding at Peck. "And my deal isn't looking very good right now."

"I can't just drop it. I've got to pay my lawyer."

"You should have thought about that before you filed this silly lawsuit," Gil said.

"It was my wife's idea."

"Sure, throw her under the bus."

"I'm telling the truth. She said I had to do it."

"Then she can come up with the money for your lawyer."

"Come on, Gil, give me some slack. I want this to go away too. All of us do. The school is insured. We thought they'd quickly settle and it would be all over."

"But then Gil came into some money," Peck said, "and that changed everything. Right?"

"Something like that. Please, can you get off me?"

"Okay," Gil said. "But you need to start talking some sense."

Gil nodded to Peck who finally hoisted himself up using Kite's chest as a springboard and wiped his hands, still hovering over his victim.

"Do you even care that you've ruined his family, ruined his reputation?" Peck said. "You should know that if Gil doesn't pitch, he doesn't get paid. And if Gil doesn't get paid, you don't either, even if you win the lawsuit."

"But the photos tell the truth."

Peck nodded to Gil. "We have some photos of our own." Gil reached into his pocket and slipped out a folded piece of paper, then handed it to Kite who opened it and studied the picture.

"That's your daughter, in case you can't recognize her," Peck said. "She's jumping on a trampoline. Not something a teenager with a serious concussion would be doing."

"But---"

Gil held up his hand. "I don't need to hear an explanation. We know you lied about the extent of her injuries. Now why don't we see if we can't put this behind us."

Kite closed his eyes. "Okay, what if we go down to a hundred grand?"

"Are you crazy? I didn't do anything wrong, and you know it."

Snot was oozing out Kite's nose, and he vigorously sniffed it back in. "I can't just let you walk. It's more complicated than just the money."

Gil stooped down until he could smell Kite's stale breath. "The players' union. They got to you, didn't they?"

"I can't say."

Peck raised his clenched fist in a sign that he still meant business.

"It's time to start talking," Gil said.

"Please, you don't know who you are dealing with. I can't

simply drop the lawsuit, as much as I would like. I'd rather have Peck knock all my teeth out than risk what they could do."

Gil nodded to Peck to back off his threat.

"I knew it," Gil said. He stood and rested his hands on his hips. Kite was being incentivized to keep the pressure on Gil. They didn't want him to settle. "That's your problem. I need out of this lawsuit, and I don't really care what kind of arrangement you have with them."

"Please, at least pay me something so they will think I have a real settlement."

"How much do you owe your lawyers?"

"Sixty already, but if they get out of this with fifty, they'll be happy."

Gil looked up to the sky, paused in thought. "Okay, but I'm going to need you to publicly state that you're withdrawing the lawsuit because it doesn't have any merit."

Kite shook his head and wiped his nose. "I won't mention the money and just say that we've settled our differences. That's the best I can do."

Gil looked at Peck, who rolled his eyes, then back at Kite. "I don't know why I should do anything to protect you, but I feel sorry for what might happen to your family. So, I'll pay you the fifty and you keep your mouth shut. That's the deal. Okay?"

Kite nodded. "I guess we have a deal."

36

GIL FELT LIGHTHEADED as he approached Cindi's home. She had left three messages, urging him to come see her mother before it was too late. But with the Rockies on the road, there was nothing he could do. There was so much he'd wanted to tell her since they'd last met, about how he'd followed her advice and really began to live.

The sun was blaring down, and wet stains had already formed under his arms. He had never witnessed death firsthand. He wiped his brow and steadied himself on the porch.

When the door swung open, he was stunned by the scene he entered. There lay Melvelene in a monster of a bed, with its shiny metal rails, taking up Cindi's entire front room. His lightheadedness came rushing back, and he reached out for the wall to stabilize himself.

This was a hospital bed, not her cozy mattress tucked away in her bedroom. He just walked in the door and there she was.

The room was spinning. He went to his knees to keep from passing out. He paused then he removed his shoes.

"Melvelene," he whispered through dry lips.

Her daughter escorted him to her bedside. Shaun, her son now home from Afghanistan, stood behind them. Gil grabbed the rail and clung to it.

In silence, Gil watched as Melvelene reached out into thin air for some unseen being.

"Mother," she called.

"It's almost over," Cindi said. "That's what they do. The hospice nurse said it's common in a person's last days to cry out for a close relative."

"Sure," Gil said, pretending to know all about what Melvelene was experiencing.

Her face was pale and gaunt, her hands black, her breathing raspy, just a faint figure of her former self.

"Is she in pain?" he asked.

"We don't think so. Thank goodness for morphine."

Gil reached out and softly laid his hand on her shoulder. He couldn't help himself as he leaned over her ghostly face, now devoid of any smile. Nor was there any more laughter. He kissed her forehead. "I will miss you," he whispered.

They'd had their last laughs together. Now there was only a sacred silence.

Quietly, he wished her well on her own new phase of eternity, then slipped out into the blistering sun. As soon as he reached the porch, tears filled his eyes. He was going to miss his new friend.

At home, the image of Melvelene in that cold bed, reaching out to some other realm, remained etched in his mind. Mindlessly, he shoveled in Keri's meal.

They had just finished dinner when Gil felt his phone buzz in his pocket. He excused himself and went into the bathroom. Cindi broke the news. Melvelene had just passed away. No plans had yet been made, but she'd be sure to let him know.

* * *

When Gil arrived at the ballpark, the press was so thick that the Denver police had to escort his car through the melee of bodies and equipment. It had been two weeks since the photos had been published, and Gil had yet to make a statement. With the lawsuit behind him, he was ready to fire back.

He rolled down his window and three microphones were poked inside. An officer stepped forward and pulled them back.

"It's okay," Gil said. He shut off the engine and got out of the car. "I only have a few minutes, but I'd like to answer as many questions as I can."

"Is it true that you are pitching toward your death?"

It wasn't the question he'd been expecting. Gil chuckled. "I think everyone is. I mean isn't every step you take another one closer to your own grave?"

Several reporters laughed with him.

"What I meant is, do you have a disease, ailment, I don't know what to call it, but something that is causing your muscles to become more dense, and that if you keep pitching, that may take your life?"

Gil removed his sunglasses. "It's true I have something, as you call it, but the doctors don't know what. And it's also true that if they can't find a cure, my life could be shortened. By how much? Nobody knows."

"But pitching will accelerate it."

"We also don't know that, but it's easy to jump to that conclusion. My family and I decided that I will finish the season, and we will reevaluate after that."

"What about your lawsuit?" another reporter shouted.

"It's been dropped. I'd love to comment further, but you know lawyers. That's all they will let me say."

37

A WEEK HAD passed since Gil had last spoken to his father. By now, he was hoping Pastor Ron's piety had subsided. They'd gotten over rockier times before. But he wasn't here to apologize.

He found his father in his office, Bible opened, and a single bulb lamp shining on the worn papers. His bifocals were perched on his nose.

When Gil entered, the pastor didn't stir. After a moment, he ran his finger along a verse on the open page.

"I came to tell you that I'm taking a break from church for a while."

"So I see," his father said, without looking up. "People have been asking where you've been."

"I've had a lot going on."

"I do what God expects of me, and so should you."

"I think God wants me to play baseball without being a religious icon, some kind of a public spectacle."

"You're being childish. I'd put you in the class with Slider."

"That's not going to change my mind."

"If you're trying to hurt me, you need to realize you are only hurting yourself and your family."

"Church doesn't speak to me like it does to you. I need some time off, to be away for a while, to figure out life on my own terms."

Pastor Ron nodded at the chair across from his desk. "Sit down."

Gil obeyed and rested his arms on his thighs. He knew what was coming. He'd listened to decades of his father's sermons.

"How can you say that God doesn't speak to you? You've never given it a chance, always wanted to kick against the pricks."

"I think God does speak to me, just not through organized religion. Look, I'm not here to pick a fight. I just wanted to say that church doesn't mean the same thing to me as it does you. I need some time away to experience life in a different way. It's something I should have done years ago."

Pastor Ron spun his head, his eyes narrowed. He pounded his fist on the table. "You can't leave the church. You can't run from God. Why don't you give an apology for this little incident, then see if you can't get another teaching job."

"You're not hearing me. Church doesn't speak to me like it does to you."

"Because you never let it speak to you. You've always done things your way. And look where it's gotten you. That alone should be a sign you should come back and confess your sins."

"I'm not alone. Lots of people can't relate to organized religion. That's why our churches are empty."

Pastor Ron stood and paced.

"So then, you're going to be an atheist, profess faith in nothing but yourself."

"I didn't say that. Don't put words in my mouth. All I said is that I need a—"

" . . . yes I heard you, *a break,*" Pastor Ron interrupted. "You want to know why churches are empty, Gil? Because Satan has created false churches. People worship evil: actors, athletes, and musicians.

"Think about your own sport, Gil. Baseball is a system of modern day opposites and symbols, used to mimic those of God. Fair and foul, strike and ball, safe and out, all these little rules that provide this microcosm of opposites so we can compete on the field. And we build massive stadiums, cathedrals, to worship. We make pilgrimages to billion-dollar sports facilities. Can't tear down the old ones fast enough.

"Our sports stadiums, that's where all the churchgoers have gone. No more bread and wine, just hot dog buns and beer. It's pure counterfeit. Satan's followers have created a set of rules so there will always be a winner and a loser, just like in real life, but with no God in the picture. And they've created this culture, all of these rituals that teach us incorrectly about how to deal with modern life. Instead of clergy robes, we use uniforms. And fans show up donning their favorite player's jersey. It's just like going to church in your Sunday best."

"Dad, don't you think you are stretching things a bit. And aren't you being a hypocrite? You've been pushing me to play ball, to use my God-given talent. Now you're telling me I'm evil for doing what you've wanted since I was in college."

Pastor Ron ignored Gil's words and continued his rant.

"If you win, you get to baptize your coach in Gatorade."

"I'd prefer champagne."

"Please don't mock me. You've got guys giving the sign of the cross, kissing their fingers and raising them to heaven."

"Come on, it's just a way to relax and enjoy life for a bit."

"No, you can't avoid the fact that people attend these events to see who's going to win. Two teams war with each other under a system of rules to see who will conquer. It's all calculated to steal people away from true religion where there are real winners and losers."

"You mean the ones who will end up going to heaven or be cast down to hell."

"That's right. And you were to show them by your example. Until—"

"To me, baseball is more than about winning or losing. It's about being on the mound, digging deep into yourself to find out who you really are. It's about discovery."

"You're missing the point. You play this little game of baseball, feeling what it's like to experience opposition, and the exhilaration that comes when you win, to become a great sports hero that everyone worships. You replace that feeling with the real purpose for being here on this earth.

"We don't want to spend the effort to understand what the old symbols mean. Instead of trying to reinterpret them, we have converted them into pop culture, into sports rituals so they are easy to understand. But our sports symbols aren't giving our souls the right message. All they seem to do is to turn people inward, to put the focus on themselves. It's all about notoriety and money. They should be telling us to lead a spiritual life, outside of today's world of electrical gadgets and television, to turn outward to help others, not inward to self-centeredness. They simply don't want God to lead them back to him."

Gil stared past his father's probing eyes. "Look, I don't have all the answers. All I know is that I'm on a journey, and I'll let you know when I finish. I've got to play baseball right now to figure it out."

"Satan is deceiving you. If you keep pitching, you're going to die. You'll end up dying in vain."

"I don't think so. I think God did this to me so I could discover the meaning of life for myself. And I'm going to keep pitching until I find out, die or not."

"I'm warning you. Don't tempt God. If you try to fight Him, you'll learn what he has in store for you. That I can promise you."

"I'll take the risk."

"Fine, have it your way. God works in mysterious ways. One way or another, you won't be pitching for long."

Gil stared coldly at his father. "It's time for you to stop meddling with my life."

"This strike could settle, you know. Then this little charade would be all over."

"I think it's time for me to go."

38

GIL HAD JUST finished tucking in an extra pair of socks into a side pocket of his gym bag when Keri appeared in her robe and tossed the morning paper at his feet.

"They're out there again," she said with a smile. "I'm glad you get to deal with it." Keri turned and silently disappeared. Gil looked at the headline then pounded his chest with his fist. A sharp pain stabbed somewhere deep within him, and he struggled for breath.

The media wasn't going to leave him alone. With all the advertisements and special sections, the Sunday paper was nearly an inch thick, but all Gil saw was the bold headline:

CONSERVATIVE CHRISTIANS CALL FOR GIL TO STEP DOWN

The full story ran in section E, the weekly detail on religion. Gil's hands were shaking, and the papers rattled as he opened the full spread. He scanned the article, picking up key words here and there. It was something about several right-wing Christian organizations calling for a boycott of every Rockies game where Gil took the mound. For what? The allegation was that he was a fake Christian, that he'd been secretly teaching his high school students that there isn't a heaven. They had a direct quote, taken from his science fair, "that there wasn't a heaven," and he thought "everyone was a fool to believe in such a place."

In a rage, he threw the paper aside and scampered toward the front door. He flung it open, ready to take on the first reporter. A mad scramble ensued as three different camera crews jockeyed for the best shot. One ran up, not much older than high school age, and shoved a piece of paper in his face. "I've been asked to deliver this to you."

Gil was furious that he'd taken the bait. He should have ridden out the storm in the inside.

"That's the letter," she said when Gil snatched it from her, "but there's the message." The punk pointed to Gil's front lawn.

His eyes widened and his chest tightened. In two perfectly carved out trenches a foot thick was the shape of a cross. Someone had removed sections of sod then had chalked in two intersecting lines as if these were baselines on the baseball field.

Gil couldn't help himself. He yanked the letter from the envelope.

You're no role model for our youth, just a Satan worshipper. May you burn in hell—a place you'll soon believe in.

The camera lenses kept clicking. Gil had an uncontrollable urge to punch someone. That was what they wanted. All he needed was another well-placed photo.

A female reporter in jeans and a light cotton sweater stepped forward, lowered her microphone, and signaled behind her for the cameraman to cut filming.

"This is nonsense. How could you stoop so low? This isn't news." Gil foamed.

The reporter nodded in apparent agreement. "I'm not talking about all of this noise." She swept her arm in a full arc.

"Then why don't you all pack up and get out of here?"

She stepped closer and moved her brightly painted red lips close to his ear. "I know about your illness. I know about Dr. Kusha. I don't care about your religious preference. This story is so much bigger than whether your agnostic beliefs are ruining America's youth. This is even bigger than performance-enhancing drugs. Do you want to comment before we run the story?"

"You don't know anything," Gil said through clenched teeth.

"I know enough, and if you don't comment I'll write it with my own spin on it. I've consulted experts, Gil. The disease could be transmittable. Look at what HIV did to Magic Johnson's career."

"You're wrong," Gil said. "Don't go there. I'll sue you for defamation. None of it's true. I'm perfectly healthy."

She didn't budge. "I'm not here to be spiteful," she said. "America is all about baseball, and you're one of their heroes. If their knight in shining armor is going to die in battle, don't you think they have a right to know?"

Gil reached for the door handle. "Don't run the story, not until we have medical evidence. It won't be good for me, for baseball, or America. You understand?"

The reporter kept her blue eyes focused. "I'm sorry Gil. Your fans have a right to know."

Keri was standing in the front room, her sash tightly wrapped about her waist. One hand was full of Kleenex.

"I can't take this anymore. Gil, it's not fair to me, or the kids. We can't live like this. Can't we have our lives back?"

Gil opened his mouth and raised his finger, like a politician looking for a sound bite. He let his hand fall. "I know. I'm going to take care of this," he said, picking up his gym bag.

Gil shoved his truck in reverse and squealed the tires in the driveway, daring any spectator or news crew to halt him. In the street, he punched the gearshift and slammed the gas pedal to the floor, waiting for his tires to spew gravel. In his neighbor's yard, he saw four men with familiar faces—elders at his father's church. But they weren't looking at him. They had their baseball caps removed, placed over their hearts, and stared steadfast at the cross etched in his front lawn.

I knew it. Pastor Ron strikes again, saving his flock from the wolf in sheep's clothing.

Gil clamped down on his brakes, jerked the transmission into reverse and spun backward, smelling his plume of smoke. He craned his neck and squinted, trying to understand what could be capturing their attention.

Then he knew. He pounded his fist on the steering wheel.

Why didn't I see this before?

His father's warning, the cross in the lawn. His anger subsided as did the pain in his chest. No, this was all good. His father had opened his eyes. He'd done him the biggest favor of his life. *I grew up believing that this life was all about doing good and avoiding evil. Righteousness is good, sin is bad, that kind of stuff. Life was all about going to heaven—and avoiding going to hell. I was destined to a place where the streets are paved with gold, or to this place of eternal burning with the Devil.*

Now he knew that wasn't true. It was all right in front of him, just like Preacher had said. Opposites are not ends but means to accomplishing something else, like the opposite ends of a magnet being used to generate electricity, or water falling over a wheel to grind wheat, so that the goal in the physical world isn't to be at one of the opposites, but to use them to generate power. The world of religion should be the same as the physical world. The goal in life isn't to try to die and go to heaven—or to avoid going to hell—because those are opposites and being at one of the opposites doesn't do you any good.

Growing up in my father's shadow, that's all I thought about—going to heaven in the next life and whether I'm going to make it.

No longer. Staring at the cross, he threw the notion out the window like Galileo when he discovered that the earth revolved around the sun, or Columbus when he found out the world wasn't flat.

But if life isn't about going to heaven, where does that leave me?

The cross told the whole story. Opposites exist to generate an inner, spiritual power. By transcending opposites, you move to your center, where your heart is. That was the real meaning of the cross, to change your heart and live a life of compassion.

He felt a giant burden being lifted. I'm not here to earn points, or to win, or to go to heaven. I'm here to learn, to have the experience, to transcend, to be driven, and hopefully to help someone along the way.

Gil sat subdued in his truck thinking of Melvelene, the happiest person he knew. She laughed in the face of death because she was there to save him. He was going to do the same—for his father.

39

FALL WAS IN the air, and along with it, cool mornings and refreshing afternoon breezes. Austin was back in school, ending any chance of him attending another road game. Most of the home games were scheduled at night, a calculated attempt to increase attendance by not competing with work and school.

The Rockies were gaining ground on the Giants after their mid-season slump and were hoping that their home stretch would get them in contention for a wildcard spot.

They were playing the Yankees for the second time that season. The last time they'd met, Slider had taken out their second baseman. This time they were ready.

The sun had lowered past the rim of the stadium casting a shadow over the infield, but Slider kept on his sunglasses. Gil watched as Slider frantically tossed around anything in his sight in what looked like a desperate search for his batting gloves. His hands were shaking.

"You okay, Slider?" Ratcliff said.

"Leave me alone. Just find me my gloves."

Ratcliff's eyes and mouth simultaneously shot open but no words came out.

Slider's right foot began to twitch. "To hell with it, I'll bat without them."

He took the first bat he could find and pranced up the stairs and onto the field. One of the ball boys fished through Slider's cubby, found his gloves, and bounded after him.

Slider ripped them from the young man's grasp, tried to tug on the first one, but his hands were so jittery that he couldn't do it. He threw both of them to the turf. When he entered the batter's box, it was from the left-hand side, closest to the Rockies' dugout.

"Slider's not a switch hitter," Ratcliff said as soon as he saw it. "Why is he batting left-handed?"

Slider took an awkward, off-balanced swing at the first pitch, a clear half-second behind the ball.

"Want to take off those sunglasses?" the pitcher said. He was the same player Slider had unsuccessfully tried to bulldoze his way over at their last meeting.

"Shut your hole," Slider said.

"How about the other side of the plate?"

Slider stared blankly at the catcher then back at the pitcher. He adjusted his helmet then stared at the umpire in confusion.

"I'm a switch hitter now."

Seeing the confusion, the pitcher put two fastballs right down the middle of the plate, and Slider was behind them both.

Slider set up for another pitch. "Go take a seat," the catcher said.

He took another practice swing and waited for the pitch.

"That's three," the umpire said.

Slider didn't move until Boclin came to the plate. "Slider, my turn," he said with his Brazilian accent.

Slider slipped off his glasses and blankly stared at Boclin. His pupils were dilated, and he blinked rapidly.

"No kidding?" Slider said.

Boclin placed his hand on Slider's shoulder to lead him back to the dugout, but Slider shoved him away. "Don't jerk me around that like. I only swung at two pitches."

Seeing the commotion, Ratcliff bolted from the dugout. "Slider," he called. "Come on. You'll get them next time."

Grabbing his bat at both ends, Slider cracked it down on

his leg, shattering the shaft into pieces. He tossed the remnants onto the dirt and stomped away from the plate. Ratcliff strode after him and spun him around. "Wrong dugout, Slider."

"Yeah, yeah, I know."

"Gotta take a pee," Slider said, tossing his helmet to the batboy. He turned and headed for the locker room.

It was then Gil noticed the back of Slider's uniform.

"He really did it," Gil said.

The entire team watched as Slider stumbled through the dugout, their eyes focused on the black letters on his jersey. The familiar "TREYZ" had been replaced with "ME."

"That's his new name?" Manzi said to the general manager.

Ratcliff resumed his position on the railing. "Legally changed it yesterday. I couldn't keep it off the uniform."

"Was that a tattoo on his cheek?" Gil said to Preacher.

"I think so. He's crying out for your attention."

Melendez spoke up. "My father was the same way, but I didn't end up like that. I know just what it's like to have your father abandon you then come back into your life just because you get famous and have money."

"Maybe you should be the one to help him," Preacher said.

"Believe me, I've tried," Melendez said. "But he won't talk to me. He hates everything I stand for: married with a nice family, fancy home in the 'burbs with the rich folks. I don't think anyone can help him right now. He's unreachable."

Gil pitched a scoreless first inning. In the second, the batter took a check swing, trying to foul off one of Gil's low fastballs. The slight contact lifted the ball down the right field line and into the corner where the ball's motion suddenly died. Juarez, hobbling with his bad knee, skipped toward the back fence. By the time Juarez got to the ball, the batter was well on his way to third. The Yankees' coach spun his arm like a propeller, waving his batter toward home.

Juarez still had his arm, and he rifled a shot to home plate. His throw from right field was perfect, and Preacher's glove was stuck just in front of home plate.

It was payback time for what Slider had tried two months ago. But the batter didn't try to smack into Preacher. He was too small. So he dropped onto his buttocks and slid, lifting his right cleat into the air. It cleared Preacher's glove and sliced into his arm, leaving a six-inch gash that immediately began oozing blood.

Out of his peripheral vision, Gil saw Slider tearing down the left field line. He'd already shed his glove and his fists were clenched. Gil intercepted him, throwing both arms around Slider's chest. "Easy, Slider. We're going to need your bat today. We can't afford to have you getting tossed."

The umpire ejected the Yankees' runner, and that seemed to settle Slider. Gil let him go and walked him back to third. Gil put his arm around Slider's shoulder. His shoulder muscles were twitching. "You okay, Slider?'

"Hey, don't ask me any more questions, okay? I know what I'm doing."

Gil let go and ventured toward home plate where the trainer, Briscoe, was attending to Preacher with his first aid kit. Preacher shooed away his trainer and began arguing with the umpire.

"Naw, you've got to sit out a bit and get that stitched up," the umpire said.

Briscoe agreed and began to escort Preacher off of the field.

The game remained scoreless until the fourth inning. Juarez got a double, but Gil struck out, leaving him stranded at second. Slider passed Gil on the way back to the dugout. "If you can't get the job done, then I guess I'll have to do it."

Slider took two quick strikes, staring into empty space. Confident, the pitcher threw another fastball over the plate, and Slider pounced on it, punching the ball into left center. Juarez easily scored, and Slider was held up at first. But he didn't stop. He was ready for a repeat. His stocky legs spun, and he wheeled his way to second. The throw was in plenty of time, and the second baseman, fully expecting Slider to try to take him out, blocked the base, steadying himself for a collision.

When Slider lowered his shoulder, the second baseman jumped out of his way, tagging Slider on the arm and avoiding the collision. The umpire stuck up his thumb and called him out. Slider skidded, widened his eyes at the umpire then flipped him the bird. His nostrils began to flare, and he turned to keep running the bases, but he became disoriented and his line angled away from third base and into the outfield. Upon realizing that he was going to miss the plate, he changed directions toward the closest Yankees player, the beefy left fielder. When Slider was within five yards, he started wildly swinging his fist.

The Yankees' left fielder deflected the first round of punches with his glove then landed his own right hook dead center in Slider's face. His nose popped, and blood sprayed from his nose. By now, the center fielder had arrived and lunged at Slider, taking him down with a full body slam. In a matter of seconds, most of the Yankees had piled on, punching and kicking Slider from every angle.

None of the Rockies came to Slider's aid. The entire security detail descended and broke up the melee. In the end, five Yankees players were ejected. Slider, his face bloodied, curled up on the turf and shook uncontrollably. He was carried off the field in a stretcher like a football player being courted off the gridiron. With her head hung low, Slider's mother silently crept out of the stadium.

Gil pitched the following inning then went straight into the locker room. Slider was still in uniform, curled up on the exam table, still shaking. An IV was stuck in one arm and the doctor was monitoring his heart rate.

"Just trying to stabilize him," the doctor said. "Then he's off to Swedish Hospital. The ambulance is ready to go. It would help if you could get him to tell us what he ingested."

Gil kneeled down so that his eyes were level with Slider's. His pupils were the size of saucers.

"My season's over, Teacher. They're going to ban me when they see all the gunk in my blood."

"Why, Slider? You had so many things going for you."

"Why? You, of all people, you should know. It's because of you. I couldn't compete with you. I'm supposed to be the star of the team, but you come out of nowhere and steal everything. I figured you were doing drugs, and I needed to keep up."

"You got it all wrong, Slider. I'm not on drugs. What the papers said is true. I've got this wacko disease that most think is going to kill me. Trust me, you don't want to compete with me. I may not even be around next season. The team will be all yours."

Slider reached out for Gil's hand. "That's the truth?"

"The truth. You've got to clean yourself up. Fall on your

sword. Maybe they'll let you come back. We're going to need you if we're ever going to make the playoffs."

Slider let go and curled up tighter. Gil could see the goosebumps on his skin. "I never asked you about Melvelene's funeral."

"It was nice. I told the story of our first visit. If it wasn't for you, I'd have never met her."

Slider closed his eyes.

"Time to go," the doctor said, "and you've got to get out on the mound."

Gil looked up at the television monitor. The inning had ended, and he was up.

* * *

That evening, the doctor led them down the hallway. Gil's shoes slid along the glossy, white floor tiles. The smell was familiar, a pungent odor of antiseptic and body odor fused together. As he passed the heavy wooden doors, he peeked through the cracks. He wished he had time to make a surprise visit to some unsuspecting patron, just like he'd done with Slider when they discovered Melvelene.

They found Slider robed in a cotton shield, his arms bare and an assortment of tubes were pumping mysterious fluids into his bulging veins. Gil could see his tattoos better now—a cross on his cheek, a skull and knife and his right shoulder, and a broken heart on his left.

Slider's eyes were closed, and he was breathing with the rhythm of the ventilator, which, through a nosepiece, injected oxygen into each nostril. His eyelids flipped open the moment Preacher thanked the doctor. Once wide as saucers, they'd shrunk to the diameter of a pencil lead.

Gil walked to the far side of the bed, leaving Preacher closest to the door.

"Thanks for coming, guys," Slider said, propping his head to focus on his visitors. "Sorry you have to see me this way. I guess I finally hit rock bottom."

"I was just thinking about the last time we were at Children's Hospital, about how we snuck out."

Slider smiled. "I remember. Now I'm the patient." He swallowed and focused on Gil. "Do you know how much I hated you? Sorry, but I did."

Gil slid a chair next to the bed. "Don't worry. That's all behind us now. We just want you to get better. We're like family. We need you back."

Slider closed his eyes, and a tear seeped through his eyelashes. "The drugs. I started taking them to give me an advantage, but then the drugs kept getting better. I went way past steroids. Coke, acid, you name it. It took me to this place I never wanted to leave. I could run from my past, from my future—now that Gil Gilbert was snuffing out my career. I wanted what you had, the experience you felt when you pitched your no-hitter. I won that game for our team as much as you did, but nobody even mentioned my name."

"It's funny," Gil said. "Right before that game, I had a long discussion with Keri. I wasn't sure I wanted to pitch, but she said I had to, even if it killed me. She said that she finally realized that if I didn't pitch I'd die inside, and she couldn't stand to see that happen to me."

"But you didn't take drugs."

"Slider, don't give up on yourself. We'll get you cleaned up. You can get there."

"He's right," Preacher said. "Don't beat yourself up over this. Now you've experienced the worst that life can dish out, you're ready to have your experience."

Slider wiped his nose, sending a half-dozen tubes swinging from the IV bag. "I don't know how I'll ever do it. It was so easy with the drugs."

Gil put his hand on Slider's wrist. "We're not giving up on you, not now, not ever."

40

DR. BABAK KUSHA arrived at Coors Field three hours before the first pitch against the Arizona Diamondbacks. The gates were still closed and the security guard, apprised by Gil, escorted the doctor to the glass doors just to the south of the iron fence barring the main entrance.

Dressed in his knickers and a white T-shirt, Gil was leaning on the receptionist's desk.

"Dr. Kusha," he said, holding out a Rockies ticket, "this wasn't easy to get. Come on back. I'll give you a tour."

Gil led him through the main tourist attractions, the locker room, training facilities, press rooms, then down an empty hallway to the storage room filled with the cardboard boxes. He lifted two of them off a stack. "Have a seat."

The doctor patted the brown corrugated material and gently sat down. "I guess we're alone."

"Absolutely." Gil slapped his thighs. "So, tell me what I'm facing."

Dr. Kusha stroked his chin. "It's not good, Gil. You ready for this?"

"We are sitting down," Gil said with a nervous grin.

"The bottom line is that I don't have a definitive answer. No absolute diagnosis."

Gil smiled. "You're a doctor. What other answer would you give me?"

"When we last met in my office in Minnesota, I conjectured that any physical exercise might be accelerating your tissue density."

"I remember."

"Well, now we have another month's worth of data, and the picture is becoming a little clearer. Thanks to your wife, I have your physical measurements."

"Yes, I know. She's been mapping me out."

"And your nightly cardio data, that's been extremely helpful. Where I wish we'd made some more progress is at the genetic level. The enzymes in your blood are all over the place, and they definitely change on the days you pitch. The best way that I can explain your condition is that your disease is like a good cancer. It just keeps churning out good cells, not bad cells. It's almost the opposite of cancer. But too many good cells is also a bad thing. You're going to be so healthy, it will kill you."

Gil kept his eyes focused on his physician.

"Well I won't keep you waiting. I probably don't need to tell you this, but your breathing is becoming more labored. I suspect you are having difficulty breathing at night."

Gil nodded. "Maybe a little."

"And your chest is getting tighter because your pectorals are getting more dense, as well as your bone structure. It's just like I suspected. You have some type of neuromuscular disease that continues to progress. I wouldn't be surprised if you start pitching even faster, but I have to warn you, it is killing you. I'm pretty sure that every pitch is leading to your death. If the tissue density continues to increase, you are going to suffocate yourself."

"You're sure?"

"I'm sure it's progressing. It's getting worse, not better. But as a professional, I can't tell you that you're going to die. I just don't know. I've consulted with several experts all over the world. I've come up with a few similar cases, but nothing that matches identically."

"And what happened to those people?"

"Some lived, some died."

"But you didn't give anyone my name?"

"Of course not. I never mentioned pitching, baseball, or anything that could give you away. You already have enough problems in the media."

"That's for sure. I know I asked this before, but I'm going to ask again. What's your prognosis?"

"Hard to say, but if you keep up the same physical routine, I mean if you keep pitching on the same schedule, and if it keeps progressing at the same pace, it could be another year—or less. I just don't know. I'm sorry that I don't have more. We're working on it, and someday I think we will have it figured out. I just hope it's in time."

Gil bit his lower lip.

"What I can say for certain is that your pitching is aggravating your condition. We've analyzed your breathing pattern and the stress placed on your heart for the last three months, then overlaid it with the days you pitch. It's clear that you really struggle to breathe every night following a start on the mound, and your heart is working overtime. That much stress on your system isn't good. My initial prognosis is proving correct. Your muscles and bones are becoming denser, thicker. You are suffocating in your own success."

"So if I stop pitching, the disease will stop progressing?"

"I don't think we can say that. I said pitching is aggravating the condition, but probably not accelerating it. The issue is that excessive exercise causes a huge amount of inflammation, and the body hates inflammation. If the disease keeps progressing, and you aggravate it, it could collapse your lungs, or even stop your heart, then it would be all over."

"Is there anything I can do to stop the inflammation so I can keep pitching?"

"Ibuprofen is good. It keeps down the inflammation, and it's not a banned substance. Icing down also helps. You should take an ice bath after each outing. But even with all that, I must say that the most effective remedy is to stop pitching, or at least go longer between starts."

"Okay, I understand the doctor part of you wants me to stop pitching. But if you were in my shoes, what would you do?"

Dr. Kusha removed his glasses and rubbed his eyes. "Who

wouldn't want to be you? I think everyone would love to have your outgoing personality, your ability to connect with people, not to mention be the most famous athlete in the world."

He looked into Gil's eyes. "My whole family comes over when you pitch. We have dinner together, all the neighbors come over, and we have a great time. When they flash the speed of your fastball, we all start jumping up and down and cheering like we're all crazy. It's like you've changed all of our lives. I'd feel selfish if I said I wanted you to keep pitching."

With his hands steadied on the cardboard, Gil began to push himself up. "I guess I have my answer."

"Wait, Gil. There's one more thing. How are you doing, really? I mean—"

"You read the papers?"

"Don't need a paper. It's running every hour on ESPN. I'm sorry, Gil. I can't imagine what it must be like to have your father turn against you."

"He's certainly stirred up a hornet's nest. From what I hear, he's told the players' union that Slider's on drugs, that I'm a pedophile, that the whole institution of baseball is a tool of the Devil to ruin the American fabric." Gil shook his head. "It's classic Pastor Ron."

"Lots of people are really worried about you. I'd like you to see someone."

"No, no shrinks. I'm fine. Really, I am. You don't know me very well. I have the will to beat this."

"I understand, but as a doctor, I think you should at least go see a professional. Your neurotransmitters are all messed up."

Gil shook his head. "No drugs. I'm at a good place right now. You know what I finally realized? It can be just as dangerous to think that you always need to be happy as to avoid being depressed. That's because life will make sure that you can't always be happy, and then you get depressed when you can't get where you think you're supposed to be. Happiness can't be a mental goal any more than sadness. Those people are called bipolar. Life is about how to experience both, yet be able to traverse them to them to lead a full, balanced life."

Dr. Kusha stood. "The world could use a few more people just like you."

41

RATCLIFF CALLED A mandatory team meeting at ten in the morning. He gave the team a mere thirty-minute notice.

"I wanted to tell everyone before you hear it on TV," he said when the team had assembled. "It looks like the season is over."

"What?" Biondi said, jumping up. "We're almost to the playoffs. That doesn't make sense. The replacements have more fans and are generating more business than the regulars ever did."

"That's only true for the Rockies, but that doesn't really matter," Ratcliff said. "The owners and the players' union came to an agreement early this morning to end the strike. Bottom line is that the Rockies won't be needing your services as of tomorrow. I'm sorry, really sorry. You deserve to finish the regular season. You're as good as any team I've ever managed."

"Better," Gonzalez said, his head lowered.

Biondi was still standing. "So what, just like that, and our season is over?"

"I'm afraid so. The regulars are going to finish the season."

"But the season's almost over. They can't just step in. They haven't played in nearly a year. Can you imagine what it's going to be like?"

"Probably like when we all started," Juarez said.

"I can't believe it," Biondi said. "We were going to be in the playoffs. And with Gil, I was dreaming about the Series."

"I'm sorry," Ratcliff said. "We made a good run of it. I couldn't ask for a better group of guys."

"But the papers said the owners weren't going to back down. Why did they cave?"

"They didn't. The players did. Every week, ratings continue to climb. They are afraid that if they don't come back now, their careers might be over. Your success made them come crawling back. They may even be facing pay cuts. I'm sorry."

"I guess this is it," Gil said to his teammates.

"I'll get the final word tonight after the formal vote. For now, why doesn't everyone go home and spend some time with your families. You'll get official letters with your final check tomorrow. Come back at ten, we'll have a final team meeting, and you can clean out your lockers."

Ratcliff slipped out, leaving the players with their heads down. A depressing silence hovered over the dejected players. Gil finally spoke. "I can't accept this. It can't be over. We've all worked too hard, sacrificed too much to have it end this way. It's not right that we've played ourselves out of a job."

Preacher reached over and put his arm around Gil's shoulder. "I guess it's the end of the line for both of us. This will be better for you anyway. Go home and get some rest. Your body needs it."

"No," Gil insisted. He flipped Preacher's arm off and bolted upright. "This team is good enough to keep playing. We all wanted to get to the Series, and we're going to get there."

* * *

At ten o'clock the next morning, the locker room was buzzing with speculation. Preacher was sitting in front of his locker stuffing some shorts into his bag when the news broke. Gonzalez was sitting next to him, digging some dried-up turf out of his cleats. Gil stood against his closed locker, arms folded. Defiant.

"You're not going to believe this," Ratcliff said, storming into the room. "The players rejected the contract. It's time to play ball. We've got a game tonight."

"I knew it!" Gil said, slamming his hands against the locker.

Ratcliff held up his finger. "There's a catch."

The cheering halted. Gil stroked his chin, wondering what they had conjured.

"Instead of taking the deal, the players' union filed for an injunction to stop the games. They've scheduled a hearing for tomorrow morning, but that doesn't stop us from playing tonight."

"An injunction," Gil said, "based on what?"

"You're not going to like this. They are claiming that the replacement players are ruining the game. If they can get a judge to agree, they can get their jobs back and demand more money for next season."

"Ruining the game?" Juarez said, shrugging. "They're just jealous we are better than they are."

"They can't have a legal basis," Preacher said.

"That's right," Boclin said, hands on hips. "Your American legal system is crazy, more crazy than in Brazil."

"I agree," Ratcliff said. "The claims do seem quite silly, but anything can happen in our court system."

"Does this have anything to do with me?" Gil asked.

"Some of it. I haven't read the court documents, but I've heard their lawyers are going to argue everything from tainting the game with reality television all the way to rampant drug abuse."

"Slider," Juarez said before Gil could react.

"I'm sure that will come up, along with his on-the-field antics. Playing bulldozer instead of baseball can only help their case."

"What about Gil?" Preacher said.

Ratcliff hesitated then locked eyes with Gil. "From what I understand, Gil's father has issued a sworn statement testifying that Gil has been using illegal drugs to make him pitch faster."

Gil's mouth fell open. "What? That's impossible. He'd be lying. You all know I'm not on drugs. It's preposterous. I can't believe my father would stoop to that."

"I'm sorry, but that's what I was told," Ratcliff said. "I guess that since Slider was caught, he's assuming you were on them as well. Anyway, the hearing is this afternoon. You've been subpoenaed to testify."

"I thought you said we had a game tonight," Biondi said.

"We do. Our lawyer said the judge could take several days to render her decision. Until then, we're playing ball."

* * *

Gil was grateful that his camera crew wasn't allowed into the courthouse. He seated himself in the fourth row and watched as the lawyers presented their cases. The thrust of the union's argument was that baseball was America's great pastime, a part of its cultural heritage, and while the players and owners were having an honest dispute over the player's contracts, the replacements had illegally stepped in and were tarnishing the game. If left to continue, they would cause irreparable harm, thus requiring an injunction until the issues could be sorted out.

The replacement players had their own lawyers, who aptly pointed out that if the union wanted an injunction, they should have filed their papers in April, not on the eve of the playoffs.

Still, the judge wanted to hear the evidence. So Gil listened as the attorneys droned on about how baseball has become a puppet of Hollywood. They had conspired to bolster ratings in order to hinder legitimate negotiations between the owners and the real players.

But the lynchpin was the use of illegal drugs. After years of cleaning up baseball for illegal steroids, the replacements came in and undid everything. They had Slider's admission. And, they now had a sworn statement that baseball's most popular player, the pitcher who defied the laws of physics, was also taking illegal drugs, resulting in inhuman speeds. While they said that they could go into other accusations made against Gil, they had decided, at least for now, not to delve into those issues.

Gil was called to the stand and questioned by the judge. She asked Gil how he was doing.

"I think that I should play tennis since it seems like I spend all my time in court," Gil said with a grin.

"You've heard the allegation in your father's affidavit. Is it true?"

Gil shook his head. "No, your honor. I wish I knew what was happening to my body, but it's not because of illegal drug use. You know that camera crews follow me everywhere, sometimes even in the bathroom. Trust me, if I was taking any kind of illegal drugs, the whole world would know."

"But Slider was on them."

"He was, but to conclude that because Slider was taking injections, I am also, is not justified. You can depose my doctors if you think I am on drugs. They are just as baffled."

The judge slipped her bifocals down her nose and snapped her binder shut. "I think that's all for now. I'll decide on the injunction before playoffs."

42

GIL HEADED STRAIGHT from the courtroom to Pastor Ron's church. He'd be late for the game, but he didn't care. He had to put this behind him. Bible study was tonight, and he'd have a captive audience. The church parking lot was half-full. Gil wondered how many would skip their weekly delve into the holy writ for an evening at the ballpark.

Gil barged into the main auditorium. Pastor Ron was at the podium, commenting on a verse in the book of St. Luke. He peered down, paused, then continued. Gil leapt up onto the rostrum and purposefully strode over to his father.

Pastor Ron again looked up and adjusted his spectacles. "May I help you?"

Gil could hear the clanging of the camera crew as they frantically set up their equipment.

"Do you mind?" Pastor Ron said, glaring down. "We are having a service."

"Do you know where I spent my afternoon?" Gil interrupted.

"I suppose off to the ballpark playing some childish game."

"No, you know where I was. I had the pleasant experience of being hauled into court, where I was put on the stand and forced to listen to your absolutely false allegations. How could you? You know I'm not on drugs."

"I have to follow my convictions."

"As do I." Gil shook his head and panned the congregants, most with tattered Bibles opened on their laps. "It's time we get to the bottom of this, and your congregation might as well hear this."

Gil closed his eyes, waiting for the wave of dizziness to subside. His chest was pounding. "You all know about my pitching," he began, "and some of you might even know I tried to pitch professionally twenty years ago. It was my father's dream for me to play in the major leagues—because he felt I was God's chosen messenger to spread His almighty word on the baseball field.

"But it didn't turn out. And you want to know why? Because Keri, who you all know, one day announced she was expecting our first child. And we weren't married. Well, that changed everything, didn't it? It's hard for such a sinner to spread the word."

Gil felt his father's glare.

"For the longest time, I couldn't get over that. I resented you for trying to control my life—all in the name of God. But looking back now, that was the best thing that ever happened to me, even though it's taken me twenty years to find out why."

Pastor Ron tried to stop Gil, shouting, "You're like a lost ship, carried about wherever Satan blows you. He has you in his chains. Those words that come out of your mouth, they're not yours."

"I have never lied, not about the photos, and not about the drugs," Gil countered. "The truth is that I have some unexplainable disease that is eventually going to take my life. My days are numbered."

Even with his father's poisoning, he knew he was among friends he had grown up with. Hushed whispers floated up as the reality of his condition sunk in.

"I think we should get on with our Bible study," Pastor Ron stammered.

"I'm not finished. You need to hear this. I know I was supposed to honor you as my father, but I just knew it wasn't right for me to use my baseball talents to cram my religion down everyone's throat. Maybe that's okay for some people, but not me. And so I have spent twenty years trying to sort out what I believe. Then this disease hits me and I wonder why."

"God called you, but you wouldn't listen."

"That's where you're wrong. You think it's a second chance to spread God's word, but I can't accept that."

"Then what?"

"I struggled with that for the longest time. That happens when you're facing death. But then it hit me. When you good people burned that cross in my lawn, my eyes were opened. The sign of that cross. I don't know why I'd never seen it before. Life is about moving to the center, the center of the cross, where your heart is. That's where you live. Not at the edges, not where it is hot or cold, not where there is a heaven or hell, but to transcend those ideas and live from my heart, at the center of my compassion. And that is why I am pitching when I know I will die. That's what my heart is telling me, and even playing in the face of death, I've never been so alive. If I have a message to the world, I guess that's it."

"Are you finished?"

"One more thing," said Gil. "I'm sorry for not honoring you as my father, but I had to do what I thought was right."

Gil reached over and placed a white envelope onto the pulpit. "It's my peace offering. For you and Mom."

43

WITH THE SEASON winding down, Gil didn't want to miss any opportunities. It was Saturday, and the Rockies had an early evening game. Gil wasn't pitching and had the morning off.

On weekends, Austin slept in until at least ten, and later if Keri let him. Carrying a bundle of clothes in his arms, Gil cracked Austin's door. The sheet was pulled over his head, an apparent attempt to keep his room dark.

Gil flipped on the light switch. "Surprise," he said.

"What?" Austin groaned, peeking his eyes out.

Gil swung the sheets off the bed, leaving Austin exposed in his underwear. "Check 'em out," Gil said, holding out his present.

Austin rubbed his eyes and stared at the white and purple jersey. "A Rockies uniform." He popped up and held the shirt in front of him. "Wait, there's pants and socks, and my name is on them."

"You're the official batboy today. I talked Ratcliff into it. He's breaking a team rule, but I guess some rules are meant to be broken."

"Really? That's so cool. I'm really going to be in the dugout?"

"Yep. We've got to get to the park early so they can train you. And we need to stop off downtown and get you some shoes."

Austin was on the floor, slipping the uniform over his boxers. "This is going to be awesome. I can't believe you did this. Hey, Mom!"

Keri was already standing in the door, her arms folded, leaning against the doorframe.

"Pretty neat. I think I'll come just to see you."

"You've got to get Alicia to come too. I'm going to text all my friends. I can't believe it. I just wish you were pitching."

Keri slipped into her son's room, put her arms around Gil's shoulders and whispered. "You're a cute dad."

Austin threw down a bowl of cereal, grabbed his cap, and bolted out into the garage.

"Think he's a little excited?" Keri said.

"A boy's dream. See you at the ballpark."

* * *

Gil and Austin stopped by a shopping mall on the drive to the stadium to get him a pair of running shoes to match his Rockies uniform.

"Might as well go all out," Gil told his son.

As they were leaving the mall, they heard a voice from behind. "Hey, aren't you that Gil dude?"

A man, missing one of his front teeth, and who had a head of matted hair that came to his shoulders, scooched himself upright. His face had the appearance of leather. He was sitting on the cement outside the mall, propped up by a brick wall. Perched on his lap was an acoustic guitar. The case was sprawled out in front of him, with a few dollar bills fluttering in the breeze.

Gil turned. "Yeah, that's me."

"I hear you play a mean guitar."

Gil smiled. He was expecting someone to ask for his autograph or a question about how he could really throw that fast. "I've been known to light up a few stages."

The man flipped the shoulder strap over his head and held out the guitar. "Why don't you pluck a few strings, see if some of these good folks won't contribute to the cause," he said, looking into his nearly empty guitar case.

"Sure," Gil said without hesitating. He stooped over, slung the strap over his shoulder, and strummed the strings. "Not bad.

What am I singing?"

"*Stairway to Heaven*, if you know it."

"Whoa, going way back, aren't you? Even before my time. I haven't played Zeppelin since I was in freshman dorms. Let me see if I can remember. A woman buys a stairway to heaven, but when she gets there, the stores are all closed."

"That's the one. You got it. No stores in heaven."

Gil plucked out the tune and sang the first verse.

By now, close to a hundred people had formed a semi-circle around the performer. Gil kept up his tune, but periodically nodded at the guitar case. A few tossed in some coins. Gil's eyes narrowed. Austin had seen those eyes before, usually when he didn't do his chores or his homework. Austin slipped off his Rockies cap, flipped it upside down and stuck it out in front of his chest, sauntering along the front row then working his way back through the crowd. "I'm taking up a collection for that homeless man. My dad would really like it if you'd help."

Gil sang enough verses to give his son time to work his charms. When Austin came back to the front, his cap was overflowing with bills. He unloaded the currency in the guitar case. "There you go, mister. I hope you have a good meal and a soft bed tonight."

The song ended, the crowd clapped wildly and in unison rushed forward for autographs and pictures.

"Austin and I need to get to the ballpark, so I can't stop for any signatures, but I hope you are all going to watch the game tonight."

The crowd respectfully parted, and the father-son duo bid their friend goodbye and headed off.

"Austin, did you bring your ticket?" Gil asked.

"Of course, you think I'm crazy?"

"You'll be in the dugout with me." Gil nodded back at the homeless man.

"Are you sure? I sit next to Mrs. Melendez," said Austin.

Gil smiled.

"Got it." Austin snatched his ticket from his jeans pocket and ran it over to the man. "Dad's not pitching today. I think DeJesus is on the mound, but the seat is really good. Dad says you can't sell it. You have to come to the game."

The man took Austin's hand in both of his, gently stroking them. "Can I ask one more thing?"

Austin looked back at his father. If they didn't hurry, they were going to be late.

Gil could sense not only the fan's gaze, but those of the cameras. He nodded.

"Can we all have a prayer together? I need all the help I can get." He pulled Austin tight into him.

"Sure," Gil said, stepping toward the man who held out one of his hands. Gil could smell the stench of body odor and stale tobacco. "We might as well make this a family affair. Whoever wants to join, just reach out and take someone's hand."

A giant smile broke on the man's face, revealing his deteriorating dental work. "I love you, man."

44

EXCEPT FOR THE upcoming decision by the federal district judge, the Rockies controlled their own destiny. Trailing the San Francisco Giants by two and a half games, if the Rockies could sweep the three-game series, they'd win the division and clinch a playoff spot. If they lost even a single game, their season was over. If the judge decided against them, there would be no playoffs, regardless of whether they won the pennant.

Gil was scheduled to start the series with the Giants. Melendez would start game two, and if he won, then game three would be laid on DeJesus' shoulders.

Gil took the mound and after his first pitch, his shoulder was on fire. His upper chest burned. The muscles in his body felt like the day after lifting heavy weights. He worked through it, allowing a run to score in the first inning. He slowly loosened up, but by the fifth inning, the burning followed every pitch.

The outfielders stepped up to save the day. Juarez's knee was hurting so bad that running was next to impossible. But his bat made up for it. He'd been hitting over .500 in the last week. He hit two homers and a single, which would have been an easy double for Slider. Boclin, his batting average hovering in the mid-200s, finally began to connect wood with leather. With a single, double, and triple, he'd helped the Rockies to score eight runs. Manzi, determined to get in the playoffs and face Chicago, chipped in another two runs.

By the eighth inning, Gil had allowed four runs, more than any other game in the season. But with a healthy lead, Ratcliff signaled for his closer. He'd let Gil rest and Tajima put the icing on the cake.

The ice baths and ibuprofen helped, but Gil had a hard time disguising his body's violent reaction to his pitching. He walked like a marathoner the day after a race.

The next evening, he gingerly found his way to the bench to watch Melendez. It was his best game of the season. He allowed only a single run, while the Rockies' lineup managed another seven points.

The Rockies needed one more win to get into the playoffs. It was up to DeJesus, whose cutter was on. Through the first three innings, the Giants remained hitless.

"How are you feeling these days, Gil?" Slider said, dressed in a pair of jeans and a Rockies T-shirt.

Gil turned. It was the first time Slider had ever called him by his real name. "I was going to ask you the same thing. You still okay with the suspension?"

Slider nodded. "I am. I think they went easy on me since I put myself in rehab and admitted everything. Counseling has been good for me. I'm just starting to deal with the pain of growing up without a father—and his sudden reappearance. You know, I did get the commissioner to let me play when we get to the Series."

"No kidding?"

Every head in the dugout turned.

Slider put up both hands like a baseball player protesting a foul call. "Hey, I'm serious. I think he was kidding at first because he didn't think the Rockies could ever make the Series, especially if I was out for the rest of the regular season and the division series. I told him we had a deal before he could go back on it, and the lawyers put it in writing."

They watched as Ratcliff made his way from the mound back to the dugout.

"Does Ratcliff know about this?" Gil said.

"Sure does."

DeJesus allowed a home run in the sixth inning. He was furiously kicking the dirt with his cleats. He grabbed his elbow then violently massaged it. After taking his stance, he hitched his shoulder.

"That's not a good sign," Slider said.

"He's like an injured horse," Gil said.

DeJesus took his windup and let the pitch go. It smashed into the dirt two feet in front of the plate. The pitcher began wildly hopping, gripping his elbow. Briscoe rushed out on the field. Gil watched from his hideout, hoping what he was seeing was merely a dream.

Briscoe waved his arm and instantly one of the batboys grabbed his first aid kit and ran it out on the field. He whipped out some bandages and concocted a sling. Melendez slipped next to Gil on the opposite side of Slider. An eerie silence crept out of the stadium and seeped into the dugout.

"If it's what I'm thinking, he's going to need Tommy John's surgery," Melendez said. "He's out for the playoffs."

They sat in silence as Briscoe and Connor coddled the Cuban off the field. When he saw Gil, he pointed to his sling. "See, one bad pitch and my career is over."

The mighty Cutting Cuban, the man who pitched for freedom, was done for the season. In the dugout, Ratcliff looked at Connor. "I've got pitchers, but nobody you want out there."

Ratcliff spit into the dirt, something he hadn't done since he was a player. He turned to study his bench. Tajima was nervously tightening a string on his glove.

"Tajima," he said.

The Japanese pitcher jumped up. "Hey, come on, everyone. Get excited. This is our season. We're not going to lose."

Ratcliff waved his hand. "I don't need you as a cheerleader. I need a pitcher."

"Anything for you coach," he said.

"Get warmed up. You're going out there."

"Isn't the next inning number seven?"

"Yeah, it's your lucky number."

"But I'm only good for two innings, at most."

"Don't ask stupid questions. Just go out there and pitch. Okay?"

Gil was tossing a ball, up and down, silently watching as Tajima grabbed his glove. Gil let the ball fall to the ground. "I'm going to the bullpen."

"Since when did you become the manager?" Ratcliff said.

"I didn't mean to overstep, but I want to get us to the playoffs. I can give you one good inning—if you need it."

Ratcliff sighed. "You sure?"

"I'm okay, but just if you need me."

Ratcliff consented, and Gil exited the dugout.

The Rockies rallied, scoring two runs. Tajima got them to the last inning with a one-run lead. In the ninth, he gave up a single, then walked the next batter. He looked to the dugout with a face of desperation.

Ratcliff jumped up and signaled to the bullpen. It was up to Gil to clinch the win.

A hushed silence fell over the stadium when Gil took the field. As he reached the mound, the clapping began. The crowd was on its feet. After the first pitch, the burning sensation came roaring back. He didn't feel tired, but like he was pitching under water. When his first pitch hit 112 and the crowd went wild, all thoughts of how sore he felt went by the wayside. He retired the first three batters he faced and the Rockies were in the history books. They'd finished the regular season with a record of ninety-six to sixty-eight, and they'd be facing the St. Louis Cardinals in the first round of the Division Series.

The players rushed the mound and surrounded their ace. Fans flooded the field. Security didn't bother to stop them. This was such a rarity; the fans deserved it.

It took thirty minutes for the grounds crew to set up a makeshift stage. The Rockies were the Western Division Champions, and the necessary pomp and ceremony was about to begin. Ratcliff was awarded the team trophy. He gave the obligatory speech. This was a team effort, they were thrilled, but knew this was just the start and that they'd be ready when they traveled to St. Louis.

Champagne followed. Calls were made for speeches. Everyone wanted to hear Gil. Boclin grabbed the microphone and in English mixed with Portuguese, announced that Gil had a promise to fulfill. "Gil doesn't know it, but his old band is here, and he's going to sing for us. And I'm going to find the most beautiful girl and show everyone how to dance like a Brazilian."

The players stepped back as Gil's amateur band members lugged their equipment onto the stage. The ground crew worked furiously to provide electrical connections and extra microphones.

Gil was handed his electric guitar and stepped forward. "Well this is a little surprise. I suppose I did promise that I'd sing if we won the pennant. So here it goes."

Gil strummed his guitar and looked back at his band. They nodded and in unison started the song.

Gil's band finished with a traditional rendition of Gil's *Take Me Out to the Ballgame.* "Come on, let's hear you sing it," he said. "*One, two, three strikes you're out at the old ballgame.*"

More champagne followed in the locker room. There were enough reporters for all the players to recant the Rockies' amazing season until well past midnight. In the excitement of the win, Gil forgot about his ice bath or taking more anti-inflammatories.

By the time he reached home, he could barely move. As soon as the garage door opened, Austin, Alicia, and Keri, followed by Peck, raced into the garage and helped him out.

They talked for another hour until Austin's head bobbed, and he slipped sideways on the couch. "Looks like it's bedtime, everyone."

Gil stayed in bed the entire day. Ratcliff had given the team the day off. Even if he hadn't, Gil wasn't about to move. His chest was heavy, like he was suffering from a severe chest cold bordering on pneumonia. The continuous coughing felt like it was ripping out his insides. Keri called Dr. Kusha's cell phone and explained the symptoms. He told Keri to have Gil stay in bed for twenty-four hours, then call him tomorrow. He kept him on the ibuprofen and a cool chest pack.

It was early afternoon when the phone rang, and Ratcliff's number popped up. He reached over to the nightstand and fumbled with the phone before Keri came rushing in and handed it to him.

"How you feeling?" Ratcliff said.

"Getting there," Gil said, scooching himself up onto his pillow.

"I figured you could use a bit of good news. You remember when the judge said she'd render her decision before the playoffs?"

Gil propped himself on his elbow. "You said it was good news."

"It is. She threw out the suit. Said it was totally baseless. The judge said that the replacement players couldn't possibly tarnish baseball's reputation because the striking players had already done a good job with that. She says she loves watching your reality show and wants to see you pitch in the playoffs—provided you're healthy enough. That means there will be a playoff and a World Series with this season's players."

Gil swung his legs over the bed and slid his fingers through his disheveled hair. "I can't believe it. A judge for a fan. Did you get her tickets?"

"She'll be taken care of. I just need to know if I'm going to have a pitcher."

"Count me in. There's no way I'm going to miss this one."

45

IT WAS A perfect autumn day, the temperature was in the mid-seventies, and the skies were filled with Canada geese making their way south. Gil arrived home just as Keri and the kids were finishing lunch. Team meetings didn't start until four o'clock.

"Let's go to the park," he told Alicia. "We can get caught up on what's going on in your life."

She closed her book. "Really? We haven't done that since I was in grade school. Remember when you used to push me on the swing so high that I'd nearly fall out?"

"I think we should see if I can do it again."

A minute later she was in her shorts with a Rockies cap over her pulled-back hair. Her ponytail poked through the back hole.

They drove to Red-Tailed Hawk Park with their entourage close behind. With the elementary schools back in session, the playground was deserted. As soon as she closed the car door, Alicia turned and waved. "A seesaw. I haven't been on one of these in years. Come on." She began jogging then stopped and waited for him. He was moving gingerly as if he were walking on broken glass.

Alicia bounded to the far side of the seesaw and hopped on the seat. Instantly, it bottomed out on the pebble gravel. Gil reached up and pulled her down.

"Still as light as a feather. When are you going to put some meat on those bones."

"You always know how to make a girl feel good, don't you?"

Gil shimmied his way onto his seat and sunk his weight into the beam, causing his daughter to shoot up into the sky.

"Wow, kind of puts butterflies in my stomach."

"Ever hear anything from Conklin?" He extended his legs and soon he felt the same sinking feeling in his stomach as he flew to the top.

"Not much. After I broke things off, I got a few texts, usually after you won a game. Nothing recently."

"After this season, you're going to need to get back to school and meet some more people."

"It's going to be hard. People will think differently of me now that you're famous."

Gil stopped at the bottom, keeping Alicia in the air. "Really?"

"Of course. My life will never be the same. Hey, it's kind of fun being up here." Gil could see her gleaming white teeth as she twirled her head around. She held out her arms as if she were a bird. "It's almost like flying."

Gil was squatting. Her weight wasn't enough to lift him up. "Well, it's not too fun being down here. Want to stay up there all day?"

"That's okay. Hey, did I tell you about Peck liking girl things? It's really weird. He comes off like this tough guy, but underneath he's got this feminine side. The women at the games adore him. He fits right in."

They chatted until Gil finally realized they were both standing, the teeter-totter balanced between them.

"Okay, so let's get serious," Gil said. "Father-daughter stuff. How is your life, really?"

She twisted up her mouth and shrugged her bare shoulders, still deeply tanned. After pausing for a minute, she said. "Kind of like this seesaw. In neutral, just not doing much. But that's okay, I needed some time off, remember?"

"The summer's been good for you."

"It has, but you're right. I'm getting ready to move on. Remember our discussion about how when I got to the top of the mountain, that I'd know? And that's when I could jump and fly?"

Gil tried to remember, but it seemed like another lifetime. He nodded.

"Well, I think I'm to the point where I'm ready to start hiking again. It's no fun being stuck in the middle."

"Well, I think you're right. Now you understand why I need to pitch."

She scrunched her nose. "Maybe, but you know what you want to do. For me, I'm not sure. I loved school, but I'm not sure it's right for me."

"Then why don't you do something crazy, like join the Peace Corps and go to Africa? Or maybe study abroad in Italy. We should have the money. Put yourself on a good journey."

"I'll think about it."

When they finally left the playground, Alicia walked over to her father and took his hands in hers. She looked up into his eyes. Her lip was trembling.

"Dad, I know."

"Know what?"

"The real truth about what's happening to you."

Gil looked down at her tearing eyes. "Really? You're probably the only one on the planet. Tell me what you've divined."

"This isn't the time to kid around with me." She burst into tears and threw her arms around him. He felt her body convulsing beneath his powerful arms.

"You're acting like I'm going to die tomorrow. Now come on, let's sit down and talk this thing out."

He grabbed her hand and led her to the swings. "So tell me what you're worried about." A hawk flew above them, and Gil craned his neck to watch.

She reached up and turned his face back. "I need all of you here right now."

"Okay, I'm sorry. What's eating you up?"

"I know what you have is really serious, and they've been saying that someday you're going to die, but Mom told me about your last visit. I know what Dr. Kusha said."

"He's a good doctor, isn't he?"

"Oh, please stop. I'm your daughter, and I'm not a little girl anymore."

He reached and stroked her cheek. "And a very pretty one at

that. Have I ever told you what a beautiful woman you've grown up to be? You remind me so much of your mother when she was your age."

"Dad, I know your tricks. We all know them. You love to talk, but never about what's really important. But you can't avoid this one. I know the truth. Your pitching is killing you. You're going to die."

"Yes, but we're all going to die."

"Stop it! That's not what I'm talking about. It's the pitching that's doing this to you. This could be your last game. Every pitch you take is bringing you closer to death. You can't pitch anymore. You could die on the mound. The more you exert yourself, the faster you escalate your condition. You can't pitch anymore."

"Alicia, that's not what Dr. Kusha said. And besides, we all get closer to death with every breath we take. Do you want me to sit in a wheelchair the rest of my life? If I did what you're suggesting, you guys would need to feed me because lifting my fork is going to make me die. That's not life. That's not living. Being on that mound, living my dreams—that's life, that's why I'm here. I'm sorry Alicia. I gave up my dream once before, and . . . "

Shaking, she buried her face into his rock-hard pectoral muscles. "I know about that too," she sobbed. "You got mom pregnant in college and quit playing so you could support us. I know. Mom told me." She paused, then looked into his eyes.

"But that wasn't a mistake. I wanted to be with your mother always, and I did the one thing I knew that would keep us together. And you're the result of that decision."

Alicia nodded her head and sniffed. "I know. Mom told me that too. That's why we can't live without you. I can't see you die on that mound. I'd never get over it."

He lifted her cap and smoothed her hair. "You and Austin are the best things that ever happened to me. I wouldn't change anything that's happened to us in the last twenty years."

She wiped her nose. "So why do you have to keep pitching? Let's just keep on with how things are."

"This is something I have to do. I can't explain it other than to say I feel it in my bones. I need to be out there pitching. I can't let everyone down. Think about Austin. He can't wait to see me out on that mound. That's his dream, to see his father win the

Series. What's so wrong with that?"

"Because that's the last he'll ever see of you, that's what."

He wiped her cheek. "Alicia, I feel fine. I'm going to finish off the season, then we'll all sit down and decide about next year. Tell you what. We'll take a vote. If you all want me to give up baseball, then that's what I'll do. Fair enough?"

"What if this is it? What if I never see you again?"

"That won't happen. I promise I will not die on the mound. I'm feeling fine. Dr. Kusha gave me some good suggestions, which I am going to follow. I have at least one more season in me. That is, if you let me come back another year."

She sniffed and focused her gaze on his eyes. "You promised," she whispered in his ear. "You promised that this won't be the last time."

"I did. Now we should probably get going."

46

WHEN GIL TOOK the mound in St. Louis, he felt better than he had since the All-Star break. "I feel really good," he told his family when he awoke in their hotel room. It was the first time he'd traveled with all of them. For every other road game, he had a room to himself. At first, he wasn't sure if it was a good idea to break routine, but the thought of waking up next to Keri was too irresistible; and to see Austin's face, eyes wide with excitement, as he went over the Cards' lineup, couldn't be missed.

Ratcliff pulled Gil after eight innings. The outfielders' bats remained red hot, and Ratcliff figured Tajima could hold on to a three nothing lead. Tajima gave up a run, but that was good enough. The Rockies had stolen the first game on the road.

Gil had started to feel fatigued after the fourth inning, but thought nothing of it. As he watched Tajima finishing off the game, the same tightness he'd felt during the pennant race came roaring back. His chest felt like it was compressing in on itself. Hunched over, Gil snuck into the locker room. Connor already had his ice bath ready. He slipped on a pair of shorts and plunged into the icy waters.

The shock of biting cold made him gasp, but he slid down like it was a steam bath on a frigid day. The numbing cold relieved the pain. Connor pulled him out after four minutes.

"No press conference for you. Keri's outside waiting. We're getting you to your room."

"I thought they were expecting me. If I don't make an appearance, they'll start to talk."

"I thought you were past that," Connor said.

"I guess you're right. Bed for me."

In the hotel room, Gil kept up his hunched walk.

"You look like Grandpa before he died," Austin said when he saw his father.

"Funny," Gil said. "Just a little twitch in my back. I'll be okay in the morning."

Melendez started the next day. He gave up a respectable three runs, but Juarez struck out twice, and the rest of the outfielders followed suit. The Rockies lost three to one and headed back to Colorado.

At home, Dr. Kusha completed his phone examination. His diagnosis remained unchanged. Rest was best. Gil needed to listen to his own body. His research team was still feverishly working on trying to unlock the mystery behind his illness.

* * *

Feeling better, Gil was ready to go on two day's rest. In front of a cheering home crowd, he retired the first six batters he faced with a total of eighteen pitches. But in the third inning, the stiffness returned. No runs scored, but he used up twenty pitches. He asked the trainer to rub his shoulder while he sat on the bench.

By the fifth inning, his chest was so tight that he struggled for breath after each pitch. The irony was that the harder it became to breathe, the faster he pitched. He finished another scoreless inning, sucking in air as he exited the field.

Ratcliff sat next to him. "You sound like you have asthma. I'm going to pull you, Gil. We've got a four-run lead, and I need to save you for game five if I need you." He slapped Gil's leg. "You okay with that?"

Gil nodded. "At least Keri will be happy."

The reliever gave up a run in the seventh and two more in the eighth. Tajima pitched well, but gave up a homer. With the score tied, Ratcliff was facing extra innings. That all changed when Juarez homered in the ninth. Game wise, the Rockies were up two to one.

After the game, Keri asked Peck to stay with Gil. When Gil walked out of the locker room hunched over, Peck insisted on driving him home. Keri had his ice bath ready, pouring a week's worth of stored ice cubes into their bathtub.

"Whew!" Gil said when he plunged in.

"How do you do that?" Keri said, watching goose bumps explode over Gil's skin.

"Take the plunge? Kind of like our getting married. You just jump into it, and there you are."

"Just like that?"

"Uh huh. Don't believe me? Why don't you try it?"

She didn't hesitate. Still in her jeans and Rockies jersey, she plopped herself into the tub beside him. "Didn't think I'd do it, did you?"

He looped his head sideways and kissed her. "I'm glad we took the plunge twenty years ago. We've been good for each other."

The tension in Gil's upper body made it impossible to sleep. Keri spent an hour massaging Gil's chest and shoulders until Gil was softly sleeping. His shoulders and chest by now were massive. He looked more like a professional bodybuilder than baseball player. His neck was about as thick as his head, and his thighs stretched his pants legs like leotards.

* * *

Alicia found her mother kneeling next to Gil, kneading his shoulders with her fists. Alicia was in her pajamas, rubbing the sleep out of her eyes.

"You look tired, Mom," she said.

"I'm okay, just trying to loosen up this fighter."

"Dad, you're making me nervous. I can't wait until the season's over."

"Dad's going to take the Rockies to the NLCS." It was Austin. He charged in and hopped on the bed. "The Cubs are up three zip in their series. Dad, if you can get the Rockies one more win, we're off to Chicago. Here, can I help?"

Austin crawled to the other side of the bed and began working on Gil's other shoulder.

"I think I'm good," Gil said. "Why don't we get breakfast— out of bed."

* * *

Melendez pitched game four in front of a screaming home crowd. But he was pitching on two day's rest, just like Gil. He threw tired and the Cards clobbered him. The team would be travelling back to Missouri for the final game, and Ratcliff knew he had a problem.

The changes in Gil were now obvious to just about everyone. His body was swollen with muscle and his breathing labored. Ratcliff felt torn. On one hand he needed Gil to help the team win and he didn't need to worry about ruining him for next year, because there would be no next year in the majors once the strike settled. On the other hand, Ratcliff liked Gil and deeply respected his grit. The man never complained, never asked to be taken out, even when his breathing was labored and muscles stiff with pain.

Gil can't go nine innings. I'll pull him after five or six or use him as a reliever, Ratcliff reasoned. *That'll give him recovery time.*

Ratcliff's concerns were moot. By the sixth inning, the Rockies had a ten-run lead. Ratcliff pulled Gil, and the Rockies coasted to victory and their first trip to the National League Championship.

* * *

Ratcliff faced a major problem. The NLCS had a format that didn't lend itself to letting any starting pitcher get in three games. The Rockies would play their first two games in Chicago, then return for three games at home. If needed, they would return to Chicago for the last two games. The format meant that, with a travel day between games two and three, he could have Gil and Melendez pitch the first four games with two day's rest. But game five presented a problem. Neither pitcher would have enough rest to start. His bullpen wasn't deep enough to start one of his relievers. He'd be forced to start the rookie, Sewell, who he'd recently called up from the minors after DeJesus threw out his arm, and he knew they'd lose.

As much as the Rockies tried to hide Gil's condition, the press still got wind of how he'd been hurting. He was filmed hobbling into his truck when Peck drove him home. His back was arched and he was clutching his chest as he gasped for air.

Ratcliff, Connor, and the Rockies' front office knew they had a potential disaster on their hands. They needed Gil to win the pennant and Series, but what if he was permanently harmed—or worse, what if he died? The Rockies' manager and coaches would be crucified in the media, and probably by the fans.

"We've got one choice," Ratcliff said. "We leave the decision to play up to Gil—and we make sure everyone knows it."

Keri kept silent, leaving the decision to Gil. He knew how she felt. "Don't risk your life. We need you," she had told him.

* * *

Game one against the Cubs had the air of a fight rather than a game. Slider, still struggling with his emotional imbalance, knew he couldn't face being on the same field where he'd had his breakdown. He chose not to travel to Chicago.

Manzi, scandalized in the press for his supposed indiscretion the year before with the Cubs, had to relive his nightmare one more time. He played like a man possessed. He made it on base three straight times, scoring twice, the only two runs put up by the Rockies.

Gil stayed on the mound until the sixth inning. His muscles began to seize up like an engine with no oil. He could feel his control going and walked the first batter. Then his arm froze during the release of a curveball. It hung like a feather floating in the air. The batter, looking for an off-speed pitch, guessed right and slammed it over the left field fence. Gil looked to the dugout, and Tajima started throwing in the bullpen.

"That's never happened," he told Connor when he got to the dugout. "I mean, yeah I've been sore, but just shutting down, that's never happened. My arm just wouldn't work."

Tajima got them out of the sixth with a two-to-two tie, but in the ninth gave up a homer to drop the first game. The odds makers were silenced when Melendez took the mound in game two and threw a shutout. It was his best game of the year, and he went all nine innings. A depressing silence fell over the Cubs stadium when he struck out the last batter. The Rockies had broken even and now were heading home to Denver for three more games.

Ratcliff lingered in the dugout, watching as the sullen Cubs fans emptied out of the stadium.

"You thinking the same thing I am?" Connor said.

"Probably. We should be worried about how we can get Melendez to pitch three games, not Gil."

"He's still pretty banged up after yesterday's outing. He says he feels fine, but watch him when he's sitting on the bench."

"Yeah, I've noticed. He breathes like he's having an asthma attack."

When the Rockies returned to Denver and Gil claimed to be rested, Ratcliff came up with a new plan. If Gil could pitch the first home game, Melendez could pitch game four. He'd give up on game five, letting both Gil and Melendez take a much-needed rest. If the series went back to Chicago, he'd start Gil, and if it went to a game seven, Melendez would be called on for a repeat.

* * *

Between Alicia's relaxation sessions and a day at home, Gil felt ready for another day of combat. When he awoke, his arm and chest felt fine. Still tight, but he wasn't facing the labored breathing that seemed to shut him down.

The new problem was his eyes. Everything looked foggy, like he had glaucoma. He rubbed them, but nothing worked. When he looked into the mirror, nothing seemed out of the ordinary. He took a shower, but the hazy appearance wouldn't disappear. He snuck into the kitchen, took a few ice cubes from the freezer and rested them on his eyes.

Keri caught him lying on the couch before he could slide the cold packs onto his shoulder. "What's going on?" she said.

"Nothing," Gil said. "Just experimenting."

"By putting ice onto your eyes?"

He wanted to tell her he had a little bit of a headache, but knew she'd eventually get it out of him. "I feel really good this morning, but my eyesight is a little bit hazy. I'm fine now, back to twenty-twenty."

Keri picked up the phone.

"You're not going to call him?" Gil said. "We've bugged that poor man to death."

"He wants to know of any new symptoms."

Gil shrugged his shoulders and flipped on the television.

Dr. Kusha noted the change, asked to speak with Gil, and then ended the conversation by telling Gil he'd look into it.

By the time the game started, Gil's symptoms had vanished as mysteriously as they began. At game time, the announcer read through the list of distinguished guests. When he concluded by saying that the entire top three rows of the rockpile had been reserved for the Rockies' biggest fans, Gil stopped his warm-up and looked to the bleachers above right-center. It was a sea of turquoise, with orange caps. Prairie Ridge High School. As the camera zoomed in on the fans, he saw Peck crammed in with more than two hundred high school kids. Those were his kids. They were feverishly waving, hoping to get Gil's attention. He removed his cap and waved it back.

Gil peered into the dugout. Getting 200 seats for a playoff game must have cost a fortune. Ratcliff merely shrugged. He looked to Preacher, then to Biondi, who did his traditional waddle to the mound.

"We all thought it would be nice to have your former students come see you pitch in a playoff game."

Gil pitched all nine innings, giving up a single run in the fifth. Boclin and Juarez continued their long bomb attack and generated three runs between them. The average speed of Gil's fastball was 110. He'd silenced all of his critics.

The celebrations were short-lived. Melendez got pounded in game four. Six runs had scored by the fourth inning. Four more scored in the fifth. Ratcliff decided to pull him, saving his arm for one more attempt if they had to go seven. Trista Melendez didn't say a word the entire game.

Ratcliff called game five amateur day. He could have used one of his relievers to start, but then he'd be short a reliever when the team returned to Chicago. The rookie, Sewell, went back on the mound.

Sewell's second outing was respectable but predictable. Ratcliff kept him in for six innings. He allowed eight runs, and the Rockies dropped another game. In Chicago, the Rockies would need to win both games. With no other pitchers, Gil would be his next starter, and if they could miraculously pull out a win, Melendez would be called on for the final game seven.

With the day of travel, Gil was awarded four days of rest. He felt like a Marine, going into a skirmish, beating up on the enemy then getting a pass for some R and R, only to come back and face reality. The Yankees had already finished out the American League series with a lopsided smashing of Boston. Nobody wanted a chance at the Yankees more than Juarez. They cut him thinking he was a has-been, assuming his injured knee was career ending. The orthopedic surgeon who'd looked at his knee said nearly all of his cartilage was gone, that he was scraping bone on bone with every step. He said he didn't care. If Mickey Mantle could do it, so could he.

And he did. In the final two games against the Cubs in Chicago, he batted over six hundred. Gil's streak continued, allowing only two runs in eight innings. In game seven, Melendez, ready to redeem himself, gave up three runs in seven innings. But with a grand slam by Juarez in the eighth, even Tajima couldn't blow the lead.

The Rockies were going to the Series.

47

THE WORLD SERIES followed the same format as the League Championship Series. Ratcliff gave Gil the home start.

Dr. Kusha made a special trip to Denver, not only to see the World Series, but to check on his most popular patient. On the morning of Gil's start, Dr. Kusha paid a personal visit to the Gilberts' home. He spent the morning working Gil over, poking and prodding him, taking more blood and urine samples, listening to his heart, reviewing his records from the past four months. Keri stayed by his side.

When he was finished, Gil asked Dr. Kusha for his professional opinion.

"Same thing," he said. "Both your muscles and bone tissue are more dense. The disease is progressing, and we still have no way to stop it. You run the risk of shutting down your organs if you put too much stress on them."

Gil searched Keri's eyes. "Gil has two more games to pitch," she said, "maybe three if they play all seven. What are the risks?"

Dr. Kusha shook his head. "I just don't know. The fact that Gil needs to hunch over and gasp for breath isn't a good sign. If his lungs shut down or his heart stops, I'm not sure we could get him back. I mean, I'll certainly be there with some muscle relaxants, and we could even put down a chest tube if we had to."

Keri turned her head and shut her eyes. "That's enough. I get the idea. Gil, you're the one that's going to have to decide. You'll be the one to know when to call it quits."

Gil stood and began buttoning his shirt. "I'm feeling okay right now."

"I suppose that's right," Dr. Kusha said. "The longer you wait between starts, the more time your body has to recover. I really wish you had five days."

"Ratcliff could start Melendez today," Keri said.

"He could, but he won't. He's already announced me as the starting pitcher."

Keri looked at Dr. Kusha and pursed her lips. He folded his arms and sighed. "Alright, but if anything funny starts happening, like if your vision starts getting hazy again, you get off that mound. You won't need to call me, because I'll be right there watching."

Gil had just tossed his gym bag into the back of his truck when the familiar sight of his father's Lincoln pulled into the driveway, blocking his exit. Gil looked at his watch. As usual, he was running late.

At first, Gil wondered whether this was another ploy to keep him from pitching. Gil swung his door open and rested his boot on the runner. He could always trek over his front lawn and jump the curb.

"No, wait," his father said, scurrying up the driveway, waving his arms like a football referee trying to stop a play from scrimmage. "I have something to tell you before you pitch today."

Gil obeyed and faced his father, his arms folded. His heart began to race.

"It's not right we aren't speaking."

Gil instantly relaxed. This wasn't what he expected.

"Keri called me early this morning. She reminded me that we've been best friends our whole lives and that we shouldn't let this go on any longer—in case something happens to you."

Gil nodded. "Keri is usually right about these things."

An awkward silence followed. Gil waited for his father, whose head was now lowered, staring at the concrete. After a few moments, he looked his son in the eyes. "It was real nice what you did with that homeless man. It made me realize I was doing things for the wrong reason. I'm here to apologize. We may never agree about who God is or the right way to worship him, but ruining our relationship over what we believe is wrong. I could never live with myself if I didn't come see you pitch in the World Series. You're my son, and fathers are supposed to brag about their kids. Will you forgive me?"

Gil threw out his arms and embraced his father. "Of course, but only if you'll come see me pitch tonight."

Pastor Ron reached into his coat pocket and retrieved the envelope Gil had left on the pulpit. "Your mother and I are going to take you up on your offer for free tickets, if it's not too late."

The two men embraced again. Gil could feel his father's bony arms patting him on the back. "Of course. They'll be waiting for you at the Will Call window."

"Tell me about your health."

"To tell you the truth, I'm struggling a bit, but I think I have enough in me."

"Keri's worried about you."

"I know. I hope she understands."

"She's probably the only one who truly understands you. She's your biggest fan. Nobody is pulling for you more than she is."

48

COORS FIELD WAS so decorated that Gil hardly recognized the place. Banners hung from the outfield walls, and the grass was painted with the World Series logo. An F-18 fighter and a B-1 Bomber roared over the unsuspecting fans. Carrie Underwood sang the national anthem, and Senator Udall threw out the first pitch.

Ratcliff paced uneasily. He feared all the extra celebrations were going to throw his team off their rhythm. The Yankees, who made regular appearances at such events, seemed unfazed.

The pageantry finished, the Rockies took the field. Trudeau led the charge. On his way to second base, he defiantly glared into his former team's dugout.

Manzi, feeling vindicated after beating the Cubs, took his place at shortstop.

Juarez bolted his way toward right field, legs extended like a sprinter, showing no signs of pain from his blown-out knee. The last player out of the dugout was Slider. He emerged into the bright lights with no fanfare, his cap pulled low, ready for business. Most sports writers thought his sentence too lenient and that the commissioner had been rash in his promise. Slider took a grounder from Biondi and whipped it back to first base.

In his windup, Gil watched as Slider sucked up another ball. He held up his hand to Preacher and went over to third.

"What are you doing?" Gil said.

"Warm-ups, just like we always do."

"Are you kidding me? This is the World Series."

"And?"

"You're Slider and you're in the World Series and you're throwing balls to first base. What's wrong with this picture?"

Slider smiled. "But I can't."

"What do you mean you can't? I can't pitch if Slider's standing behind me not being Slider. That guy over there on third, well, he's not Slider, and I can't play without Slider."

"The commissioner will toss me."

"For what? Being Slider? Now get back to the dugout and come back as Slider."

"Okay," he said. Slider twisted his cap to the side as he traversed the infield.

"What's going on?" Ratcliff said when Slider reached the railing.

"Gil said I wasn't being Slider, and he wasn't going to play unless you put the real Slider on third."

Ratcliff scowled at Gil. "What on heaven's earth is he talking about?"

"Are you okay if I'm Slider?'

"Quit being stupid and get out there," Ratcliff said, "before I kick you in the butt."

"Okay," Slider said, and sprung off at a full sprint. When he reached the pitcher's mound, he spun around, whipped out four running backflips, and landed square on third base. His teeth glistened through his broad smile. Gil lifted his thumb, and the crowd went wild. *Welcome to the World Series.*

Gil glanced out at the crowd, intent on their beaming faces. They'd booed him during the summer, and now they prayed for him. The cheering was so loud that his ears were ringing.

It was time to give them what they came for. He took the signal from Preacher, lined up his two fingers along the seams and whipped out a 111-mile-per-hour fastball.

"Steeeerike!" the umpire yelled, and the Series was officially underway.

In 1956, Don Larson had not only pitched a perfect game in a World Series, but he was the only no-hitter in postseason history. Speculation was rampant as to whether Gil would be the second.

Gil felt like he was on air, floating along until the seventh inning. The fans had energized him in a way that made his illness disappear. He was in another world where that disease didn't exist. He'd given up three walks, but no runs. He was two innings away from a no-hitter.

But the crowd couldn't carry him forever, not with his ravaging disease. By the end of the seventh inning, the temperature had dropped to the forties, and the rigor mortis began to set in. Gil watched from the bench as Slider scored after he was driven in by a sacrifice fly from Manzi. Trudeau, still determined to make a statement to the Yankees, hit a double, then stole third. Juarez brought him home with a sacrifice fly to center.

Gil decided to face reality. He stood and tapped Ratcliff on the shoulder, and both men understood. This wouldn't be his no-hitter. A rumble fluttered through the crowd when the lanky Japanese closer took the mound. Tajima allowed a run in the eighth then held off a ninth-inning charge and game one went to the Rockies.

The following day, Melendez pitched another good game, but not enough to stop the hired guns of the Yankees. They managed four runs, two more than the Rockies, and after two games, the Series was even.

The question on everyone's mind was whether Gil would start game three in New York.

Ratcliff still hadn't announced his starting pitcher for game three when they arrived in New York the evening of October 26. Ratcliff did not endear himself to the New York press. Not announcing a pitcher was not just bad taste, it was un-American, and unforgivable. But Ratcliff didn't have a choice. Gil hadn't given him a decision. Dr. Kusha was meeting Gil in New York to reevaluate his condition.

The news wasn't good. What nobody knew was that Dr. Kusha had been waiting for Gil in the Rockies' locker room the moment he stepped off the mound in game one. Most figured Gil had disappeared for ten minutes to take a bathroom break, but it was really for a real-time evaluation.

Dr. Kusha was now certain that Gil's disease had progressed to the point that it was placing an undue burden on both his circulatory and respiratory systems. His blood pressure skyrocketed, and his oxygen saturation plummeted. Both would return to safe levels when Gil relaxed, but the levels reached while pitching were critical. Dr. Kusha felt the same thing had been happening all season. On the same day in the morning, Dr. Kusha reevaluated Gil, focusing on his pulse rate, blood pressure, and oxygen saturation. All had significantly improved.

"So I'm okay to pitch if I limit the number of innings?" Gil said.

"I think we're down to the number of pitches," Dr. Kusha said. "You've got to limit your pitch count."

"How many?

"Twenty."

"Get serious, doctor

"I'd say fifty."

"Sixty-five and you have a deal."

Dr. Kusha shook his head. "Hopefully, your teammates' bats are hot today. I'll be in the locker room after the fifth inning."

Connor stood next to Ratcliff as they watched Gil work his magic. Gone were the amateur indiscretions of earlier in the season. Gil didn't waste a pitch. Every throw was a strike, placed precisely where Preacher called it. By the end of the fourth inning, Gil had pitched a perfect game, tossing a mere fifty-five pitches. Even some of the Yankees' fans applauded him as he exited the field. But in New York, anything and everything was expected. The calls to "get the druggie off the field" lingered after each inning.

"Have you thought more about next season?" Connor said to Ratcliff as they watched Gil finish his warm-ups at the bottom of the fifth.

Gil threw another 111-mile-per-hour fastball. Ratcliff shrugged. "Things have changed a little bit, haven't they?"

"You know my fortunes are with you. You hang it up, so do I."

"I think I hang it up when Gil does."

"Do you think he'll be back?"

"You know I'm too superstitious to answer that." Ratcliff nodded at the mound. Gil struck out the third batter, ending the fifth inning.

"How's the arm?" Ratcliff asked when Gil slipped onto the bench.

Gil opened his mouth to answer, but the only thing that came out was a gurgle. Briscoe tossed him his water bottle, and Gil took a sip. His body violently reacted, and he began to cough and sputter. He held up his hand to signal he was okay. He finally gasped and sucked in a deep breath.

"Sorry, my mouth is a little dry."

Briscoe looked at Ratcliff and narrowed his eyes. Ratcliff came off his perch and seated himself next to his ace. "I usually ask how the arm's doing, but I feel I should ask how the lungs are doing."

Gil massaged his chest. "I'm a little tight."

Ratcliff looked out at the scoreboard. The Rockies had a two-nothing lead. He turned to Connor, and they locked eyes.

Tajima spoke up. "If Gil can get us to the eighth, I can handle the last two innings."

Nobody thought of going to the bullpen. They all knew.

"Yeah, I can go one more," Gil said.

Gil retired the first batter with a pop-up fly. The second batter fouled off the first pitch. When Gil came out of his stance, a numbing pain raced throughout his lower throat, just below his collarbone. When he went to breathe, nothing happened. It was as if someone had shoved a cork down his windpipe. His face turned crimson red, and he clutched his throat. Preacher rushed out to the mound.

The ferocious New York crowd seemed to gasp in unison, and the wild screaming fell to a hush. Gil tried to stay calm and portray a collected demeanor. The last thing he wanted was the front page of the *Times* with another prognosis of his ailment.

"You okay, Gil?"

Gil rested his hands on his thighs and arched his back. It was enough to loosen his muscles and let air rush into his lungs. He sucked in a few more breaths. "Felt like I got the wind knocked out of me," Gil said.

Preacher looked into Gil's eyes. His pupils were dilated, and the veins over his temples were bulging. "I think it's time to call it a day."

"I'm okay," Gil said, straightening up. "Just two more batters."

Preacher called for a change-up, an off-speed pitch to give Gil a breather. The batter grounded it to Slider, who tossed it to Biondi at first base for the out.

The third batter Gil faced was famous for locking in on anything off speed, favoring curveballs. Preacher called for a fastball, and Gil whipped it in with his might. Preacher watched as Gil came out of his stance, lifted his chin, and paused. It was a few more seconds before Gil began to breathe. Preacher held the ball in his glove, giving Gil a chance to recover.

Preacher hated to call for another fastball, but he did it anyway. The batter swung and missed. This time, Gil pounded his chest then sucked in another breath.

"He okay?" the umpire said.

"Yeah, bad case of heartburn. He ate a bad burger for lunch."

Gil's hands were on his hips, waiting for Preacher to return the ball. Preacher didn't dare signal for a curveball, so he ordered up another fastball. Gil delivered and the inning was over with the batter's bat still on his shoulder.

"What happened out there?" Preacher asked as soon as they disappeared into the dugout. His glove was over his mouth, blocking the cameras.

Gil shook his head. "I dunno. Scared me to death, though."

Ratcliff called up a pinch hitter for Gil, signaling to the Yankees that Gil was done for the evening. The batter managed a walk, and Slider cranked a triple, giving the Rockies a three-run lead.

Tajima raced onto the field at the top of the eighth. His awkward, lanky delivery was spot-on. It was his best showing of the season. He kept the Yankees scoreless, and last year's worst team in the league now had a two-to-one lead in the only series that mattered.

The entire state of Colorado was ecstatic when the Rockies won game four with Melendez on the mound and took a two-game lead. Game five stayed in the Empire State, while Gil, under Dr. Kusha's orders, flew back early to Colorado. His condition failed to improve.

The celebrations back in Colorado were short lived. With Gil unavailable to pitch, Ratcliff was forced to start Sewell, the rookie. As in the league championship series, everyone knew the outcome even before the first pitch. The Rockies packed their bags and flew back to Colorado with a three to two game lead, still needing a single win to take the Series.

49

ON THE DAY his team was flying back from New York to finish the series, Keri planned a quiet dinner at home. It would be Gil's favorite: steaks on the grill, with corn on the cob and a fresh fruit platter. Peck and Gil's parents joined them, trying their best to keep Gil remaining calm, now that the series was so close. Everyone present felt the pressure that was crushing Gil.

Keri sent the men outside to man the grill. Jostling an armful of plates, silverware, and plastic glasses, Keri pushed her way out the door and onto the patio. Smoke was billowing from the barbecue grill. "Quit chewing the fat and put out the flames," she said through the smog.

Peck saved the T-bones from desiccation and toted them to the outdoor table, and Gil rounded up Austin and Alicia.

"You know," Peck said, after sitting down, "I can't tell you how much I've enjoyed getting to know all the players' wives this season. Feels like it's been one long reality show, and I don't want it to end. I mean, all the drama with Trista when you started pitching better than Melendez, and Rosie's meltdown after DeJesus blew out his elbow, me having to judge hair styles, and plastic surgery—"

Keri held up her hand. "Not today, Peck."

"Right," he said, and an awkward silence followed.

The phone rang, and Austin bolted out of his seat. "It's Ratcliff," he yelled through the screen door.

Gil took the call inside.

"So how are you feeling?" Ratcliff said.

Gil knew Ratcliff needed an answer about whether he could pitch. He needed to announce tomorrow's starter. The door cracked, and Keri slipped inside and held her ear up against the phone. The door banged. Trailing Alicia and Peck, Austin had let the door clap shut behind him.

"I want to win it all tomorrow," Gil said, "but my shoulder muscles won't loosen up. I think Keri's fingers have arthritis from all the massages she's given me." He winked at his wife. "How's Melendez?"

"Itching to get the start tomorrow."

He studied Keri's face, the worry in her eyes. His father too, was intently focused on Keri's reaction. "As much as I hate to let Melendez get on that mound tomorrow, I'm afraid I need more rest. With how he's pitching, I think the Rockies are going to win it all tomorrow night."

Austin rushed over. "Are you sure you can't pitch? Why don't you wait until tomorrow and try again? Come on, go to bed right now. I'll wake you up when it's time."

Gil put his arm around his son's shoulder. "You mother's right, Austin. I need another day off. And don't you dare pray that Melendez will lose tomorrow night."

Austin looked up and frowned, the corners of his mouth drooped deeply. "I hope they lose, because you deserve to pitch the final game. And you don't have to sit next to Trista Melendez and hear her brag about how her husband's the best pitcher on the team. I can't take it anymore."

Peck shrugged. "The boy's not lying. I love that woman to death, but it's true."

Melendez got the start for game six, and the Rockies lost. But it wasn't due to Melendez. He got them to the ninth inning with a one-run lead. Tajima stood on the mound as jittery as a mouse when the lights are turned on. The pressure got to him, and he walked the first two batters, then threw a change-up that was wrapped with a bow on it. It sailed into deep center and over the fence. The Rockies managed another run in the bottom of the ninth, but it wasn't enough. The Series was now tied at three each, with one game to go.

"Gil's pitching all nine tomorrow," Connor told Ratcliff as the ball sailed over the wall. "Looks like the season's come down to Gil. Who would have thought?"

50

KERI BOUNDED DOWN the hallway of their home with two dozen red roses cradled in her arms. She skipped into the bedroom, expecting to find Gil stuffing the final pieces of clothing into his gym bag.

Instead, she discovered her husband lying on the bed, the blankets tucked beneath his chin. The lights were dimmed. The flowers slipped out of her hands, and she rushed to his side. She felt his forehead. It was cold and clammy.

"Gil, are you okay?"

"Yeah, just taking a quick rest. Trying to focus."

She smoothed his sweaty hair back. "I'm not so sure about that." Keri glanced at the clock on the nightstand and stroked his pale cheek. "You're late. I've never seen you in bed after you've shaved and dressed."

"Ah, it's nothing, if that's what you're thinking. Just a little meditation. Trying not to get caught up in all the frenzy. Keeping myself mentally tough."

She leaned over and smoothed the hair she'd just ruffled. "The gas tank is empty, isn't it?"

He knew he couldn't lie to her. And even if he did, she wouldn't buy any of it. "I am feeling a little bushed. Pitching three games in a week and a half may be a little too much. Frankly, I'm kind of looking forward to just doing nothing for a few months." He scooched himself up and a wave of dizziness washed over him.

"You're not going to break your promise to Alicia, are you?"

He smiled. Nothing was secret between this mother and daughter. "We've already discussed this. This is my dream, everything I've ever wanted. There's just one more game. Life isn't worth living if I can't make my own music or dance my own dance."

"I understand, but if you can't even make it into your truck, how are you going to pitch a World Series game?"

He took her hands in his. "I think we should dance."

"I know you too well, Gil. Trying to change the subject, because you don't want to talk about it."

"No, I want to dance with my wife. You'll never dance with me, so here's our chance." Gil flipped off the covers and fumbled on the nightstand until he found Keri's iPod, shoved it onto the speaker, and slid his finger over the screen. "Perfect," he said as he pushed the play button.

The song was *I Will Wait* by Mumford & Sons. It was the last concert they'd attended.

She didn't like concerts. Enduring Gil's gigs was all she could handle. But Gil loved them, loved the artists, their passion, the way they took him to another place. Maybe that's what his band was all about, a way to escape, to feel something he could feel in no other way. But now he had baseball and being on the mound with the music of thousands of screaming fans. That was the same way—no it was better. That was indescribable.

Gil grabbed Keri about the waist and began spinning her around the bedroom. Twice they crashed into the closet doors, but that didn't stop Gil. He spun her around faster then dipped her nearly to the floor.

"You need to save your energy, Gil. Twenty-seven outs is a lot of pitches."

"Just need twenty-seven throws with how I'm feeling right now."

She put her nose against his and rubbed it back and forth. "Remember when we used to do this?"

"No, but I do remember the month after we were first married and went to your parents for Christmas. They put us in that tiny room with two twin beds, thinking we'd be able to sleep away from each other. We nearly crushed that rickety old bed. Not sure how we both fit on that thing for an entire night."

She softly kissed him. "We've had a good marriage. I've never had a single regret. Not one. And for the record, I'm glad you gave up your career for us, but now it's time for your dream. I need to stop being selfish. I want you to pitch your heart out."

He gently touched her lips with his fingers, feeling their delicate lines. "No, I'm the one being selfish."

She shook her head. "I don't think so. You need to finish your dream, to make your own music, the music your band never did." Then she took the lead and spun him around. She slipped her hand behind his back and dipped him toward the floor. His body weight was too much, and he crashed to the carpet, carrying her on top of him. For a moment he lay motionless, then gasped.

"Gil, are you okay?"

Slowly, a smile crept over his face, and he raised himself up and kissed her. "Never been better."

"That's gross!"

They turned in unison. Alicia and Austin were perched in the doorway, arms folded. Austin shook his head. "Save it for the bedroom."

"We are in the bedroom, Austin," Keri said.

"Oh, yeah. Then do it with the door shut."

"Your father has a little extra energy. We needed to take the edge off. You know, so he doesn't throw any wild pitches." She pushed herself up, smoothed her shirt, and tucked her hair behind her ear. "He's going to do great tonight. The Rockies are finally going to win their first Series."

Alicia rolled her eyes then scowled. Gil winked at her. "But I do need to tell you all something. Just for the record. And this one stays in this room . . . this is my last game."

"But, Dad," Austin screamed. "You're going to be the greatest pitcher ever—the Hall of Fame, Cy Young, MVP, and all that stuff. You need to pitch more than just one season."

"No, I just decided. This is it, and I'm going to make it count."

Austin flung his arms down. His sister tried to put her arm

around his shoulder, but he shrugged it off.

"Think of it, Austin. Now I can be your coach. You'll be better than me. Like Ken Griffey Jr. or Cal Ripken Jr. The sons are always better." Gil stood and strode over to his son, crouching to his level. He put his arm on Austin's shoulder. "Will that be okay with you? If I'm you're coach?"

"Well, I guess we can talk it about it later. But I'm only okay with it if you win tonight."

"Good, now I'm late. You all need to come down to the field after the game for the trophy presentations. I have your passes, so you're all set."

Gil kept himself loose by joking around, keeping up the same antics the players had performed all season. He paid little attention to all the fanfare surrounding a World Series game.

* * *

The press boxes were stuffed with reporters and sports writers of all shapes and sizes. None of them could resist rehashing the bizarre season, all focused on Gil Gilbert. They bantered about whether he was on drugs, or could he really have a one-of-a-kind disease, impossible to diagnose? Some even surmised that the strike was a conspiracy to get Gil into the game. They downplayed the yellow journalism about how his pitching was marching him to his own death. "It's like the days of Hearst and Pulitzer," one announcer said. "The Rockies organization has found a way create a sensational story to save their ailing ball club. When it's all over, what are we going to believe?"

The announcer's colleague replied, "All we know for certain is that the league has cleared him to play, but the Rockies are taking a big risk. If it turns out that Gil is using a banned substance, they could forfeit their entire season."

Others were more kind, saying that people should quit talking about the cause of Gil's success and enjoy the piece of art in front of them, one they will likely never see again.

The Yankees drudged up their own scandals, attacking the Rockies' other players—how Manzi was a walking lawsuit, about how Trudeau was such a whiner they had to release him, and on and on. Their starting pitcher told the press he wondered whether he should refuse to pitch against Gil until Gil could prove his own legitimacy. "He's not eating spinach to get an arm like that," he told a live TV audience right before taking the field.

The one game changer, everyone agreed, was the ominous weather forecast. A powerful cold front was sweeping down from Canada. The Colorado fans understood what could happen if moisture-laden clouds slipped over the Rockies at the same time the temperature plummeted. If the forecasts were accurate, they could all be driving home in a ferocious blizzard. If the game went into extra innings, things could get interesting.

If Gil heard any of this, he didn't let it show. By the time he closed out the top of the sixth inning, he'd thrown a perfect game. No hits, no walks and no runs. Slider had managed a single, but the Rockies also remained scoreless.

As Gil took the field for the top of the seventh, the entire stadium was on its feet. The roar was deafening with every pitch. Most pitchers had thrown close to a hundred pitches, but Gil was at seventy. He'd completed games with over a hundred in his pitch count a half a dozen times. He knew that tonight, he could never reach the century mark.

Walking back to the dugout, he unconsciously rubbed his chest. It was tight, and his breathing was labored. Unlike previous games, his entire core hurt, down to the bones. Even in the cool evening air, he could feel sweat trickling down his chest. Every pitch was taking more out of him. The familiar sounds of *Take Me Out to the Ball Game* rang through the stadium speakers during the seventh-inning stretch. Gil paused at the warning track in front of the Rockies dugout and flashed his famous smile. Leaning against the railing, he sang with them. This was his dream, and he wanted everyone to live it with him.

Following the song, he collapsed onto the bench, and the batboy slipped Gil's jacket over his chest. Briscoe kneeled down in front of him and lifted his hand. Placing his two fingers over Gil's wrist, he checked his pulse. "It's faint," he said, shaking his head. "What were you doing up there singing?"

"I'm okay," Gil replied. "Just two more innings, and it's all over."

Ratcliff descended from his perch at the railing. "Gil, you're up to bat second. We can pull you, put in a pinch hitter, and let Tajima close."

They all knew Tajima's record against the Yankees. They had his number. All eyes turned to Gil.

"Really, I'm doing fine. Let me swing away. If I can loop one in the outfield, I'll have a chance at making first."

He didn't. He took three miserable swings and was called out. Slider passed him on the field and held out his fist for Gil to knock.

"Take it easy, Gil. Let me do the talking with my bat. I'll get us a run, and if you get us six more outs, we're in the history books."

The Yankees' pitcher challenged Slider with a fastball, even though every serious Rockies fan knew Slider loved to jump on the first pitch. Slider smacked it, and the ball sailed into the right field corner. Slider was off to the races. He turned the corner at first with his legs spinning like the Roadrunner's. His hat flipped off as he reached second. Ten feet in front of third, Slider did one of his famous headfirst slides, curving left to avoid the tag. The Rockies had their first-base runner in scoring position.

Juarez confidently strode to the plate. His normal limp was gone. It was as if his bungled up knee had miraculously healed itself. Ratcliff knew better, but he also knew that Juarez didn't need to make it to first base, he just needed to lift a fly ball far enough into the outfield for a sacrifice fly. With how fast Slider was running, a shot anywhere into the outfield would be good enough.

The Rockies' right fielder quickly took two strikes. Juarez battled the Yankees' pitcher, fouling off five more pitches and taking three balls. With the count full, he lifted one into center. It was a high floater and wasn't anywhere near the warning track. The center fielder was in shallow center when he set himself to make the catch. The moment the fielder caught the ball, Slider took off.

The throw was a rocket, and it bounced once, just to the side of the pitcher's mound. The catcher sat up, putting his knee in front of the plate to block Slider's hand. In so doing, he shifted his body between the umpire and the corner of the plate where Slider's hand was slithering along the dirt. Slider had started his slide ten feet in front of home base, and he hooked his body outward so that just his fingertips caught the exposed corner of the plate. Instantly, the catcher's glove passed over, but it was too late. Slider had beaten the throw.

He popped up and spontaneously did a backflip. The crowd went wild.

But then the umpire threw up his fist, his thumb extended to the heavens. "You're out!" he yelled over the roar of the crowd.

Slider cocked his head, wondering if he'd heard correctly. He spun around. The umpire was already scribbling on his notepad, ignoring the hum of boos that raced through the stadium. Ratcliff tore out onto the field, shoving Slider aside.

"You're crazy," Ratcliff screamed, his voice hoarse from calling to his players over the racket of the crowd. "He was safe. You couldn't see to make the call." He pointed to the third-base umpire. "Ask him, he saw it."

By now, the instant replay was being shown on the stadium screen, with a vivid depiction of Slider's fingers on top of the plate before the glove reached his arm.

"Look," Ratcliff said, pointing to the screen. "He's safe."

The sound from the disgruntled fans became deafening, but the umpire refused to change his call. Slider, now brushing off his uniform, straightened up. Ratcliff threw his hat on the ground and continued his rant. Slider came up from behind him, put his arm around his shoulder, and tugged him back to the dugout.

"We'll get the next one," he said. Ratcliff was so startled by Slider's reaction that he could only follow Slider's cue and head for the dugout. "We've got two more innings, and they're going to need to switch their pitcher. Juarez wore him out."

Boclin grounded to second, and the inning was over. The game remained scoreless. When Gil attempted to get off the bench, his knees buckled beneath him and he crashed back down. He stared at his cleats like he'd slipped on something. He again pushed himself up and gingerly made his way onto the field. His body felt like setting cement. The bright stadium lights now looked hazy, and he shook his head to clear his vision.

With the arriving cold front, the winds had picked up and the temperature was dropping. Gil hopped up and down to get his blood moving, hoping his constricting muscles would relax. Instead, they acted like rubber bands, contracting but refusing to expand. The first warm-up pitch barely made it to home plate.

It took four more before he could get any velocity.

Preacher trotted out to the mound. "You okay? Every inning it's taking you longer to get warmed up. Tajima is a good closer. You sure you don't want him to take over?"

"I've got a perfect game going in the last game of the World Series. Six more outs are all I need, then I'm done. I'm hanging it up."

Preacher ripped off his mask. "Come again?"

"You heard me. I told Keri and the kids earlier today. Just help me get through two more innings. I think that's all I've got left in the tank."

From her seat in the stands, Keri focused her binoculars. She couldn't read Gil's lips, but she could see the swelling of his face, the glaze in his eyes.

"I'm worried," Alicia said. "Why's Preacher staying on the mound that long?"

"He'll be okay," Keri said nervously, shoving the glasses into her purse.

"Come on," Austin yelled. "Six more outs, and you'll have the second perfect game in a World Series. Hey, everyone, my dad is going to pitch a perfect game!"

Alicia tugged on his jersey, signaling for him to take a seat, but Austin shooed away her hand. Peck stood up next to him. He kept rubbing his palms on his jeans. Pastor Ron put his hands together and lowered his head, mumbling a silent prayer for his son.

"I'm a nervous wreck," Peck said. "The suspense is killing me. Come on Gil, you can do it."

Ratcliff took a deep sigh when Gil popped up the first batter on the second pitch. His eyes shot to the clock: 112. If he could keep that up, the Rockies would shut them out. Nobody could hit Gil when he was throwing that hard and Preacher was calling the pitches.

Gil threw back his shoulders then rounded them over and over.

"He's tight," Connor said. "I can see it. It's like I want to run out there and give him a massage. I wish it weren't so darn cold."

"The cold is actually helping him," Briscoe said. "Keeps down the inflammation. It's like a portable ice bath on the field.

The only problem is that he's so stiff it's hard for him to throw."

Gil heaved another fastball that missed its mark, but the batter swung wildly anyway. As he came up out of his follow-through, his throat closed off and he clutched his neck. He closed his eyes and thought of lying on a nice, warm beach in the Caribbean. Slowly his windpipe relaxed and the air rushed back into his lungs. But the fact that his breathing could stop scared him.

He waited for Preacher's signal, a curveball inside. It was as if Preacher understood he needed an easier pitch. The batter was a full half-second in front of the pitch. It had taken Gil a mere six pitches, and he had his second out of the inning.

Preacher called for a high four-seam fastball. The batter guessed the pitch and made solid contact, shooting a line drive through the infield. Manzi dove toward second base and nabbed the streaking ball at the tip of his webbing. The top of the eighth inning was in the books.

Gil gingerly walked like an old man to the dugout trying to avoid any further exacerbation of his condition. He wanted to keep his head down so that he would not be distracted by the crowd, but that only made breathing more difficult. As Slider came beside him, Gil rested his arm on Slider's shoulder. "Would you mind helping me a little? Just don't make it obvious."

Slider stood a little higher, slowed his pace, and allowed Gil to rest his full weight on his shoulders. "You've got to stop," Slider said. "Let Tajima close."

"Three more outs. I could do it in three pitches if I get really lucky."

Slider escorted Gil into the dugout, down the stairs and to the bench, where Gil collapsed. A batboy handed him a cup, but he waved it away.

"Slider, I'm going to rest my eyes a little. Can you nudge me when it's time?"

Gil dozed while the Yankees took care of business, taking out the Rockies next three batters in turn. Slider poked Gil in the ribs. "Okay, boy. Time to go make history."

Gil's eyes sprung open, and he shot up from his seat like he was twenty years old. "Let's go do this, then."

He trotted to the mound, getting his blood pumping, trying

to reenergize his rigid body. It was impossible to describe, but pain was emerging from every cell in him. He ignored it, and swung his arms like a swimmer getting ready for a big race. The field looked dark, and he wondered why they had dimmed the lights. He looked up and noticed the clouds as they floated across the starry sky. The storm was arriving.

After winding up, he stepped off the rubber, motioning for Preacher to approach. "Let's just play catch for a bit until I warm up."

With Preacher midway between the rubber and home plate, the two men gently tossed the ball. Each time, Preacher took two steps back until he was at his position behind the plate. Then Gil let go on the velocity. The pain that shot through his chest nearly blacked him out. But the pitch was still wicked fast.

His chest tightened, and he gasped for air. Waiting helped, and soon he could breathe. But the pain wouldn't stop. He wondered if this was what Keri had experienced when she'd given birth to Alicia and Austin.

Gil composed himself and nodded. The umpire called the Yankees player into the batter's box. "Let's play ball."

In the dimness, Gil could barely discern Preacher's flashing fingers. He let Preacher repeat the signal three times until he was sure it was a low fastball. Gil whipped it in at 111 miles per hour and the crowd went wild.

As Preacher tossed the ball back, Gil lost his focus. He held out his glove hoping the ball would somehow find its way inside. At the last second, he saw the ball and lifted his glove, but not high enough. The ball ricocheted to his left, and Manzi scooped it up from his position at shortstop and walked it back to the mound. Manzi didn't ask whether Gil was having problems, he just laid the ball in his glove and tapped him on the rear. "You got it, Gil."

Preacher signaled a second fastball. The batter caught a piece of it, enough to shoot it straight in the air. Gil tried to find its trajectory, but in looking up, a huge wave of dizziness overcame him. He put a knee to the ground. Preacher zeroed in on the fly ball, staggered into the infield, and waved off Biondi at first. The ball fell safely into Preacher's sure hands, and Gil was two outs from victory.

Gil arose, but couldn't stop his world from spinning. He tried to pick out a single object to focus on in hopes that might calm his mind. He searched for Keri. That was a bad idea. She had her hands covering her mouth, and Alicia had her arms tightly wrapped about her mother.

"Two more outs," he told himself. "Then I'm done—for good."

Gil resumed his stance and waited for Preacher's signal. Either Gil couldn't see between his catcher's legs or else no signal was forthcoming. Gil leaned closer and squinted. Nothing from Preacher, he was sure of it. Preacher was sitting in his crouch, and his hands weren't moving. He'd stopped calling any pitches. Gil stood up erect, stretched his back, and again took his stance. Nothing.

Gil studied the batter, remembered he'd had luck with his slider in the fifth inning, then he shot off a diving pitch at close to 110 miles an hour. The batter swung and missed. Gil could feel spasms in his chest as he finished his follow-through. A cold sweat was not only dripping down his chest, but now trickling down his cheeks.

This time, Gil thought things would be different, but Preacher's hands were still. For some reason, Preacher had stopped calling the shots. Gil wound up and threw a slider for a strike.

The constant pain in Gil's core hadn't gone away. As Gil stuck up his glove to catch the ball, the pain was overshadowed by the sense of constriction that had overtaken him the game before. This time it was more than his throat, but it felt like his whole chest had collapsed. The blood drained from his head, and the stadium began to spin around like a Frisbee. He took a knee and closed his eyes, fumbling with his shoelaces to hide his predicament. The swirling somewhat subsided, and his chest slightly loosened. Gil slowly stood and tried to regain his composure.

Preacher was still in his squatting stance, waiting for Gil to finish tying his shoes. When Preacher failed to signal, Gil let go of a fastball. The batter swung and missed and the roar of the crowd let Gil know it must have been at record speed. He felt his chest tightening, and the spinning resumed. There was no doubt now. He'd reached his limit. If he kept throwing, he was going to suffocate himself, just like Dr. Kusha predicted.

He focused his gaze back on Preacher, who once again sat

motionless. In a moment of silence, he thought of Alicia's arms tight around his neck.

Slowly, so that he wouldn't upset his balance, Gil gazed into the stands. Keri's hands were still covering her mouth, now wide open enough for him to see past her fingers. He'd seen that look before. She was terrified. She knew.

Alicia was clenching her mother's shoulders, while Austin, oblivious, was jumping like a Mexican jumping bean.

Gil tried to think, but the cheering of the crowd made that impossible. It was like standing behind a jet engine as it took off. The vibrations of the pounding feet thumped him like a loud speaker at a rock concert.

Think, he told himself. But he'd been thinking all his life. Maybe it was time for him to stop thinking.

The moment he let his mind go, he remembered his promise to Alicia. He thought about Keri, shaking from fear of his death. And then he understood why God had done this to him. This day was not about winning. Winning wasn't his dream. His dream was in the stands. He had to make a choice, but the decision was easy. He'd give all he had left to her.

Gil stepped off the rubber. The mass of humanity before him wanted him to finish, to put himself into history. But the image of Keri's frozen face wouldn't leave. He had to calm her fears.

He began to focus on his breathing, that cold, wet breath that came deep from within. It was raspy and labored. As he let everything else go, a warmness shot up from his very center. In that moment, he remembered Melvelene and how she'd given her last strength for him—that was her last sacrifice. Maybe that was her way of telling him that he needed to do likewise, that his transcending event would be to give his last strength to his family. That would be his own golden moment. That's when he would really know if he could fly.

Salty sweat streamed down his face and he wiped it off with his shirtsleeve. He knew he could muster a few more pitches, maybe even hit 113 and send the crowd into ecstasy. But that wasn't why he was here.

Gil took one more gaze at the screaming fans. He flashed his now-famous smile. This was it. His final moment.

He took the ball out of his glove, rolled the seams along his finger then sat it down in the dirt.

When Gil left the mound, everyone presumed he was going to the dugout. But his trajectory was off. He veered left of the dugout, toward the stands. He motioned the grounds crew to open the gate. When it swung open, he began to ascend the stairs, ever so slowly.

The screaming crowd instantly fell silent. They had expected him to remove his cap, take a bow, then have Ratcliff send out Tajima from the bullpen. But why, when he was only two outs from a perfect game in the World Series, and the game was still scoreless? What if the Yankees scored on Tajima?

Gil's eyes couldn't focus. He knew their season tickets were on the eighth row. Counting always helped. He planted both feet on each step, figuring if he counted to sixteen he would be close enough. A few kids flooded to the aisle, holding out their hands, hoping for a chance to touch their idol. He didn't notice any of them, just the counting in his mind and the struggle to breathe with each elevation of his feet as he progressed up the stadium.

When he'd counted to sixteen, he looked down the aisle. The unmistakable bulk of Peck's form told him he was at the right place. He squeezed past the first four fans, letting their hands stabilize him as he blindly wandered toward his family.

The roaring of the crowd was gone, and a hush settled over the stadium like a fog rolling in off the ocean. A few flakes of snow drifted down, a foreshadowing of the powerful storm that would strike later that evening.

Peck grabbed him by his shoulders and looked into his eyes. His pupils were dilated and unfocused.

Pastor Ron put his arm around his son and with a penetrating gaze could only squeeze harder. Both men understood.

Gil kept his slow pace, struggling to reach his son. He held out his hands in front of him like a blind person groping for direction.

"Dad, what are you doing?" Austin said as soon as he squeezed past Pastor Ron. "Only one and a half batters. A perfect game in the World Series. You can't stop. Come on, let's go." He grabbed his arm to tug him back out onto the field.

Gil softly smiled, straightened his cap, and lifted his chin. "No, this is better."

Then he put both arms around Alicia. "I remembered my promise."

"But that was only if—" she stammered.

"This is my goodbye," he said. "I saved my best for last. I will miss you. Watch out for your mother and be patient with Austin. It's going to take him a long time before he'll understand."

He smiled once again, and she smiled back amid her tears. She hugged him tighter.

Gil struggled for breath and she let him go, feeling the weight of his body coming down on her. Quickly, she stepped aside and let him collapse into her chair. He fell like a limp noodle, yet slammed into the plastic seat. His body slouched, and he groaned as he exhaled.

"I just need a little rest." Gil curled up, his head perched atop the plastic seat. Keri took her seat beside him. She put her arm behind his head, and he adjusted his position so that his head slid down her shoulder and over her breast. He nuzzled himself into her, with his ear centered over her chest. The rhythm of her heartbeat soothed him. "I love you, Keri," he mumbled. Then his eyelids slid shut.

The field cameraman had followed Gil up the steps, fully expecting him to provide some romantic moment, like giving his wife a juicy kiss and some brilliant flowers, then returning to the dugout. The gigantic screen captured every moment, even adding superimposed hearts in the corner of the display. Live television carried the same video feed.

"What a romantic," the announcer said for the television crowd.

Keri stroked his hair, feeling his clammy skin. She felt the tenseness of his body against her shoulder. His chest slowly rose and lowered. Then suddenly the movement subsided. The sound of his breath went silent. Gil's entire body twitched violently, then fell still. Not even his stomach moved.

Keri understood he was gone. He had given his last goodbye. "I love you, Keri," was his parting farewell. For a moment, she thought about reviving him. Calmly, she acted as if nothing unusual had happened. She kissed the top of his head then looked to her two children. Tears were streaming down Alicia's cheeks. Austin's gaze turned from his lifeless father to the baseball diamond, where eight Rockies players silently waited.

"Kiss your father goodbye," she said to Alicia, "then put your blanket over him."

Alicia placed her hands over her mouth. "No, Mom. He's not. No, he can't be. Call a doctor."

"No, he's gone. Let him die as he wanted." Out of the corner of her eye she sensed that all cameras were still focused on them. "If they'd only cut the cameras."

The reality of what just happened finally struck Alicia. She threw herself onto her father. "I love you, Dad. Don't leave us." Her body shook uncontrollably. Yet, he'd kept his promise.

When she sat up, Keri took her blanket and slipped it over the corpse, blocking any access to any more pictures.

Alicia took her little brother's hand. "Come say goodbye."

"He's not going to pitch anymore? He's got one more inning. He can't stop now."

Keri wanted to hold him, to explain what had just happened, but Gil's body was still resting on hers, and she didn't want to let him go.

Alicia lifted up the corner of the blanket. "Kiss him goodbye," she told Austin.

Alicia rustled her fingers through his hair like Gil was fond of doing. "He wanted to spend his last minutes with you. That's why he put the ball down."

"But I wanted him to win, to be the best pitcher." Austin's lip quivered.

"His strength was gone. He had to make a choice. He could keep playing or spend it with us. And now we all know what meant the most to him." She threw her arms around her brother and let him cry, blocking his face from view.

51

THE MLB COMMISSIONER hastily ended his phone call and slipped his phone into his jacket. Security opened the gate, and he hurried onto the field, approaching the head umpire. The two spoke, nodding, looking up as two more medical personnel wearing white shirts lugging a stretcher made its way down the aisle toward the Gilberts' row. The umpire faced the field and raised both hands, officially halting the game.

Ratcliff, his cap lowered, approached the men in gray uniforms. Preacher stepped next to him. The commissioner spoke first. "We're halting the game for at least thirty minutes. In view of the unusual circumstances, we're evaluating what to do next."

"I assume Gil's dead," Ratcliff said.

"Yes, I'm afraid so," the commissioner said. "The medical personnel officially pronounced him deceased just a few minutes ago. They are bringing the stretcher to take his body to Swedish Hospital, where I assume he will undergo a full autopsy."

The Yankees' manager approached. "What is the precedence for cases like this?"

"My team is researching," the commissioner said. "Because of my respect for Gil, my preference is to suspend the game until tomorrow, but in view of the incoming storm, that does not appear to be an option."

"We need to finish tonight," the Yankees' manager said.

Preacher grunted and stepped forward, but Ratcliff pulled him back. "Let's wait thirty minutes and see what your folks come up with. I'd like my players to stand at attention on the baseline to give their last respects."

"I think that's appropriate," the commissioner said. "We'll reconvene here in thirty minutes for an update."

Ratcliff called for his team to huddle, explained the situation and had them line up along the first baseline, caps removed and placed over their hearts. Taking the cue, the Yankees emptied their dugout along the third baseline and follow suit. In a somber voice, the public announcer came over the loud speakers saying that Gil had died, and that the game was temporarily being halted until further notice from the commissioner. He then asked them all to stand, remove their hats, and wait while Gil was taken from the stadium.

Everyone stood in shock, eyes fixated on the white sheet covering the lifeless figure. Nobody even whispered as the two paramedics hauled the empty stretcher from the main concourse and down twenty rows of stairs. Slider, who'd bolted from his teammates and sprinted up the stairs in a fleeting attempt to say his last goodbye to his only friend, helped Peck to keep the blankets spread, a feeble attempt at sparing Gil's family from the encroaching cameras.

Wrapped in the blanket, the medical personnel hefted Gil's body out of the seat and onto the padded stretcher. They covered him with another blanket, then securely strapped him and ascended back up the stairs. Slider took Keri in one hand, Alicia in the other and escorted them along the procession. Peck and Austin followed close behind. Occasional snowflakes softly floated down, glistening in the bright stadium lights.

It sounded like the stadium sighed in unison when the stretcher disappeared. The Yankees players broke ranks and returned to their dugout, while every Rockies player remained at attention. Preacher was the first one to step forward. He signaled for his team to remain in place while he approached the assistant commissioner who, under orders from his boss, remained on the field.

"I'd like to have a prayer," he said. "Can you please round up a microphone?"

The official was more than happy to break the uneasy silence and in a minute had secured Preacher a microphone.

In his deep, baritone voice, Preacher informed the crowd that he was going to have a prayer and requested that they take hands and join him. Complete strangers took hands and lowered their heads in respect. "Let us pray," Preacher said.

It was a traditional Protestant prayer, asking Providence to be mindful of Gil's family and to help them all understand the meaning of what had just happened. He thanked Gil for blessing all their lives, then blessed them all with a safe journey home as if the event were concluded and the season was over.

Another awkward silence followed. The public announcer had no additional information to provide and there was no appropriate music to play over the loudspeakers.

Then, from somewhere high up in the rockpile in right field, the sound started. Somebody started singing. It was Gil's song, the one he sang to himself during every windup when he tapped his glove three times. *Take me out to the ball game.*

The volume began to crescendo as more joined the tune. The choir expanded to the center field bleachers, then rolled into the infield seats and the upper balcony. The fans took up hands again, swaying back and forth as they sang.

Buy me some peanuts and Crackerjack. I don't care if I ever come back ...

It was a perfect segue for the commissioner, who returned to the infield toting a dozen league officials. He waved to Ratcliff and the Yankees' manager. As Ratcliff left the dugout, Preacher followed, muttering to himself. With eyes once again focused on the field and the upcoming announcement, Slider went undetected as he slipped from the locker room back to the Rockies' dugout.

"Are we ready to play?" the Yankees' manager said. "If we wait too much longer, this storm is going to let loose and we'll all be stuck in a foot of snow."

The commissioner turned to Ratcliff as if the decision were now up to him.

"What have you done in situations like this before?" Ratcliff said.

"We're still looking, but there doesn't appear to be any precedence, at least not in recent MLB history. Only two MLB players have ever died because of a game. Mike "Doc" Powers in 1909 and Raymond Johnson Chapman in 1920 after Carl Mays threw a spitball and hit him in the head. But we don't know if they suspended either game."

"Well, in football they die all the time," the Yankees' manager said. "They just cart them off and keep playing. I say let's play. The Yankees came here to win, and we're ready to do just that."

Ratcliff's jaws were flexing, but he kept his cool, his arms folded. He looked to the commissioner. It was his decision.

"If the elements weren't against us, I prefer to postpone the game until tomorrow, out of respect for Gil and his family. Baseball has never had, and never will have, another player like Gil Gilbert. This is a tragedy of such proportions, I can't imagine playing right now."

"But—" the Yankees' manager stepped forward.

The commissioner held up his hand. "Let me finish. This storm is going to dump enough snow that we can't play tomorrow, probably can't play for several days. I just spoke with the local meteorologists. They are expecting at least three feet of snow. That happens when you're in the Rocky Mountains. So, postponing just isn't going to work. And we can't delay the game any longer tonight. The fans are getting cold, the players' muscles are tight, there could be injuries. But beyond that, the fans have come here expecting us to declare a winner."

"That's right," the Yankees' manager chimed in. "We need a winner. These fans, they need something to make them happy after this. If we just leave things as they are, everyone will go home depressed. At least we can get half of them to be happy. Gil would want them to continue."

The commissioner focused his gaze on Ratcliff. "I'm sure you agree. It's got to be this way."

Ratcliff dropped his arms. "I suppose so."

"No," Preacher said, expanding his chest and forcing his way into the circle. "You don't understand what Gil stood for. You don't understand what he just taught us. We can't finish this game. It would be a mockery. Gil's death will be in vain. Pronouncing a winner is antithetical to his last act of sacrifice."

The Yankees' manager's jaw dropped, and he craned his neck forward, his face quizzical like he had no idea what this madman was talking about.

"I'll go let my players know," he said to the commissioner and turned toward the Yankees' dugout.

"Come on, Preacher," Ratcliff said. "You need to get Tajima warmed up."

Preacher wouldn't budge. His nostrils were flaring. Ratcliff reached out and tugged his jersey. "Let's get this over so we can go see Keri."

In the dugout, Preacher spastically threw on his gear, sliding two pads over his chest. When he barged onto the field, he was lugging the biggest bat he could find. And he didn't go to his place behind home plate.

Ratcliff had called Tajima from the bullpen, where he'd been warming up. He was jogging onto the field as the commissioner was explaining to the fans why he'd made the decision to continue, apologizing that they couldn't delay until tomorrow, and that he hoped they would understand why they needed to finish the season before the storm struck. The crowd stood and clapped their approval. The game had to be concluded. There was a time for everything. They would all mourn for Gil another day.

As the Rockies took the field, the applause grew. Without Gil, the Rockies needed an extra player.

Urged on by the crowd, Tajima picked up his pace, sprinting through the outfield. Preacher took his walk to a jog, then also began to run. It was a race to the mound.

Preacher claimed the territory before Tajima could reach the infield. He planted both cleats on the rubber and repeatedly slapped the bat in his hands. He protected the sacred ground like a hen over her nest.

"The guy is a freakin' gladiator," the Yankees' manager shouted to the umpire, pointing at Preacher. "Get that nutcase off the field. Let's put them out of their misery."

The catcher set himself. He wasn't moving until the commissioner changed his decision or the snow forced them all to go home for the season. This game he loved, that he'd lived his entire life for, the game that made men heroes, that made them winners, was now something else. Gil had just made him understand. There couldn't be a winner or a loser, at least not this season. He understood what it meant to go between, to transcend. He'd just witnessed Gil find his way, and wanted everyone to know what Gil had obtained.

Ratcliff remained perched at the fence, arms folded, refusing to intervene. Tajima, focusing on the task at hand, assumed Preacher was waiting for him, ready to hand him the game ball and give a few words of encouragement. But as he passed second and saw Preacher slapping the bat in his hand, he stopped in his tracks. Manzi slipped in front of him and held him back.

Preacher kept slapping the bat in his hand, daring anyone to take him on. The tie, the place between winning and losing, was, for this season, going to remain, for today, for tomorrow, forever.

The head umpire slipped on his facemask and begin striding toward the mound. Barely situated in his seat behind center plate, the commissioner shot up, rushed through the gate and onto the field. He waddled as he jogged to intercept the umpire.

The commissioner held up his hands. "Wait, let me talk to him."

"As you wish," the umpire said. "You're the boss."

Preacher was slowly turning, like the second hand on a clock, studying the field of battle, deciding who would be first to try to take him on.

The commissioner pulled out a white handkerchief and began waving it in the air, to the amusement of the crowd. With the cloth in front of him, he timidly approached the mound.

"Preacher, what's going on here? This is baseball. You know the game. If you don't let Tajima pitch, your team is going to forfeit, and you don't want that to happen, not after what—"

"Don't go there, Commissioner. I'll lay my life down here, but you're not going to continue."

"You're not making sense, Preacher. Gil would have wanted this. The whole reason we had the season was to have a world champion. We're only an inning away. The fans are cheering. They're ready to go on. This is how life works. The game must go on."

Preacher shook his head. "Doesn't anybody get it?"

Slider, observing from his position at third base, sprinted over. "Preacher, I get it. I know exactly what Gil was telling us." He held up his fist. "I'm with you, Preacher. This season is over. We don't need a winner. We need to follow Gil."

Biondi joined them. "It took me awhile, but I've been watching Gil all season. I'm ashamed it took me this long, but now I understand. I agree. Let things stand as they are. We can start afresh next year. Let's go home and reflect on what Gil left us. We can break tradition this one time."

Soon, the entire team, Ratcliff included, was standing on the mound. Snowflakes were steadily falling. The Yankees' manager made another appearance. He insisted they begin before the weather got worse and they had to finish the Series in Florida.

Preacher handed the ball to Slider and put his arm around the commissioner, shepherding him off the mound. "You know, Commissioner," he said, "I used to think a win would make me happy, just like I thought going to heaven would make me happy. But not anymore. Don't you see? That's what Gil was trying to show us. Maybe you need to think about it. Let's take the rest of the season off and think about it without worrying about today's outcome. Let's leave this tie as a memorial to Gil so we can always think about what Gil gave his life for."

The commissioner gazed into the seats, where Gil had passed away. The crowd was bundling in their blankets, hushed as they waited for an explanation.

"I have a duty to all the baseball fans."

The commissioner looked straight up into the sky, letting the crystals settle on his face. "Let's suppose you're right. What am I to do?"

"That's your decision, but if it were me, I'd do just what Gil did. I wouldn't follow any rules. I wouldn't follow duty. I'd simply follow my heart. That's what I'd do. And besides, this is a different season anyway. We're not real players. This isn't a real season."

The commissioner stared deep into Preacher's brown eyes. "Transcending between winning and losing."

"That's right. Gil could have finished the game. He had it in him. But giving his life to win? No, that's not what Gil was about. Keri and his family meant more than winning."

The commissioner folded his arms and gazed over the restless fans. "I understand," he finally said. "Can I borrow that bat?"

Preacher shrugged and handed him the stick. "She's all yours."

The commissioner went back to the mound, parting the players that were now all congregated, silently waiting for a decision. The players parted to let the commissioner ascend the mound. He laid down the piece of wood, making a cross on the rubber, then stepped back to admire his creation.

"I'm declaring the season over. No winner and no loser. I think we've all learned something important here today about ourselves and about this game. I'll see you all next season."

52

KERI DECIDED TO have the memorial service where Gil played his game. Three days later, when all the snow had been cleared by hundreds of laborers and a healthy dose of sunshine, they all returned to Coors Field. The weather once again turned warm, the sun shone.

Pastor Ron gave the eulogy, making certain everyone understood Gil's message.

"How can you be weak and strong at the same time? How is strength made perfect in weakness? That's what Gil taught us all. The answer is that you experience a state of grace when you pass between them, when you cross through your strength and weakness. When Gil put down that ball, he put down his strength and became weak. But he regained his strength the moment he climbed into these very stands. He let his heart go and found grace in his arms—and it's that grace that lifted him up so that he could fly."

Pastor Ron paused and gazed about the stadium. "His gift to us wasn't his fastball—although I loved to see him throw. Boy, did I like to see the speed on that ball—no, what he gave to us was himself. And what Gil told us was that no game, no moment of glory, is more important than family."

* * *

The Rockies held their annual post-season banquet a week later. Breaking tradition, Ratcliff catered the dinner at his own home. Lonely without his wife, Susan, he felt it would be good to bring a little life back to where he'd spent so many happy years. With invited spouses, his dining room and kitchen were bursting at the seams.

Keri was his guest of honor, and she took her place at the head of the table. "This has been the greatest season of my life," Ratcliff began. "What happened to each of us has meant more than anything, even when I won the Series as a player. Many of you know how difficult it has been for me since Susan passed away last year. I never realized how much I loved her until she was gone." He paused and cleared this throat. "I think all of you knew how much she loved her school in Guatemala. Well, I think I'm going to take some of Gil's advice. As of tonight, I am retiring. I'm going to pick up where Susan left off. I'm now the new PE teacher for elementary school kids in Guatemala. If I'm lucky, maybe I'll teach them how to play a little baseball."

www.ingramcontent.com/pod-product-compliance
Lightning Source LLC
Chambersburg PA
CBHW020356120726
47904CB00002B/593